Civilization: The Serpent Cult

Volume XII

Todd Andrew Rohrer

iUniverse, Inc.
New York   Bloomington

Civilization: The Serpent Cult
Volume XII

iUniverse books may be ordered through booksellers or by contacting:

iUniverse
1663 Liberty Drive
Bloomington, IN 47403
www.iuniverse.com
1-800-Authors (1-800-288-4677)

Because of the dynamic nature of the Internet, any Web addresses or links contained in this book may have changed since publication and may no longer be valid.

ISBN: 978-1-4502-0480-4 (sc)
ISBN: 978-1-4502-0481-1 (ebk)

Printed in the United States of America

iUniverse rev. date: 12/29/2009

I Perceive:

11/2/2009 1:49:08 AM – A child is born with a clean slate mentally, a sound mind. A child is the product of their surroundings. I had the impression civilization was careful to treat children properly and to not abuse children because the children are the life spring of the species. The logic being, if an adult abuses a child they fail their duty as an adult because the future of the species relies on the children. I was not aware civilization mentally hinders children on a scale that is far beyond one's ability to believe or perhaps even imagine.

There is no law or justice to address this mental hindering of children because it transcends law and justice. The nature of the cult, which is called civilization, is so diabolical it is hard for many to even understand.

It is important to understand how a cult operates. The most important rule of the cult is to keep the cult members in line and that is done by keeping cult members unaware they are in a cult. A cult thrives when the cult members are ignorant. This basic reality is what keeps the cult in power. What a cult member does not know about the cult ensures they will not be able to leave the cult. Simply put, one cannot leave a cult if they are not aware they are in a cult. For this reason it is important the cult makes it appear bad things are believed to be good things. The cult must make bad things appear as good things so that bad things become acceptable. The cult disguises mentally hindering children as a good thing so that people in the cult will go out of their way to mentally hinder their own children, and then suggest they do good things. It is difficult for a person to do a bad thing but it is easy for a person to do a bad thing they believe is a good thing. For this reason the main goal of the cult is to make bad things look good and make good things look bad.

The easiest way to do this is to create a value system or a system of standards. The cult creates a system of standards that makes bad things valuable and good things dangerous. The complexity of this reality is the cult must first make the cult members afraid. Using fear tactics is the most effective way to control someone who is prone to fear. Fear tactics do not work on the fearless so the fearless are a threat to the cult and thus a threat to the system of the cult. The cult uses bad things to instill fear and then disguises the bad things as good things and this encourages everyone to take part in the bad things and thus they become prone to fear.

X= child
Y = fear indoctrination tool
Z= fearful cult members
X + Y = Z

The power in this equation is achieved when Y is disguised as something good. Once the cult convinces everyone Y is good then they have the potential for gaining unlimited fearful cult members (Z). Anyone who speaks poorly about Y is a threat to the cult. The cult defends Y because without Y, Z is in question. This is why Y must be disguised as something that could not possibly have flaws. The entire cult must never question if Y has flaws. If Y comes into question by the cult members the cult itself is in danger of collapse. For this reason the cult will never allow anyone to question the merits of Y. For that reason alone anyone who questions Y must be fearless and that is why Y creates or instills fear. This creates a failsafe for the cult.

U = cult collapse
V = exterminate Z
W = fear creation tool secure
X = cult members
E = the fear creation tool exposed
Z = a cult member that breaks free of the fear induced by E

Z = E
If Z then E. Because of this X is always looking to eliminate any Z because X is only concerned about W and wishes to avoid E.
Z + V = W
Z + E = U
If a Z exposes the fear creation tool (E) the cult collapses (U) because the "scam" is exposed. The cult members are not willing participants in the cult they were simply indoctrinated into the cult by their parents unknowingly and they want to be free of the cult but first they must become aware they are in a cult.

A human being wants to be free and think for their self and because of this it is important for the cult to get to them at an early age. This is why Y(fear indoctrination tool) must be disguised as a good thing.

A = grandfather
B = Father
C = Son
Y = fear isndoctrination tool

If the cult can convince A, Y is good for them then A will administer it and encourage it on B and in turn B will encourage it and administer it to C. This is why Y must be packaged to look good. The most effective way to make Y look good is to attach luxury to it. If one has enough Y one gets luxury or an easy life. This is very complex.

A gets Y. A gets fearful. The fear in (A) encourages them to encourage Y in B. Y makes (A) afraid and that fear makes (A) unable to stand against the wishes of the cult.

F = Cult member (fearful)
G = Cult collective
H = Ex-Cult member
I = danger
J = determination

H + I + G = J

(H) loses fear, becomes aware of the cult because fear keeps one confused so they cannot detect the cult. (G) tries to warn (F) to avoid (H). (H) is at risk (I) because (G) does not want (H) to warn (F) about the cult so (J) is what determines if (H) is successful in warning (F). (I) determines the (J) of (H) so (H) must forget about (I) in order to achieve the (J) to speak with (F).
 (G) will do anything to keep (H) from communicating with (F) and this is what creates (I). For this reason (H) must be willing to die to communicate with (F) because (G) will kill (H) to keep them from communicating with (F). The (J) of (H) must be vast because the (G) is willing to do anything to stop (H) from communicating with (F).
(H) breaks free of the cult and (G) must keep (H) from communicating with (F) because (H) may convince (F) they are in fact in a cult.

There are only two kinds of people in the world. Ones who break free of the cult, and ones still in the cult. There is a small number who never were in the cult but their numbers are marginal.

The ones who break free of the cult are the only ones who can assist ones still in the cult to break free of the cult, because ones in the cult are not even aware they are in a cult. If the ones in the cult were aware they were in a cult, they would quit the cult and that is why they are not aware they are in a cult. A human being does not like to be controlled and so the cult must never let the cult members think they are being controlled.

One important goal of the cult is to make everyone in the cult perceive they are free. The cult must always have the law on its side and for that reason, only people who get the (Y) (fear indoctrination tool) are allowed to administer law. Once the cult has law on its side, it automatically has law enforcement on its side, and this means no person who leaves the cult can get in the cults way. Because of this aspect the cult will always appear righteous to the cult members. This is why anyone who leaves the cult cannot fight against the cult because that would bring the law upon them and they would be vilified and appear to be an outlaw.

The cult members are going to defend the cult because they do not even know they are in a cult, because the cult members are indoctrinated into the cult when they are children. A child is trusting and the cult understands that. A child perceives they are being raised, but in reality they are being indoctrinated. A child is not aware of the cult, they are only mindful that their own parents certainly would not indoctrinate them into a cult or harm them. This is why the cult goes back over 5000 years. The cult only had to indoctrinate a few people into the cult and in time everyone indoctrinates their own children into the cult and perceives they are raising their children "properly" when in reality they are indoctrinating their children into the cult like they were indoctrinated into the cult.

A child is not free if they are indoctrinated by their parents into a cult under the guise of being raised properly. This is why it is the paramount goal of the cult to disguise the indoctrination tool as something good and acceptable to the parents. No sound minded parent is going to harm their child willingly. A parent will harm their child if they are told by an authority figure or by a peer crowd that harming their child is good. A parent will allow a Doctor to stick a needle in their child's arm and in turn harm their child if that Doctor can convince that parent it is for the best. The cult can convince a cult member to harm their own child if that cult member can be convinced it is for the best. This is simply peer pressure. A government can convince a parent to sacrifice their child for some foreign war if the government has a convincing argument. Simply put, a parent will kill their child to achieve a sense of acceptance by their peers. A parent will harm their own child if they can be convinced it is for the best. Because of that fact it is wise for the cult to keep all parents sedated or mentally hindered. It is far easier for the cult to convince the parents to harm their children if the parent is mentally hindered, sedated.

It is nearly impossible to keep a parent from harming their child if that parent is of sound mind so the cult must ensure the parent is as of unsound mind as possible. This all is relative to the cult making bad things look like good things. The cult must keep everyone in the cult sedated or there will be problems. - 3:32:18 AM

11/3/2009 2:13:55 AM – The cult is fool proof on every level except one. There is only one flaw in the armor of the cult. Anyone who finds this flaw and escapes the cult only has two choices. The first choice is to keep their mouth shut about the cult and the second choice is to speak up about the cult and risk getting punished for doing so. The cult does not play games when someone leaves the cult and starts speaking poorly of the cult. There is too much power on the line for the cult and the cult is not going to give up its power just because a person found the flaw in the cult's armor.

In order for the cult to survive the cult has to keep the persona of righteousness. There is only one flaw in the armor of the cult and everything else is airtight. A little probing is not going to harm the armor of the cult. The cult has had thousands of years to make sure it armor is airtight. For thousands of years there have been humans who have tried to probe the armor of the cult and they have failed. There is a good chance you are in the cult as in a 99.999% good chance. Perhaps you do not remember signing up for the cult. Perhaps your parents signed you up for the cult. Your belief or disbelief of that is not even important at all. You will not understand you are in the cult because everyone you know is in the cult and that is an indication of how few have broken free of the cult.

There are some who have broken free of the cult and they go underground, and they tend to keep their mouth shut because they do not want to perhaps be murdered. It is impossible for one who is in the cult to understand they are in a cult unless someone breaks free of the cult and proves it to them beyond a shadow of a doubt.

The problem with that is the one who is doing the convincing perhaps risks their life because ones in the cult are questionable in relation to they may be agents of the cult and not even know it. The reality is a person is indoctrinated into the cult when they are child and the cult is all they know so they will perhaps kill for the cult and not even know it. This is an indication of how "good" the cult is, as in good at disguising itself as righteous. If one looks around and thinks everyone they see is in said cult they will be dumbfounded at how large the cult is, so they will deny the cult could be so large and so far reaching. The cult transcends everything in society. A better way to look at it is the cult does not turn down anyone for membership into the cult.

It is important to understand this word civilization. One definition of civil is polite, but in a way that is cold and formal. The word civilization means a society that has a high level of culture and social organization. A cult from a society point of view is a self identified group of people who share a narrowly defined interest or perspective. The cult of civilization is one way to look at it but civilization is more relative to an adjective than a noun. It would be along the lines of cult of the cold yet polite. The cult of the socially organized, with a narrowly defined interest or perspective that is cold yet polite. Cult of the cold would not fly so using the word civil gives it a "can't do anything wrong" feel. One is certainly civil if they are in a group called civilization. It is like being in a club that is called "We are great". Who does not want to be in a club called "We are great." One feels better about joining a cult that has a nice flashy name that makes one feel good when they say it.

The antonym of civil is militant. What this means is anyone who is against civilization is automatically a militant. A cult has a narrowly defined interest or perspective and anything that falls outside of that narrowly defined interest or perspective is deemed a threat and in this case a militant. One cannot be civilized and be against civilization so anyone against the narrowly defined interests or perspectives is automatically a militant, an outlaw, a pirate or an outcast.

If civilization instead took the word "good" to label itself and someone said something against this group called "good" then they would automatically be assumed to be bad. This is a complex mind game. The cult labels itself a pleasing name so anyone who speaks against the cult is assumed to be the opposite of that pleasing name and that name is a displeasing label. If one calls their self "good" and someone speaks against them then that person must be bad.

So civil means cold yet polite. One definition of polite is socially superior and refined. So anyone who speaks against civilization is socially inferior and the antonym of refined is vulgar or Neanderthal. The moment the label civilized is thrown on anything, and it is attacked, the attacker becomes vulgar. This is why the cult has no flaws in its armor except for one. It's not possible one can attack something that is called polite and come out looking polite. The label civil in civilization relates to one thing alone. At one time there was not a civilization and then there was civilization and it was considered superior to everything else or to what was before civilization. If one wants to start a cult simply call it "superior to everything else" and everyone will jump on that boat.

The problem with civil is it has that word polite associated with it and polite has the words socially superior relative to it and superior is relative to the observer. Anything a human being does that is not accepted by the narrow minded views of civilization is socially inferior. If civilization accepts cutting down a forest to make money and any human being in the world speaks out against that they are deemed socially inferior. This is just a generic example of how labeling something to be good means anything that doesn't fit into that label is bad. The cult will never suggest it is bad because then if someone attacks it, that person will be considered good. The cult suggests it is civil so if anyone attacks it they will be considered militant. This strategy is how the cult keeps its members in line. If you are not civil then you are militant or vulgar. That is not reality because the most civil person has moments of vulgarity and the most vulgar person has moments of civility and because of this the word civilization is not accurate.

As long as the cult members are fed the proper words they keep dancing and so the words are part of the control mechanism. Many cult members would kill their self if they woke up tomorrow and saw the newspaper headlines that said their name followed by evil. 'So and so is evil." Many cult members would also kill to wake up and see their name in the headlines, "So and so is a saint." What a person has to do to be labeled a saint tends to be evil.

In some wars of civilization, soldiers are labeled heroes for killing so many of the "enemy". Some cops are labeled heroes for arresting so many of their fellow citizens. Relative to some, civilization rewards people for being evil.

The CEO of a company in civilization may get great rewards for opening a sweatshop in a third world country and saving the company millions of dollars because they only have to pay people in the factory twenty five cents an hour.

Civilization is not so much superior as it is dominate. The law in the world is based on civilizations laws and so any laws that are not accepted by civilization are deemed inferior laws not because they are inferior but because they are inferior laws because civilization has taken the word civil law. The very word civil suggests everything is proper and polite.

Civilization can destroy everything in its path and those deeds will be understood to be righteous and polite just because civilization is socially superior to everything else, and even if it is not socially superior it still is socially superior because it is called civilization. The word themselves are simply mind tricks that work on weak minds. - 4:06:43 AM

11/3/2009 2:56:28 PM – Relativity is one of the most interesting concepts in the universe. Relative to the vast majority of human beings on the planet I am a fool. Relative to the vast majority of human beings that have mastered the written language rules, I am retarded. I find that fascinating and true. It is important to understand why I am retarded, relative to the vast majority of human beings on the planet. If I was just retarded since birth that would be one thing but I am not retarded from birth. I didn't get into a major car accident and smash my brain in and lose my ability to use written language. I didn't experience physical trauma and then lose my ability to use written language properly relative to the accepted norms in civilization.

I had a split second experience mentally and then I became retarded relative to the vast majority of human beings on the planet, relative to using the written language "properly". There is a quality about that reality that does not add up. Whether what happened to me is a miracle or a nightmare is strictly relative to the observer. It is perhaps difficult for a person to conform to a world that judges a person's intelligence based on how well that person can use a manmade invention called written language.

Written language is not a naturally occurring thing. Nature does not adjust a person's genetics so they will be able to use written language and this is why written language must be taught. Written language is a new invention and so a person is not prone to be able to use written language so they must be conditioned to use written language.

There is something about written language that is abnormal to a human being and because of this it requires many years of conditioning to get a human beings mind comfortable with using the manmade invention written language.

A small child will sometimes write a written language character backwards. A teacher will notice that character and scold that child and explain to that child that character is backwards or improper. Improper is a huge word because proper and improper is relative to the observer. So that child writes a character backwards and that is improper relative to what? That character is improper relative to the norms of civilization. If that child does not write characters properly relative to the norms of civilization that child is vulgar or inferior or retarded, hindered mentally.

Civilization does not send children to school to become proper relative to being absolutely proper but only to become proper relative to the norms of civilization, the cult.

I had a split second mental experience and I became retarded relative to the norms of civilization. Relative to one who can no longer use written language properly, I became retarded. I became one of the most retarded human beings in the history of mankind accidentally, relative to my ability to use written language properly, based on what civilization has determined is properly. Another way to look at it is, I negated the many years of conditioning called education and I reverted back to sound mind and those with a sound mind are not able to use written language properly because the ability to use written language properly is a symptom of an unsound mind.

That is a pretty big can of worms. There is no bigger can of worms in this universe and my middle name is can of worms. How much money should I be asking for? How much money is a fair amount to compensate me for being brainwashed into mental hell by civilization under the guise of education? Will 100 trillion dollars compensate me fairly for 35 odd years spent in mental hell induced by civilization under the guise of education? Relative to me I was retarded and now I am wise and relative to you I was wise and now I am retarded. Relative to a blind man, I am blind because I see. - 3:31:32 PM

5:41:22 PM – If a person drinks a bottle of vodka it alters their perception until the vodka wears off. This altered state of perception is called drunk. One can argue that drinking a bottle of vodka alters perception temporarily. If a person drinks a bottle of vodka everyday for a year and then stops drinking for a year, at the end of that second year they will not be drunk because the vodka would be fully out of their system. So this class of perception altering things, drugs in this case, is a temporary altering of perception.

There is another class of perception altering things and these things alter perception permanently. In this instance permanently means there are no drugs involved so the perception altering is essentially permanent. This is what some would call brainwashing. Brain washing is essentially altering a person's perception without using drugs so that when the altering of perception is achieved it is essentially permanent or requires a great shock to negate. One can accidentally become brain washed if they experience a traumatic event and from that point on when the experience a similar traumatic event they may react in odd ways.

If a person has a bad experience with heights when they are at heights they act strange. If a person has a bad experience in a car when they get in a car they may act strange. If a soldier has a bad experience in combat with loud sounds when they hear loud sounds they may act strange. So brain washing is not only intentionally altering how one behaves but also accidentally altering how one behaves. So in this case these people act strange when certain stimuli is encountered because they had a traumatic experience relative to said stimuli.

So the reaction these people have around said stimuli is forever altered unless they do something to condition their self out of the accidental brain washing.

Altering a person's perception intentionally to achieve an end goal is what tyranny of the mind is. If a person is conditioned to be afraid permanently then that person can be controlled using fear tactics. If a person has their perception altered so they are afraid permanently they can be controlled permanently using fear tactics. What exactly would that be considered on a scale of a crime against a person?

If it is a crime to put a hit of LSD in a person's drink without them knowing and it alters their perception temporarily, then it must be a greater crime to alter ones perception permanently, but it is not a greater crime in fact it is not a crime at all relative to civilization, the cult.

If I spike your drink with LSD and you end up harming yourself it is my fault and I am accountable. If I condition you so you do not think clearly, using non drug method's, and you end up harming yourself I am not responsible or at fault, relative to civilization, the cult. Something about that does not add up. One can get a urine test to prove someone spiked their drink with LSD but someone cannot prove their perception was altered using non drug methods.

How would you know for a fact you were not brainwashed as a child using non drug methods to permanently alter your perception? The only way you would know is if you accidentally cancelled the altered perception or broke free of the altered perception, brainwashing. If one accidentally broke free of this brainwashing they would wake up to the fact they were brainwashed but outside of that there is no other way to tell one was brainwashed as a child.

If one gets brainwashed a child they cannot tell because they never felt what not being brainwashed is like because they never got a chance to mature mentally before they were brainwashed. So I will ask again. How do you know for a fact you were not brainwashed as a child? Are you going to suggest you trust everyone around you that they would not brainwash you as a child? Who on this earth would brainwash a child? Whoever would brainwash a child must be the most vile evil sinister persona in the universe. Is that your logic for knowing for a fact you were not brainwashed? Do you think evil is obvious or evil is subtle?

Would you submit if someone did brainwash you as a child and it totally altered your perception permanently they could be considered evil? If a child is given something that alters their perception permanently is it the child's fault? What I am suggesting is as a child something altered your perception to such a devastating yet subtle degree nothing you have done in your entire life since the perception altering conditioning is what you would do, or think, if you did not get the perception altering event as a child. What that means is every single thing you have done since about the age of twelve or earlier is a direct symptom someone or something altered your perception permanently and you do not even know it.

Certainly one such as I could not discover something accidentally that would shatter your entire universe. For a one such as I to discover something that would alter your perception of the world forever would be on the scale of impossibility. It would be on the scale of a miracle that a one such as I could discover something accidentally that would shatter your perception of the world to such an extreme you would deny it was true to save yourself from imploding mentally.

What would you do if civilization was simply a cult that alters children's minds so they can be easily controlled using fear tactics and you are one of the children that civilization has altered? Who exactly would you call to complain? Would you be calling the police, the government or the court system? They are all part civilization. Are you only using 10% of your mind because that is how nature intended it or because that is how one's mind is after they get the brainwashing from civilization, the cult, as a child?

The only way you would ever know your were brainwashed as child is if one your friends woke up from the brainwashing by accident and tried to explain to you that is the reality. That is your only hope in the universe that one of your friends wakes up from the brainwashing and tries to let you know you were also brainwashed.

The cult would not have brainwashed you in the first place if they gave a dam about you to begin with. Would something evil condition a mind that is at 100% power down to 10% power or would something good condition a mind that is at 100% power down to 10% power? That is a philosophical question. Relative to a slave master it is good to condition a mind down to 10% power so that person, slave, is easier to control.

Perhaps you first have to ask if I am writing these books to control your mind or free your mind. You do not know me and you certainly will never see me and I only have a high school education so there is no reason for you to believe anything I say ever. I do not even know how to use commas properly since the accident. I do not even know how to use the written language properly. Every single poorly disguise thick pamphlet diary I write would be given an F by an English teacher.

I published this book so that essentially proves I am not wise because I am picking a fight with civilization by doing so. I am trying to communicate to six billion people this written language invention actually hinders the mind drastically and in turn, does not make one wise. I do not even write books about anything but that, and that proves something I am quite certain. - 6:47:52 PM

9:01:18 PM – How does one go about making a sound mind sound? Education is based on the premise the mind is unsound and after its gets education it is sound. One can play the details and suggest the mind is not as sound as it should be, so one gets education then they have a sounder mind. One can also suggest when a human is born they are stupid and then they get education and they are wise. Education as in written language and math is manmade and that is a big red flag or it should be.

It is easy to understand many manmade things have good sides and bad sides. There is a long list of things mankind has invented that started off having only good side effects and ended up having lots of bad side effects also. Mankind invented liquor. Mankind invented guns. Mankind invented nuclear energy. Mankind invented penicillin. Mankind invented chain saws. Mankind invented pesticides. Mankind invented religion. Mankind invented politics. Mankind invented prisons. Mankind invented written language. All of these things have good aspects to them and all of these things have unintended bad aspects to them, except written language.

Written language is the one invention that mankind is convinced has no possible bad side effects at all. That is a huge red flag. It seems quite strange mankind could actually invent something that only has good aspects and no bad aspects at all, because that sounds pretty supernatural to me. It must be a miracle of all creation that mankind could invent something that has all good aspects and not one single bad aspect to it. Written language must be the miracle of all miracles. Mankind must be supernatural because they created something that is perfect in every way possible. Mankind split atoms but that had some bad side effects called nuclear waste. Mankind invented politics but that had some bad side effects called taxes and revolution. Mankind invented religion but that had some bad side effects called holy wars and religious persecution. Mankind invented chainsaws and that was fine until people started leveling forests that took fifty years to grow, in a week.

Mankind invented pesticides and that was fine until the pesticides leaked into the water supply and harmed anything that drank that water. Seems to me mankind screws things up as well as they screw things down when they start inventing things. But then we have written language and there is nothing that could possibly be bad about that. If there was anything bad about written language we are screwed because we are encouraging everyone to eat of it, so to speak, so there better not be anything wrong with written language. There better not be anything wrong with education because if there is, we are doomed. - 9:21:41 PM

When words are illegal thoughts are illegal so revolution is legal.

When a law makes words illegal it makes thoughts illegal which makes that law unlawful.

A law can discourage one from stealing but cannot discourage one from thinking about stealing.

When thinking is discouraged slavery is complete.

One who is afraid of their thoughts is afraid of everything.

One cannot be expected to censor their words and thus their thoughts because of how someone else may or may not react to them.

One who fears words should be avoided because you may use a word they are afraid of and they may in turn deem you to be a threat.

If a group of words are illegal to say then whoever invented them should be punished when they are used.

Doing improper things properly tends to be less costly than doing proper things improperly.

Rules do not make one safe because they limit ones options and this makes one unsafe.

11/4/2009 2:16:11 AM - Marie Curie was a scientist and she was pleased to experiment. She worked with elements that were radioactive. She died of a condition called aplastic anemia and that is a condition where the bone marrow does not create sufficient new cells to replenish blood cells. This condition can be caused by radiation exposure and in her case was certainly the cause of her death. Marie Curie was not aware experimenting with radiation without protection could lead to death. The effects of ionizing radiation were not yet known to anyone so it was not that Marie Curie was ignorant to understood knowledge it was really she was not aware because this knowledge was not understood by anyone at that time.

Cause and effect relationships are not uniform. For example if a person puts their hand on a stove they learn in an instant the cause and effect relationship. It took Marie Curie many years of working with radiation to understand the cause and effect relationship. There are many cause and effect relationships relative to mankind that are understood swiftly and then there are some that are still not understood. Some of mankind's greatest inventions are equally its most damaging.

There was one invention that started civilization and because this invention ushered in civilization it was never questioned to have a damaging cause and effect relationship. This invention is relative to being saved from a burning building by someone and then suggesting that person can do no wrong. This invention is relative to the concept of being too good to be true. The invention was so good if anyone suggested there were problems with the invention they were laughed at and mocked. This is an indication of the complexity of cause and effect relationships.

If there is a very good invention one tends to be a bit slothful in finding faults with it. There couldn't be anything wrong with asbestos because it is such a good insulator. This is just an example of how sometimes one is so focused on the good aspects of an invention they are closed minded to the fact the invention may have damaging aspects.

Written language is not a lack of awareness Marie Curie type of situation. Human beings have been attempting to suggest to the species the major damaging effects of written language and math, the tree of knowledge, for over five thousand years so it is very complex in relation to what happened to these beings who tried to explain these damaging effects, and in relation to why they were ignored for five thousand years. One issue to ponder is how on earth did an invention with such damaging effects on those who subscribed to it go unnoticed for five thousand years. Perhaps it is an illusion that it went unnoticed. Perhaps the warnings did not go unnoticed they simply went unheeded or perhaps were covered up. It is possible mankind invented something that destroyed mankind five thousand years ago. - 2:51:51 AM

5:26:09 PM-

[Galatians 4:16 Am I therefore become your enemy, because I tell you the truth?]

I am suggesting a great truth and you may not be pleased with a great truth and so you may assume I am your enemy because the great truth I speak of may perhaps shatter your world.

I am not suggesting supernatural because I am not a sorcerer. I am not suggesting you pay homage to me. I am not suggesting you follow me. I am not suggesting you tell anyone I even tell you this great truth.

I prefer you tell people you came up with the great truth on your own. I am not suggesting you pay me money for the great truth. I am not suggesting you give me awards for telling you the great truth. I am not suggesting there are rules you must follow. I am not suggesting you believe the great truth I tell you, because disbelief will not change anything.

I am not your enemy, I am your friend but the great truth may shatter your world perception and that may make you assume I am harming you, and that may make you assume I am your enemy.

I accidentally discovered the great truth so I did not do anything intentionally. My intention was not to discover the great truth but I did discover the great truth so it was an accident. If I convince the species of the great truth it will be purely accidental. I cannot try to convince you because no other being has ever convinced civilization of the great truth.

The species as a whole has never been convinced of the great truth so if I try, I will harm myself. I understand if I convince you of the great truth it will shatter your perception of the world and you may perceive that will harm you. I am not against civilization because civilization is made up of humans and humans are my friends. I am not against technology. I am not against music or words or ideals. I am not about making more rules and laws I am about making less rules and laws. All the rules and laws do is isolate us into little separate cages. I am open minded to the fact there perhaps does not need to be anymore rules and laws than there are now and perhaps maybe a few less rules and laws.

None of the ancient texts were ever about making more rules and laws because rules and laws are the fruits of the tyrant not the fruits of the free. Laws and rules do not create wisdom they encourage fear. Rules hold one back because one has a thought and then they say "That thought goes against the rules".

Are you making the rules or are you just a slave to the rules suggested to you? Is our goal a species to create so many rules we are nothing but slaves to the rules we create so in turn we make ourselves slaves? Rules are not made to protect you they are made to control you. I do not want to control you because I do not detect you need to be controlled.

Sometimes a person does something that appears to be unsafe but ends up being very safe. Sometimes a person does something that appears to be against the norms of

in your face? What if everyone was giving children cigarettes and when you warned them they laughed in your face? What if everyone was sacrificing children's minds and when you warned them they laughed in your face? What would you do if every adult in the world liked to mentally rape children except you, but they outnumbered you six billion to one, what would you do? What if six billion people we not aware they liked to mentally rape children and they had all the weapons and all the laws on their side and there was just you aware of it, and you were trying to stop it, and when you told them about it they laughed in your face because they knew you could not doing anything about it?

What if there was nothing in the universe you could do but watch the children be mentally raped by the six billion people who also were mentally raped as children and in turn did not know what they were doing to the children? What if I told you children are being mentally raped on an industrial scale and you were one of them and you were mentally blinded so you would not be able to see what was going on? Do you think your money is going to save you from this situation? A wise being once said "Health is important." That wise being was Buddha and the reason he said that is because he negated the ill effects of education and he had to watch children being mentally raped by the education every single day and he had to remind himself that health was important because all he wanted to do was get away from here. Do you know where you are at? Do you know what you are after you get the education? I am very out of context because I just assume you know everything I know and that is my greatest delusion.

I just assume everyone knows what the education does to a child's mind. That is bad for me to assume that because my perception tells me there is no time and so I find it difficult to figure out what patience is. I will attempt to explain that.

My mind tells me there is no time since the accident about a year ago relative to a calendar, so how long do you think I have been aware education mentally ruins children? What do you think I think when I hear "We have raised money to educate the children." If you have a mentally hindered, brainwashed being teaching people how to use guns, you are going to have a lot of people blowing their brains out. That is what I think when I hear "We have raised money to educate the children."

[Matthew 19:14 But Jesus said, Suffer little children, and forbid them not, to come unto me: for of such is the kingdom of heaven.]
One wise being summed it up "Suffer little children". Who exactly is making the children suffer?
[Genesis 11:5 And the LORD came down to see the city and the tower, which the children of men builded.]
The men are making children suffer. What is a man in relation to this text?
[Revelation 4:7 And the first beast was like a lion, and the second beast like a calf, and the third beast had a face as a man, and the fourth beast was like a flying eagle.]

[and the third beast had a face as a man] = man in relation to these texts is a beast.

What is a beast? Is a bear a beast? There is something in this line that is very delicate. One has to look at this line very carefully to see the slight difference.

[And the first beast was like a lion]

[and the second beast like a calf]

[and the third beast had a face as a man]

[and the fourth beast was like a flying eagle.]

Notice the word like. Like a lion, like a calf, like a flying eagle but then it does not say like a man it says had a face of a man.

This is the face of a man [Genesis 11:5 And the LORD came down to see the city and the tower, which the children of men builded.] = A man turning his children into slaves to build towers.

Does a parent educate their children for the child's sake or for the parent's sake? Isn't it every parents dream to tell their friends their child is an A student? There are bumper stickers that say "My child is an A student or is on the honor role." So a parent is bragging openly how well they have educated their child or had their child educated.

X = written language and math makes a person wise.

Y = written language and math does not make a person wise but in fact mentally hinders their mind.

Z = parents bragging about their child's grades

A = parents punishing their child for poor grades

B = bad

C = good

$X + Z = C$

$Y + Z = B$

$X + A = C$

$Z + A = B$

If X is true then Z is C. What this means is that parent who brags about how well their child is doing in education is convinced beyond a shadow of a doubt that education does this [Genesis 3:6 And when the woman saw that the tree was good for food,… and a tree to be desired to make one wise,…] Makes one wise.

I will suggest education, written language, reading and math does not make one wise but in fact mentally hinders one if taught improperly. I will suggest any parents who brags about how well their child is doing in school is bragging about how well they are mentally hindering their own child. There are only two things in the universe that mentally rape children knowingly or unknowingly or support the mental rape of children knowingly or unknowingly, a sinister persona or a lunatic. I am on the fence about whether civilization is a sinister persona or a lunatic.

One of these wise being suggested you are a lunatic. [Luke 23:34 Then said Jesus, Father, forgive them; for they know not what they do. And they parted his raiment, and cast lots. [for they know not what they do] = lunatic

A lunatic is insane and they know not what they do, so one has to be forgiving because a lunatic harms things but does not perceive they harm things, so they are without a soul or a conscience. A lunatic will mentally rape a child and then put a bumper sticker on their car and tell the world they did good. A lunatic does not have a conscience so one has to keep that in mind before making any judgments.

Now another wise being suggested a sinister persona [Genesis 3:14 And the LORD God said unto the serpent, [Because thou hast done this], thou art cursed above all cattle, and above every beast of the field; upon thy belly shalt thou go, and dust shalt thou eat all the days of thy life:]

[Because thou hast done this(learned written language and math)] = [God said unto the serpent]

This is very complicated.

X = lunatic
Y = serpent
Z = mentally hinders children
A = severe punishment
B = kept away from children

X + Z = B
Y + Z = A

I will explain this swiftly because you will you will not believe it anyway. Written language and reading and math are sequential based. Learning how to spell is simply arranging letters in the proper sequential order. ABC's are in sequential order and that is the first thing a child learns is their ABC's, the alphabet of the language they are learning. Writing sentences relies on arranging words in proper sequence, nouns, adjective, adverbs and so on. Using commas relies on seeing a sentence as parts. Sequencing and seeing things as parts are left brain attributes.

Math relies on sequencing as in 1, 2, 3…. When one is doing math they are sequencing to figure out the answer to the math equation. Both math and written language rely on many rules. Rules are left brain orientated. So we have sequencing, rules and determining parts and those are all fundamental basics for education, and those are all left brain aspects. One might attempt to use their sequential logic they have been left with after the brainwashing and suggest X amount of years of this sequencing, fortified with heavy reward systems for doing well at it cannot possibly harm the mind that much.

[Luke 17:29 But the same day that Lot went out of Sodom it rained fire and brimstone from heaven, and destroyed them all.]

Five hundred years or more after Abraham and Lot slaughtered that city and everyone in it that was encouraging this invention, written language and math on the children Luke was still talking about it. Two thousand years after Luke spoke about it I am bringing it up again. There are some in the world who understand how to apply the education properly without ruining the mind of the child. You are not one them and everyone you know is not one of them. It is more of an oral education not a written education, which is accepted everywhere of course. My intuition suggests you are not going to stop mentally hindering children. My intuition suggests if you didn't figure it out in five thousand years you are never going to figure it out. I figured it out by accident but that still counts.
[John 8:43 Why do ye not understand my speech?..]

What would do this to a person to the point where they cannot understand. I do not perceive I am saying anything complex yet I am aware you cannot understand what I am saying or understand the spirit of what I am saying. I cannot tell you what I understand because you perhaps cannot understand what I tell you. You have an inner voice and sometimes when you are sad or depressed it tells you something is not right with this world. This voice has been pushed into the background of your mind and it is a questioning voice.

I am not suggesting when you were born you were in the state of mind you are now. I am suggesting after many years of this education your mind was slowly altered and so was mine. I was in the state of mind you are now and I had to face death, which is not reasonable, to get out of that state of mind.

It is important you understand how I got out of the state of mind you are in, and I am pleased to talk about myself because I understand the alternative. The most important thing you can take away from how I got out of the brainwashing is to be mindful I did not get out of it because of physiological trauma.
I did not get hit by car or have a stroke. Nothing physiologically happened and that means something mentally took place.

This technique to break out of the brainwashing is relative to the reverse thing.
[Luke 17:33 Whosoever shall seek to save his life shall lose it; and whosoever shall lose his life shall preserve it.]
Seeking to save your life when you perceive you may die is reasonable, in reverse world.

[and whosoever shall lose his life shall preserve it.] This comment is saying one has to die to live. That does not make any sense, in reverse world. So one is sitting somewhere and they perceive they are going to die and then they do not run so they submit to dying, and then they live. That is not reasonable, in reverse world. Abraham was holding a knife over Isaac and Isaac did not run. That is not reasonable in reverse world.

[and whosoever shall lose his life shall preserve it.] Whoever dies lives. If whoever dies lives then the word [life] in the above comment is really death. Whoever shall lose his death state of mind shall preserve his life state of mind. Whoever shall lose his unsound mind, brain washed state of mind, shall preserve his sound mind.

[John 8:43 Why do ye not understand my speech?]

Simply put, you were born and your mind was in the life state of mind, sound mind, and then you got educated and your mind was bent to the left, and you went to the dead state of mind, extreme left brain state of mind, unsound mind and in order to get back to sound mind you have to trick that unsound mind into dying.

One might suggest it is quite vain to take a child of sound mind and condition them into an unsound state of mind and put a burden on that child where they have to defeat their fear of death in order to just get back to where they were before the education.

Education is inanimate. Written language and math are not alive and they do not harm on their own. Education is a tool like a gun and in the hands of a skilled teacher education is a good tool and in the hands of an unskilled teacher education is a nightmare. You are not a skilled teacher and no one you know is a skilled teacher in relation to administering this tool called education.

The deep reality of this situation is right brain has a lot of ambiguity which is doubt. I have lots of doubt since the accident. I do not doubt petty things. I doubt the big things. One of those big things is I doubt you can apply this [and whosoever shall lose his life shall preserve it.].

You understand for over five thousand years we have been educating ourselves with this tool to the extent ones who do not get this education are looked at as stupid, and discriminated against.

If you do not get education you get a slave job. You have to go to school and cannot drop out until you are sixteen. You are conditioned by about the age of 10. By about the age of twelve or so one start to gets very self conscious, shy, embarrassed and civilization calls that puberty. Kids start killing their self around the age of fourteen and some sooner. The conditioning is too much and their emotions are turned up so high and so fast one might suggest they decide not to go on with the mental rape.

I am not sad about that because I understand cause and effect and my emotions have been essentially purged at this stage since the accident. If I write these books and for example a someone who understands the mind gets a hold of them and starts doing research and figures out what I am saying is absolute truth, which it is, what do you think is going to happen relative to civilization compensating people for doing this to them?

Because of this [John 8:13 Why do ye not understand my speech?] I am in a situation where if I explain it too well I perhaps get killed and if I do not explain it well enough I fail my purpose.

My mind is unable to feel anything but neutral about that. Perhaps I should be trying to save myself by keeping my mouth shut but that response is contrary to my purpose. One might suggest if someone discovers something it becomes their purpose to explain it to others. There of course is a lot of room in that comment for magnitude. My purpose is gargantuan. I am mindful to avoid suggesting supernatural because I am dealing with people who are hardly able to understand cause and effect relationships in reality. Supernatural is out of my league.

X = 10 – 12 years of sequential heavy education which is left brain relative
Y = a child's mind that is not fully developed
Z = a very left brain leaning state of mind
X + Y = Z

Is this trivial to you? Z = a very left brain leaning state of mind

When I went to school they never told me the education would make me simple minded. When I went to school they never told me the education would make me hallucinate. Did they tell you the education would make you simple minded and hallucinate? I am curious why the government and the board of education does not at least tell the child the education makes them simple minded and makes them hallucinate.

Life is very difficult if one is simple minded and on top of that hallucinating. What are you going to do when I convince you education made you simple minded and made you hallucinate? What are you going to do after I convince you and you seek compensation for being put in this state of mind by "the powers that be" and they tell you to go to hell? What exactly did you do to upset someone to the point they conditioned you into a simple minded state of mind to the point you hallucinate? I lean to the side just being born is why they did it to me. Perhaps they did it to you because you were born. Maybe that is ones reward for being born, they get conditioned by civilization, the cult, into a simple minded state of mind to the point they hallucinate.

I should be sleeping but I tend to write my books when I try to sleep. I feel there is always one more thing I need to say or to suggest. I am working on coming up with that perfect sentences or word that is going to make the blind see. All of the good sentences have already been taken. I am not very effective because I am zero for six billion. I am zero for six billion. I have not convinced anyone to break this brainwashed state of mind the education has put them in and I have been at it for infinity relative to my perception.

I understand what John meant by this [John 8:43 Why do ye not understand my speech?] I am not telling you I am great I am telling you I am late. I do not see any reason to become physically violent over this mental child raping because I do not see physical violence will solve it because I am mindful it is too late. I do not want you to get the impression I would not slaughter people to protect children. It is just I do not see that would solve anything because whatever this education has done to our minds as a collective species is so powerful it is unstoppable.

It is beyond my ability to stop yet I cannot accept that and I will not accept that. How do I explain what I had to do to get out of this state of mind? I try to recall what I had to do to get out of this brainwashed state of mind accidentally, but at this stage it is hard for me to relate to because the time stamps and the emotions are gone from the memories.

When the sane recall a memory they have a timestamp and an emotion attached to it and that creates suffering. If you ever thought to yourself something like "I wish I was still with that person." or " I wish things were like they use to be." That is a form of coveting and also longing and thus suffering.

I recall to get out of this brainwashed state of mind the education caused I had to suffer a lot but now I do not relate to the concept of suffering. I can suggest I was depressed and suicidal at about 15 and the accident happened on my final suicide attempt at the age of 40. You may be able to understand that time span but I can no longer relate to that time span so I cannot perceive that length of suffering. It is very complex because the way I explain it makes it seem like education is the only problem but the reality is everyone gets the education and they in turn instill their "fruits" into any child they are around. You do not know anyone who didn't get the education, would be a better way to look at it. You only know people that "have it" and you can use your creativity to define "have it" even though creativity is a right brain aspect so you will not do very go at that.

You actually have to do some drugs to get any creative juices flowing because that thing in your head called right brain is essentially veiled by the time you are about 14 due to the education. Ironically that's about the time the youth starts doing drugs and kids start killing their self. Simply put at 12 to 14 is when the left brain is so pronounced from all the sequential left brain education the human being is fully of unsound mind or starts showing signs of insanity.

In reality doing drugs are simply a symptom that a person wants to feel the right brain. Creativity, complexity, deep thoughts. Some call it a spiritual experience and some just want to escape this left brain extreme state of mind the education leaves them in, and of course many end up dying because of it or worse being thrown in jail by the very civilization, cult, who put them in that extreme left brain state to begin with by way of the education being taught improperly.

You may perceive I am writing these books to save you but I am not trying to save you. I do not have any desire, so I do not have any desire to save you. Desire is relative to time. Desire is a craving. One who applies the remedy, mentally cannot sense time so they arc in thc now or the machine state so they just do without this desire concept attached.

The truth about these books I write is I do not remember exactly what I write after I am finished at all. I recall the spirit of what I write about but no details or actual sentences or phrases. What that means is you are the only one who remembers what I write in my books. I will explain that neurologically.

Left brain is very good at short term memory and right brain is like an absent minded professor or is good at long term memory. Relative to one who is brainwashed they understand their subconscious stores all the long term memories, that is right brain, but it is veiled in ones who get the education and have not applied the remedy. If one is in equal 50/50 mind they remember a small bit of short term but long term memory is fantastic. Granted that explanation sounds like I am mentally challenged yet I assure you I pray for ignorance.

Some in the reverse world would consider a person lacking ignorance rather dangerous. I can suggest I am accidentally lacking ignorance but that perhaps would not appease them.

There is a problem with me writing these books because there is a chance I will condition myself back into the brainwashed state if I write too much because I tend to try to correct my spelling and use commas but on the other hand it has not worked so far. There are people who spend their whole life and lots of money trying to reach this neutral, nirvana, sound state of mind and I am actually flirting to see if I can get out of this state of mind. My reason for this experimenting is because I have all these poorly disguised thick pamphlet diaries explaining how I can get back to this state mind if I do leave this state of mind from writing too much.

I am mindful I could make money off of this discovery. I am mindful I could go on speaking tours. I am mindful I would perhaps do better in person explaining this situation. I am mindful it may appear like I am afraid of going in the public spot light. Two months after the accident my intuition suggested I write infinite books and never show my face in public spot light and that is the decision and that is not going to change. I have an aversion to money because that is why I tried to kill myself. Somehow I hate money and I would rather die than deal in money and that is because it caused me to harm myself so that is permanent and that is my problem.

I perceive not showing my face is for the simple reason, some will want to see what I look like and I will do my best to make sure they never see what I look like and that is a nice emotional conditioning tool for them. Maybe some hate what I say and they want to see me so they can say "He looks like I thought he would." or maybe some like what I say and they want to see me so they can say "He looks like he is telling the truth." and I will do best to not allow either to say these things. I had to defeat my fear of death to break the brainwashing caused by education so all of these worldly endeavors are difficult for me to relate to at all anymore.

There is a concept about depressed or sad people being easy to manipulate. It is a strange concept because it seems to be one thing the reverse world and the real world have in common. One is not going to get out of the brainwashed state of mind if they are arrogant or content. The reason for this is one who is depressed or sad is depressed or sad because they are aware something is wrong, they are aware of the brainwashing just not consciously.

I read today about a family of four and it was what they call a murder suicide where one of the adults killed their spouse and their two children. They would have perhaps been good candidates for this [and whosoever shall lose his life shall preserve it.] and perhaps they took that technique a bit too literal. Never assume I am suggesting you kill yourself literally. You have been abused enough by civilization. You have been beaten down enough by this civilization, cult that wanted to make you wise using their proven tool called education.

I do not write my books for the arrogant and the ones who love the world. If one loves the ways of the cult, civilization, they should go have their eyes examined because I may not be able to cure that extent of blindness. I am mindful I am really only writing for people who are depressed or suicidal. I am mindful to communicate to them they are not depressed and suicidal, they are simply a bit more aware something is wrong than others. Perhaps I am trying to reach myself. Perhaps I would suggest to someone depressed and suicidal you are far more aware than most, about things. The ones who are not openly depressed and suicidal tend to be very depressed and suicidal but it comes out in different ways. The ones who are openly depressed and suicidal are starting to lose ego because they are not hiding the fact something is wrong. Simply put they tend to be past the point of giving a dam if someone knows they are depressed or suicidal and that in fact is a good sign relative to reality but is not a good sign relative to reverse world.

The ego which is pride is devastating and this is brought on by the education brainwashing. A little child does not have an ego and that is not because they are stupid that is because they have not started the conditioning yet. An adult would not do certain things a child would do because their ego or pride would stop them. I write books explaining how six billion people are in deep neurosis and that perhaps is making me lots of enemies but I do have the ability mentally to feel what that means and the worst that can happen is civilization will kill me and I do not mind repeat performances.

If one does not mind getting killed for telling the truth then there is no point in not telling the truth. Perhaps I should tone down my message but I understand that it is difficult to do this [and whosoever shall lose his life shall preserve it.] and whether I put lots of sugar on this [and whosoever shall lose his life shall preserve it.] or come out and say it, my chances of success as a whole are still zero for six billion.

I already understand everyone who ever suggested this waking up remedy failed as a whole and I have already decided to write infinite books before I realized that so I am just failing well. I will fail and make the ancient ones look like they did well in contrast. Some of these wise beings had many disciples, people they convinced to wake up, so that makes them absolute successes compared to me.

Perhaps I just write a lot but never convince anyone of anything. Perhaps I am just trying to see if I will make good on my decision to write myself into infinity. I understand some break this brain washing in different ways and some wake up fast and some wake up slow. I went from sense of time to no sense of time in about a week. It was so profound I actually thought I would not be able to function at all again. I was mentally paralyzed and that is an indication of how powerful the machine, right brain is when it comes back online.

There are many experiences in life where one can feel a mental rush but none of them compare to when right brain comes back online. There is no sensation like feeling unveiled right brain again after it has been veiled by the education. It is so powerful I drank nine shots of vodka and felt no euphoria at all. I actually had to experiment because I could not tell how powerful it was at the time. After nine shots in a matter of minutes I noticed my motor skills were diminished but my mental clarity was not altered. Some may perceive I am bragging but not being able to feel euphoria because one is permanently in a state of euphoria, took me awhile to get use to.

What I understood from that experiment is I only got drunk before to feel right brain and since I unveiled right brain I could no longer get drunk so getting drunk or high has become irrelevant.

A person only does drugs that get them high, to escape that left brain extreme suffering state of mind caused by the education brainwashing, to escape the reality of the brainwashing state of mind. When drugs do not get them high after they escape the brainwashing, apply the remedy, they do not do drugs because drugs do not work anymore. What I am explaining here is drug addiction itself is a symptom a person is conditioned into the extreme left brain state because of education being taught improperly. I am suggesting drug addiction is a side effect of a manmade invention called written language and math, and is a mental side effect of those inventions because they are not applied or taught properly by Masters who understand the bad mental side effects of said inventions. I am not talking about ghosts or aliens or lizards. I am talking about elementary cause and effect relationships. - 7:01:09 AM

9:12:49 AM – Imagine the things I avoid telling you.

10:15:27 AM – I was trying to sleep and I glanced at the television and noticed some religious program and they were offering a necklace with the picture of Jesus on it for fifty dollars. They suggested it was love offering so they could continue their ministry. I understand what their ministry is. Profit based instead of prophet based.

One of Mohammed's last words was this "We the community of Prophets are not inherited. Whatever we leave is for charity." This is a comment that is relative to that. [Matthew 10:8 Heal the sick, cleanse the lepers, raise the dead, cast out devils: freely ye have received, freely give.] I prefer to give my writings away freely and it is not because I have morals or class. If you find anything in my writings of value you take them as your own and I will never enforce my copyright. I am mindful I cannot win and that is why I give freely. I am mindful of what I am up against and that is why I give freely. I do not want anyone to think I give freely because I have morals. Applying the remedy may take you the rest of your life and besides I figured it out by accident so I cannot imagine how I could charge for it. It is not your fault you got brainwashed so no charge.

How many times does a father kill his wife and his children because he lost his job and his income? Apparently money is worth far more than life and that is what you call civilization. Apparently money is worth more than your mind because you got the education with the understanding you would have a chance at making good money. You may or may not make good money but after just a few years of the education you are simple minded and hallucinating. If you saw your friend lying in the road would you ask him for a love offering so you could help him? It's not about morals it is about your nature in the mindset you are in. Money doesn't talk unless you're hallucinating. I do not see money any differently than a peanut shell.

Considering where I understand I am at, not having money might speed up my impermanence. Not having money in reality world is a good thing; not having money in the reverse world is bad thing. In reality world people do not kill their self when they run out of money; in the reverse world people kill their wife and their children and their self when they run out of money. I didn't have this accident because I had money; I had this accident because I didn't have money.

The sooner you realize suicides are simply people trying to escape this reverse world state of mind the education put them in the sooner you will understand one thing. They are simply trying with all their might to escape the left brain extreme state of mind the education has put them in but are not consciously aware of it. Education literally kills people if it is not administered by a Master that understands its unwanted mental side effects. You are not an expert and no one you know is an expert at administering the education, so people do not die from it. I am aware there are experts but you perhaps would just laugh in their face if they suggested education in fact hinders the mind unfavorably. You laughed in this beings face [Genesis 3:3 But of the fruit of the tree which is in the midst of the garden, God hath said, Ye shall not eat of it, neither shall ye touch it, lest ye die.] and you listened to this being instead [Genesis 3:4 And the serpent said unto the woman, Ye shall not surely die:]

[Genesis 3:5 For God doth know that in the day ye eat thereof, then your eyes shall be opened, and ye shall be as gods, knowing good and evil.]

Good and evil denotes seeing things as parts and that is a left brain trait. You will notice the serpent spoke to the woman and then she ate off the tree, and I am not suggesting anything harsh against literal women, this is simply a contrast statement because Adam would not have lasted very long if he said literal men did it. This comment is revealing.
[Genesis 3:13 And the LORD God said unto the woman, What is this that thou hast done? And the woman said, The serpent beguiled me, and I did eat.
Genesis 3:14 And the LORD God said unto the serpent, Because thou hast done this, thou art cursed above all cattle, and above every beast of the field; upon thy belly shalt thou go, and dust shalt thou eat all the days of thy life:]

[The serpent beguiled me] and beguiled means to charm, deceived and to cheat. The education veils the complex right brain and leaves one with the simple, sequential left brain state of mind so one is cheated out of their full mind. If you were told the education will make you wise and makes you lots of money you were beguiled because it made you simple minded, susceptible to fear and put you in a hallucinating, suffering state of mind. If one gets this education under the auspices of being accepted they are also charmed because they sold their mind for acceptance.

This comment is made [The serpent beguiled me, and I did eat.] and the very next comment is this [And the LORD God said unto the serpent] and that is relative to this comment : [cast out devils] [[Matthew 10:8 Heal the sick, cleanse the lepers, raise the dead, [cast out devils]: freely ye have received, freely give.]

One can look at it like one gets this education and they are then mentally unsound and thus sick, a mental leper, mentally dead or possessed by the devil and these are all one in the same.

A man killed his children and his wife over money yesterday so he was either mentally sick, mentally a leper, mentally dead or possessed by the devil and no matter what answer you pick you are right.

So here we are thousands of years after this comment was written and yesterday a guy killed his wife and his two children and civilization, the cult, is asking "Why?" and here is the answer [Genesis 3:3 But of the fruit of the tree which is in the midst of the garden, God hath said, Ye shall not eat of it, neither shall ye touch it, lest ye die.] Your disbelief does not faze me.

These ancient texts only had one simple humble suggestion to the human race and that was, "Do not mess with that invention you think makes you wise." The sane will comb out a million rules from these texts and they will follow them but they ignore the one rule that these text suggested above all one should follow. The only rule that mattered was exactly the rule they missed. This is an example of the reverse world. The one rule that these texts suggested across the board is the one rule the reverse world totally missed.

Here in reality world where I am at, that one rule [Ye shall not eat of it, neither shall ye touch it, lest ye die.] is the only rule I see in all of these texts. All other rules are in vain if one does not follow this first rule. What else is there in reality that fits these traits [Genesis 3:6 … , and that it was pleasant to the eyes, and a tree to be desired to make one wise,]

Pleasant to the eyes denotes reading and also denotes the characters are pretty and that is relative to hieroglyphics and also Hebrew relative to when the texts were written. The characters are pretty and pleasing and education is thought to make one wise. One cannot really resist that charm and that deception. It is far too strong of a charm to resist. It is too strong to resist and civilization forces it on you by law anyway and if you decide not to get it you will be rewarded with a slave job and discriminated against on the basis you did not get the education. That is what is known as forced indoctrination.

One does not have to get the education but they will be punished for not doing so in every way imaginable. Because of this reality these wise beings figured out a way one can negate the unwanted mental side effects learning the written language invention created.- 11:24:51 AM

11/6/2009 2:35:33 AM –
Inventions tend to create problems further inventions are required to fix.
The written language invention created problems mankind will never recover from.
Disharmony in a harmonious system cannot last.
Observing others suffering relies on great concentration so one does not begin to suffer also. Belief in an illusion tends to lead to suffering.
The future is often determined by the present.
A harsh reality is better than a sweet illusion.
Contradictions often suggest complexity not confusion.
It is possible everything is impossible.
Frustration is caused by the inability to control what one is unable to control.
Accomplishing nothing in life is quite an accomplishment.
When one is born the world changes and one cannot top that.
Questioning acceptability is more important than accepting without question.
A question tends to lead to an understanding so question everything.
Every answer relies on ones understanding of the question.

3:50:28 PM –
If they could see what they can't see

The glory of the violent mask
The hand they hold defeats their task

The war they win will lead to more
The sorrow sought that rider's crowd
Elegance stripped the shell remains
Buried up with covered chains

 Their battle horse the steed of time
The cutlass blade unnoticed gash
The hand was strong but crippled now
Eyes yet narrow perceptions plough

The pride is sorrow of dead man's hand
He finds no solace in his wealth
His cleverness he hides with no stealth

The steed of time lessons weak
Forget the right, forget the meek
 The piercing of the cries unheard
Understood the truth yet not the word

The belt of one pulls tighter still
The gasp for breathe denies the will
Complexity yet simple light
Forget to test if it was right

Impatience is what time delights
Swimming in the harmful lights
Perception taste like bitter tea
If they could see what they can't see

See, Me, Be - http://www.youtube.com/watch?v=zihqh-oE6sQ

8:44:30 PM –
[Leviticus 19:29 [Do not prostitute thy daughter, to cause her to be a whore]; lest the land fall to whoredom, and the land become full of wickedness.] is relative to

[Genesis 3:6 And when the woman saw that the tree was good for food, and that it was pleasant to the eyes, and a tree to be desired to make one wise, she took of the fruit thereof, and did eat, [and gave also unto her husband with her; and he did eat.]

[Do not prostitute thy daughter, to cause her to be a whore] = [she took of the fruit thereof, and did eat, and gave also unto her husband with her; and he did eat.] this comment is relative to [Genesis 3:13 And the LORD God said unto the woman, What is this that thou hast done? And the woman said, [The serpent beguiled me, and I did eat.] and this is relative to [Genesis 3:14 [And the LORD God said unto the serpent], Because thou hast done this, thou art cursed above all cattle, and above every beast of the field; upon thy belly shalt thou go, and dust shalt thou eat all the days of thy life:]

X = one who gets the education
Y = one who encourages one to get the education.

So this comment [Do not prostitute thy daughter, to cause her to be a whore] is a comment spoken by one who has broken the brainwashing caused by the education, speaking to one who got the education but did not break the curse it causes, relative to [Genesis 3:17 … cursed is the ground for thy sake;]
Only a fool or a being cursed prostitutes their own child. The wise beings who wrote these ancient texts were not speaking about prostitution as in selling one's body for sex they were speaking about selling their child's mind for the promise of a few copper pieces.

Judas sold his mind for a few copper pieces and when he realized that he killed himself. Judas did not sell Jesus down the river because Jesus broke the brainwashing/ curse so in fact Judas by turning in Jesus sold himself down the river because Jesus held the key or remedy to breaking the curse. Judas also sold everyone down the river and he could not bear that guilt. He turned in the guy with the key to breaking the brainwashing. So Jesus was a threat to the cult called civilization because he knew how to wake the people up from the brainwashing.

Civilization paid Judas some money to find this being who could wake people up from the brainwashing caused by education, so they killed Jesus because the last thing the cult wants is for people to start leaving the cult.

Every parent in the universe will say one thing to their child. "I want you to get an education so you will have a better life than I had and so you will have an easy life." That's prostitution. Every parent in the universe will say to their child "You are going to get an education so you will amount to something." That is prostitution. Every parent in the universe has been told education makes one wise relative to [Genesis 3:6 …, and a tree to be desired to make one wise,]

The parents are no longer thinking for their self they are simply assuming every single person before them accepted the education and so they will never question education at all. They are nothing but a sheep prostituting their own child for the promise of luxury and a few copper pieces.

When one prostitutes their own child this is what happens [[Leviticus 19:29 lest the land fall to whoredom, and the land become full of wickedness.] So civilization as we understand it is whoredom of wickedness and that means everyone gets the education, veils their complex right brain as a result and starts exhibiting mental symptoms which were called sins at the time of these ancient texts. So I am suggesting civilization is simply a large scale brainwashing machine to keep people simple minded and prone to great fear and thus easy to control.

I do not see the mental symptoms once one is brainwashed as sins I see them as symptoms of an unsound mind as the result of being brainwashed by this invention that is understood by every "man" on the planet to make one wise.

Avaritia (avarice/greed) – First point is greed is relative to the observer. Two greedy people will not think they are greedy. It is complicated to define greed. The easiest way to look at it is a state of mind of prolonged greed and greed is in fact lust. This is only possible for one in an unsound state of mind because one in a sound state of mind, who has broken the brainwashing/curse, has right brain unveiled and it is so powerful it will not allow the mind to remain focused on such things because it ponders way to fast, so one cannot mentally stay in a mind set of greed or lust more than a moment, relative to a clock, for example.

So these sins were not suggesting anything but psychological symptoms caused by eating off that tree of knowledge and so these sins are really symptoms or mental effects of getting taught the education, the tree of knowledge, improperly, the cause.

If one does a drug that makes them very hungry then that great hunger is a symptom of doing that drug. So that great hunger is not a sin it is a symptom one has done something to alter their perception to the degree they feel great hunger. This again is cause and effect.

If one gets many years of this left brain sequential education and does not apply the remedy to negate the altered state of mind, they exhibit symptoms and these wise beings called those symptoms, sin. Living in sin means one ate of the tree and did not apply the remedy so they are exhibiting symptoms of that, and those symptoms are called fruits of their tree and their tree is their mind.

If a person does a drug and it alters their mind so their mind tells them they are very hungry they are in fact hallucinating because their mind is telling them something that it would not be telling them if they did not do that perception altering drug. This in fact is what the education brainwashing is used for in part. It alters one's mind so one exhibits the desired fruits or behaviors.

Economics relies on people consuming things they perhaps do not need. Desire for something one does not need is called luxuria (extravagance) and this is the hallmark of an economic system. People who have been brainwashed and have not applied the remedy do some very harsh things to acquire things they really do not need. People may take advantage or harm somebody to get the money they need to buy something they don't need. The whole principle of economics is to make a product popular and make people believe they need it whether they need it or not. What this creates are people who cannot afford that product, stealing it from other people because they believe they need it and that creates crime. What this means is the economic system encourages crime. The deeper reality of that is the education brainwashing encourages the economic system. So what that means is the education brainwashing encourages crime. Deeper still, crime encourages economics.

Not that I ever get off topic but, a prison system creates jobs and the police system also creates jobs. The more laws, the more police are needed, the more prison systems are needed. If there were no laws there would be no police and there would be no prison system.

X = laws

Y = police and prisons

Z = jobs

As X increases Y increases and thus Z increases.

X + Y = Z

It is in civilizations interest to create more laws because the economic system is measured by jobs. When jobs are not available then crime goes up because people need food whether they have a job or not. People do not tend to kill their self because they get hired they tend to kill their self when they get fired. This is relative to extravagance. The more extravagance one has the harder they fall when that extravagance is in jeopardy. This gives the poor an advantage because they can never fall as far as the ones who have lots of extravagance.

It would seem a poor person would be more greedy than a rich person but in fact a rich person is more greedy than a poor person. The poor remain poor because they are not as greedy, and the rich remain rich because they are full of greed. This is complex because civilization programs everyone to be greedy and that is why civilization pushes the education on everyone. It is civilizations purpose to make sure everyone is as greedy as possible because if people are not greedy the economic system will collapse and in turn civilization will collapse.

There would be no need for civilization if there was no money. There would be no economics without money. This would mean everyone would have to supply their own needs. That is dangerous from civilizations point of view because people would have to use their mind to survive and in time they may become wise. Wisdom and civilization do not mix. The wise understand the importance of freedom so they do not run for office because they do not want to control anyone. Civilization is simply a system of controls. Civilization starts off with brainwashing a child with this education invention. The parents allow it because they were brainwashed with the education and so they can attest with education one can make money, and so they never question if there are any bad side effects to this education.

The wise beings that wrote these ancient texts understood very clearly civilization was simply a slave making machine and its draw was this invention thought to [Genesis 3:6 …, make one wise,] If there was an apple that was being sold and its selling line was "Desired to make one wise", who would not eat of it?

You ate of it and that is because our parents ate of it and their parents ate of it all the way back 5000 years.

Y = child
Z = reward
A = education

A + Y = Z

Everyone was a child and that means everyone had an adult guiding them and 5000 years ago an adult told a their child to get education to become wise and since then every adult tells a child to get education to become wise and there has never been a question about why this education is so sequential based, which is a left brain trait and why there is not equal amounts of random access education, which is right brain.

Only a person that is fearless would tell six billion people they have been brainwashed by this Trojan horse called education thought to [Genesis 3:6 make one wise,] when in reality all the education has done is made one simple minded, easy to control using fear tactics and has made one hallucinate beyond explanation.

I am writing infinite books to tell six billion people how much they are hallucinating and they are hallucinating so much they mock what I suggest. Simply put six billion people got [Genesis 3:13. Beguiled..,] and because they have been charmed their mind has so much pride and they have a large ego so they are not capable of humility for one second to consider they have been beguiled.

The ground they walk on is cursed because the ground is their mind [Genesis 3:17 … cursed is the ground for thy sake;]

Every ones bottle neck is their mind, and one's mind is relative to ones perception. The education conditions the mind far to the left so one is greedy for thing's they do not need and that keeps the economic system going and in turn civilization. Everyone knows for a fact there are human beings that live in the middle of the Amazon in small groups of perhaps 5 to 8 people and they live their whole life in the Amazon and never have any extravagance and they still have smiles on their faces at the end of the day. Do you think they are smiling because they are stupid or they are smiling because they are not cursed?

I watched a show about the ones in the Amazon and listened to them communicate and I understand they do not even hardly have sentences in their language. What I mean is they usually just use one or two words at a time. What is interesting is if a human being from civilization was put into their shoes, that human being could not survive, but if a human being from the Amazon was put into civilization they could survive.

The complexity is these beings from the Amazon could not survive in the cities they could go out into the wilderness and survive without any assistance. Of course Civilization frowns on that because in order to live in the wilderness you have to own that land, and in order to do that you have to have money to buy that land so the only people in civilization that can live on their own are what are known as transients.

Civilization despises transients and demonizes them and civilization also demonizes the ones in the Amazon. What that means is the ones in the Amazon way of life is more complex than civilizations way of life and that is a symptom civilization relies on extravagance instead of relying on their mind to survive because after they get the education their mind I unsound so they are unable to live in the wild any longer so they have been domesticated and thus caged.

The truth is civilization is nothing more than domesticated animals and they must be kept in their cages because they can no longer function in the wild. The sane will actually argue that is a good thing. The sane will argue being in a cage is a good thing and being brainwashed as a child is good thing. The sane will argue brainwashing a child and leaving that child with simple minded thoughts and emotions turned up to maximum so the child is hallucinating is a good thing. This is why the sane are in the reverse world because they see evil as goodness and goodness as evil.

If education made a person wise then everyone who got educated would be wise but that is not the case. Most that get educated are reduced to slave jobs. The vast majority of people who get education are working slave jobs. I do not consider a person who is hallucinating, wise.

Once I believed a person who was hallucinating. They suggested I was not wise enough to attend college and because I believed that hallucinating person I ended up killing myself and since then I no longer pander to hallucinating fools. If I detect wisdom in any human being involved in the accepted education system I will remind them.

[Genesis 3:6 …, and a tree to be desired to make one wise,] The sane desire wisdom because the wisdom aspect of their mind was veiled by about the time they were ten because their parents prostituted them. So essentially their parent's sacrifice them to demotic, written language. That can never be changed or taken back so one has to accept that reality and look for a way to negate that state of mind they are put into by their parents and by civilization. That is as good as it gets.

The sane wish in their hallucinating minds they could just give everyone a pill and everything would be better and it would negate the brainwashing. I could just give my books to the board of education so they would understand the error in their ways but the truth is they are hallucinating and they would just spit in my face. Essentially they are mentally dead and would see truth as lies.

Civilization does not care about making anyone wise, they care about economics and that is money. People die but money does not die, so people are expendable and money is eternal relative to the sane.

If the plans of civilization ever panned out then everyone would be free and everyone would have no reason to work a slave job. The plan of civilization is to create so much extravagance no one has to ever do anything but breathe. For this reason the mind is not important to civilization. A sharp mind may get in the way of the plans of civilization. That is one of the fatal flaws of civilizations "wisdom" education. Eventually someone wakes up and negates the education brainwashing and they want civilizations head on a platter, psychologically speaking. It is not as much of a vengeance as it is a reckoning.

Right brain does not like rules because rules hinder the complexity and pattern detection which are right brain aspects. That of course is why the taskmaster veils it in children so the child does not get any ideas about escaping their cage. It is harder to escape the cage if one cannot detect the cage.

It is always a mess when a being wakes up from the brainwashing in a certain way. [Genesis 19:25 And he overthrew those cities, and all the plain, and all the inhabitants of the cities, and that which grew upon the ground.]

Moses and Lot annihilated entire cities and every single person in those cities after they woke up. That is a symptom of how difficult it is to break the curse/brainwashing and how powerful right brain is. Right brain is more valuable than an entire city of brainwashed people. After the education one is essentially a rabid animal and they make their own children rabid because they assume without education they will only get slave jobs. It is very complex but the charm of this education is very tempting. I am pleased the sane actually keep these ancient texts in circulation considering they are simply texts, in part, explaining why the brainwashed should be killed because they keep prostituting the children because they are too mentally gone to know what they are doing, they know not what they do. If they brainwash their own children eventually the whole species will be of unsound mind and the species will all suffer as a result .If I would have broken the brainwashing and didn't have these ancient texts, I would have no model for my battle plans, would I grasshopper?

I can write that in my diary because the sane are so "sane" they cannot even imagine that is absolute fact.

Right brain is relative to creativity and thus imagination and those brainwashed had their right brain veiled at about the age of ten with the permission of their parents under the auspices of money and luxury. "Let me mentally rape your child and you might get money for it later." That is what prostitution is relative to this comment: [Leviticus 19:29 [Do not prostitute thy daughter, to cause her to be a whore; lest the land fall to whoredom, and the land become full of wickedness.]

I do not suggest the land is full of whores, I prefer to call the sane, brain dead mole crickets. It has a pleasing ring to it and is just as accurate. I perceive I just ruined this diary so I will have to write another one.

Written language and math are sequential heavy, a left brain trait, and that is called education but education is really a brainwashing tool when not taught properly. If not applied or taught properly by a master who understands the bad side effects, a person's mind is conditioned into extreme left brain state of mind. Because said education is taught to children by people who have no clue about its unwanted side effects a child is thrown into this extreme left brain state of mind before their mind is even developed.

There is a remedy to negate these unwanted mental side effects but the fact civilization just keeps doing it to children and the fact the remedy is very harsh to apply, means either civilization is infinitely more sinister than the devil or civilization is infinitely more ignorant than a rock. I understand how to explain the remedy and I understand many ways one can apply the remedy and break the brainwashing civilization has forced on them, but I am not intelligent enough to teach the education and keep a person's mind intact perhaps.

I understand this comment [Genesis 2:17 But of the tree of the knowledge of good and evil, thou shalt not eat of it: for in the day that thou eatest thereof thou shalt surely die.] is very accurate. It is perhaps best not to get mentally raped to begin with no matter how much money civilization says you will get for doing so, but civilization is far too strong now so a child has to get the education by law in most places and so the remedy is the next best thing. Simply put, one has to mentally rape their child by law because these masters who can apply the education properly are few and far between. There are none of these masters in America, that's a fact, perhaps.

If civilization is possessed and unaware it is possessed by a sinister force since it does this to children, then it is best to defeat it. If civilization is just dumber than a rock it is best to keep it in a cage and away from children. One should avoid reasoning with "it". There are in fact no other possible explanations or solutions. I should be pleased I at least broke the mental curse put on me by civilization but apparently those illusions of grandeur just never panned out because I am waging war, and the worst kind of war is a war of words because words can go far and wide and oft deep. I will now discuss something important. - 10:42:29 PM

11/7/2009 1:09:45 AM – Right brain has lots of ambiguity. Ambiguity is doubt. I have doubt about some important aspects of this accident. Based on the ancient texts, written language/the tree of knowledge conditioned me to extreme left brain and veiled right brain and I never got a chance to feel right brain all the way. Now I have accidentally unveiled right brain it is so powerful I am not use to it and so I am unable to decide if that is what I did, because right brain has lots of ambiguity. It is important for you to understand the accident so you can get an idea of who you are dealing with.

I will cover it swiftly because it is not even important to me any longer.

I took a handful of pills to kill myself and when I started to get very ill I felt this heat beam go from my neck to my toes and I thought "You need to call 911 or you will die" and then the next second I thought "No you want to die." And then I just went to sleep. So what I did is this [Luke 17:33 ; and whosoever shall lose his life shall preserve it.] I had a chance to save my life when I perceived I was going to die and I did not try to save my life so I preserved it, broke the brainwashing.

I have lots of ambiguity and "preserve it" is rather vague. There are only two options in the universe preserve it could mean. Preserve it could mean I unveiled right brain after it was veiled because of the education veiled right brain and that would be in line with the ancient texts.

Abraham suggested fear not [Genesis 15:1 After these things the word of the LORD came unto Abram in a vision, saying, Fear not, Abram: I am thy shield, and thy exceeding great reward.]

I perceived I was dying and I feared not, or I saw a knife held over my heart and I did not run so I feared not and I preserved it or one can look at it like I perceived death and I submitted to it, as in Submit.

One also could look at it like I looked a Medusa's head, death, and I turned to stone. The main point is I discovered one of two things and perhaps you are going to have to decide which one it is. I either unveiled right brain, and it is so powerful, for any human being to veil this right brain in any other human being for any reason they should certainly be punished without hesitation. That's the first possibility.

The second possibility is the fear not, submit to fear, face death and defeat ones fear of death technique tricks the mind itself into believing it has died, so the mind stops registering time, and many aspects relative to life, and one is in a mental state they are looking back at life and they understand life perfectly because hindsight is 20/20. In that case I cannot be upset with anyone because I am in fact mentally in the afterlife but my body is still alive.

It was suggested Jesus defeated death. That in fact is what this is [Luke 17:33 ; and whosoever shall lose his life shall preserve it.] So here are your options for who you are dealing with. If I simply unveiled right brain then you are reading the personal diaries of a being with his subconscious moved to his conscious state of mind.

If I accidentally mentally literally died yet I physically am still alive then you are reading the personal diaries of the living dead and in that case you are dealing with something infinitely wiser than you are presently.

If you laugh at those two options then you do not stand a chance, but of course you do not stand a chance to begin with. None of the things I write in my books were taught to me. There is no human being on this planet that taught me the things I write about in my personal diaries, which means right brain is so powerful, one does not even need education at all because right brain is so swift in detecting patterns and learning for itself education is in fact vanity.

You perhaps want to lean to the fact I simply discovered an ancient method to breaking the curse of the left brain written language education mindset because if I in fact mentally died yet am physically alive that would explain why I am so vengeful. One might suggest vengeance is mine.

I would imagine after years of suicide attempts and then understanding those suicide attempts were simply the result of being brainwashed as a youth into an unsound state of mind by civilization, it is logical I would be vengeful. I perhaps would not be writing books explaining civilization is essentially a dirty whore mental rapist of children, if I was not vengeful would I grasshopper? At this point since the accident I do not even know exactly why I am still writing except for the fact I am compelled to write into infinity and although that is beyond your ability to understand it none the less is true.
[John 8:43 Why do ye not understand my speech?]

The point in part is I am writing books to bring you back to reality. Relative to you point of view you may be pleased with some things I explain to you, but relative to me I perceive it is vengeance.

If I tell you great truth and you become less ignorant then you become less blissful and that is my reckoning. Bliss is spiritual joy and I am going to make sure six billion people do not have that aspect much longer. Ignorance is bliss and before too long you will not have much ignorance and thus very little bliss and that is my vengeance. At about 1 AM is when I started to become ill from taking the pills and for some reason I like to write at night. I tend to become rather, let's say, mischievous.

When I go out in public and see people I only see perfection with the feeling through vision aspect and so I see everyone as perfect and then I wonder why I even write my books at all. Then I come home and read the news headlines or talk to people in chat rooms and realize I am in hell. I am not suggesting I am good or bad. I am suggesting I had an accident and I am an accident. I will certainly explain this remedy which is this fear not, do not save your life to preserve it, submit technique to you flawlessly and you will understand exactly what I am saying but I am uncertain if you can actually pull it off.

It is important to understand before you attempt this ancient technique you are ready to handle wisdom. The reason for that is because once you apply this remedy you cannot go back, ever. Everything you perceive right now is going to change after you apply the remedy. For example if you are addicted to drugs after you apply the remedy you will not be addicted to drugs simply because if you apply the remedy properly you won't even be able to feel euphoria at all from drugs because mentally you will be in a state of euphoria.

You may be able to feel satisfaction now if someone put a trillion dollars in front of you but after you apply the remedy you will feel nothing from things like that. The reason for this is because right brain is so powerful it transcends everything in the physical world on every level and every scale. You won't rip people off for a little money because that profit does nothing for you. You are not going to be so concerned about yourself or ego because you will no longer have one. You are not going to be embarrassed about anything or ashamed or afraid of anything no matter what it is. Right now you are ashamed and embarrassed about almost everything and also afraid of a bad haircut. Right now you are ashamed about what you do think, and about what you don't think, and you are also dependant on what others think about you. You will harm other people to be accepted by your "friends" and all your friends, after this remedy is applied are going to be reduced to illusions.

You will have what is known as brain function and so you will be a one man army or what I like to call a lone wolf. You are going to be the advisor and there is no one who is going to be able to advise you. There will not be any human beings on this planet that you will say "I wish I was as wise and intelligent as they are." You say that a lot right now. You wish you were more creative and more intelligent and you are wondering why you are not more creative and more intelligent and I will tell you why. You got mentally raped by civilization as a result of civilizations assumption it knew how to apply a sequential left brain heavy conditioning invention without ruining the mind, but it did not know what the hell it was doing.

There is no one you know that can understand what I am saying so if you cannot understand what I am saying then you are simply screwed. You are going to have to think for yourself because all of your little friends do not have the brain function to understand what I am saying and perhaps they never will. I attempted to communicate with people in civilization who suggested they are intelligent but they turned out to be intelligent relative to a rock.

I keep asking them [John 8:43 Why do ye not understand my speech?]. It is possible I am just typing the same letter over and over and that is why no one can understand what I say because if that is not the case I am dealing with beings that are not literally dead just mentally dead beyond all definitions of the words mentally dead.

In some ways I want you to apply the remedy the way I did. In some ways I want you to have 20 razor slashes on your wrist and 30 failed suicide attempts under your belt so when you wake up and feel the power of right brain you will be set for vengeance against the whores who put you in the state of mind you are in now. Perhaps I did those things to myself so I could tell you how to accomplish the remedy without doing those things. I speak to many who speak as if they are awake and applied the remedy but they are simply trapped at some stage up the mountain. I will just say you do not want to get stuck somewhere up the mountain, psychologically speaking, so to speak. - 11/7/2009 2:16:03 AM

11:15:35 PM – This is the definition of speech:
The faculty or power of speaking; oral communication; ability to express ones thoughts or emotions. Speech is relative to language and language is relative to written language relative to civilization, the cult.

A right is something that is given freely. One is born and then they receive freely, rights. This is what the bill of rights is about. What this means is no other human being can tell another human being something contrary to the rights they gain when they are born. Simply put no human being has the right to block another human being's rights freely given by being born.

No organization or group of voters has the right to deny another human beings rights. This means the majority does not rule when it comes to rights. A billion people cannot deny a single person their rights because the rights are given freely when that single human being is born. Rights are not negotiable no matter what and when they are negotiable revolution is required to reestablish the rights. This creates a certain checks and balances because even if one person is denied their rights by a billion people that one person has the right to revolt and fight against those billion people to reestablish their rights, not as much for their self but for the ones that come after them. This means relative to America, revolution in any form is acceptable when rights are denied. Laws and morals do not matter if rights are taken away because if right are negated laws and morals are negated.

This is the first amendment of the bill of rights. The bill of rights are things a human being gets freely because they are born. These rights are things a human gets for being born so they cannot ever be questioned or denied or even altered because once that happens there has to be revolution to restore them. This means the bill of rights are more important than life itself because without the bill of rights one is a slave and is in fact caged. A better way to look at it is life is not life if one does not have these rights. This is relative to give me my rights or give me death because without the rights one is a slave and in turn is dead, so to speak.

"Congress shall make no law respecting an establishment of religion, or prohibiting the free exercise thereof; or abridging the freedom of speech, or of the press; or the right of the people peaceably to assemble, and to petition the Government for a redress of grievances."

This first one is establishment of religion. Congress, voters cannot determine what a religion is. The voters cannot determine what a religion is not also. This means a human being has the right to make a religion based on anything and it is legitimate. The moment the voters or congress determines what a religion is they deny a human being the rights they have been freely given when they were born. The reason for this is no human being can determine what a religion is for another human being.

Congress cannot determine what a religion is because then they can pass laws that are biased towards a belief system and in turn outlaw that religion. Congress or voters are not intelligent enough to determine how many religions there are because a religion is relative to one who practices it. Eating food can be a religion and the followers eat certain foods at certain times and certain amounts of food and they do this as a ritual. A religion could be drinking beer and a person drinks a certain amount of beer at certain time and this creates a spiritual mindset and that is their worship. If a person is in this beer drinking religion and they wish to encourage it in their children they are allowed to no matter what the laws says about a minor drinking beer because if that is not the case that person is denied their freedom of religion.

No human being can determine what a religion is or is not for another human being. A tyrant does not like that reality because a tyrant only wants to control, and so a tyrant will pass laws that will say there certainly is a certain religion and the one your practice is illegal. A tyrant will always create control mechanisms based on a promise of security and safety. [Congress shall make no law respecting an establishment of religion] this means congress or the voters are never ever, ever allowed to determine what is a religion and what is not a religion. A person can break a law and claim it is their religion, as long as it does not infringe on another's life, liberty or pursuit of happiness, and then congress or voters cannot punish them because if they do they infringe on a humans right to practice a religion of their choice, and they also start determining rules based on establishment of religion.

Now a tyrant will deny what I suggest because if what I suggest is true, their control and power is going down the drain. If a person gets arrested for smoking pot and they suggest that is their religion and the cops says congress has not establish smoking pot is a religion then that cop is simply a minion of congress's efforts to create laws that establish religion. [Congress shall make no law respecting an establishment of religion] Congress is not allowed to create laws that establishes or de-establish religion, and cops are not allowed to enforce such laws because if either does they deny a person their rights given to them freely at birth and so they are nothing but tyrants and control freaks and hate the bill of rights.

This is why the wise beings that establish this country were very careful to make sure there was no way anyone or any group of people would form a monopoly on power because that is what a tyranny is. Of course control freaks are not going to agree with the bill of rights because all they want to is control things and control is contrary to freedom.

This is why at the time this bill of right was created there were essentially no laws. There were no drugs that were illegal. The law of the land is simply the control mechanism of the people for exhibiting mental symptoms caused by the education .

A law is control and America is land of the free and that is why America is unlike any other country established in the history of mankind. If America tries to be like any other country it simply becomes a tyranny. It appears very dangerous this concept of freedom but I assure you tyranny is far more dangerous. When one gives up their freedom and thus their right for a little safety they kill their self. If one gives away their rights and then has a change of heart they cannot get them back. Washington hated the government of America and so did the founding fathers so this bill of rights is not suggesting what a person, the people, cannot do it is suggesting what the government cannot do.

[Congress(government) shall make no law respecting an establishment of religion]

These rules are not about the people because the people are absolutely free. These rules are telling the government if it starts messing around with these rights it had better be ready for a revolution. It is not important what the government thinks or the voters think about anything because every human being is born and thus given these right freely and no human being or government can intervene with that absolute reality or there is going to be a revolution because they infringe on a person life, liberty and pursuit of happiness.

The government tries to make it appear like a person who is free better do what they say but in reality the government is expendable and the government better make sure it does not upset the people because the people have a right to abolish it on the slightest whim, and that means the government should be afraid of the people at all times, and that makes the government think very carefully before if even passes a single law.

"That whenever any Form of Government becomes destructive of these ends, it is the Right of the People to alter or to abolish it, and to institute new Government"
Declaration of Independence

What this means is the Government itself can be destroyed at the whim of the people for any reason whatsoever. The Government isn't America. That is why Washington said "the government is not reason." The main founding father of America said the government is insane. This means the government is the tyrant and that is why the people have a right to abolish it at any time and because of that the government has to walk very carefully at all times because the people have a right to abolish it totally at anytime no matter what. If the Government tries to stop the people from abolishing it they deny the people their right and so the government proves it is a tyrant and then it must be abolished. It is an infinite loop of protection and checks and balances for the people. Granted you have been brainwashed by the education and your fear level is through the roof so what I am suggesting sounds scary to you and that is why the brainwashing is used, so you will sit in your cage and watch the tyrant take every single liberty away from you, and you will never lift a finger because you are afraid of a bad haircut. Once your right brain intuition is veiled you are nothing but a sucker. You will perceive something is not right but you will have no way to tell something is not right. You are not going to be able to go read in a book intellectual, left brain, information that tells you that you being suckered. They keys to detecting a trap are pattern detection, intuition, and complexity and of course fast processing of that data and the education turns all those right brain aspects essentially off so you are a Grade A sicker and ripe for the picking. You have been mentally blinded by way of the brainwashing and so you are nothing but a pushover in every definition of the word pushover and the problem with that is you perceive you are going to be telling me what I can and cannot do. After you vote yourself into a cage I will come by and lock it for you.

When there is only multimillionaires in government then the people are simply being taken advantage of by carpetbaggers and the people can start the government over based on the initial articles that founded the nation. The government does not have a say because the people are the only determiners and they have the right to abolish the government at any time. The people can abolish the government and when the next one starts, the people can abolish it and keep doing this so there is no government because it is their right. The people choose to have a government or not so if the government gets to strong it means the people want it to, and so they harm their self. The reason for the right to abolish is because if a government lasts to long it gets to powerful and then it controls the people.

America is not supposed to be like any other country or government in the world and that is why we are free and none of the other countries are free. If America is like any other government in the world at all it means is the people have blown it and ruined the land of the free. If we try to be like other countries we will only end up a tyranny because we are the only land of the free.

The founding fathers knew what all the other governments in the world were up to and they made this bill of rights in such a way as to avoid America ever becoming like all the other governments in the world because they were all simply tyrannies. America is not about living safely, America is about living freely. If one wants to be secure they can go live in a tyranny and they cannot speak their mind nor do what they are pleased to do. If one wants to live and be free come to America if one wants to be safe and isolated go live in a tyranny. One has a choice to leave America if they cannot handle freedom. Freedom is not about safety, freedom is about living your life as you see fit and not having some control freak standing over your shoulder threatening you with jail if you do not live up to their perceived acceptable standards. A law cannot trump freedom of religion and religion can be anything a free human being determines it is. That is very scary so you need to go live in a tyranny and they will make sure you are nice and safe in your cage. - 12:06:41 AM

12:09:33 AM - One does not discover something of value and then put a price tag on it because the merit of the discovery has a value unto itself. Anything of true worth transcends the value of the person who discovered it. None of the wise beings put a price tag on their discovery because no amount of money could compensate for the value of the discovery so their choice was to give it freely.

The discovery they made transcended their own worth and value. Their own life was not more important than the discovery and many of them showed that to us. They died and at times horrible deaths because they understood their own life was not as important in contrast to the concepts they were trying to explain. This is an example of the reverse thing. Many of the sane are looking for something that will make them lots of money and make their life more valuable and these wise ones were not concerned about their own life and that is an indication of the value of what they discovered. If one discovers something of value greater than their self then they have discovered something of true value. If one is not willing to die for their discovery then it is not worth charging for and if one is willing to die for their discovery then it a priceless discovery. Sometimes explaining great truth may cost one their life but great truth is worth more than life. I may copyright my words but I could not bear to ever enforce that copyright because I have never said anything you are not already aware of, even if you are not consciously aware of it. I am reminding you of what we were, not telling you what we are.- 12:21:46 AM

11/8/2009 6:44:07 PM – There is a concept along the lines of, the more advanced civilization takes over or dominates a less advanced civilization. For example the group that is more advanced dominates the less advanced and one example would be what Americans did to the Native Americans and also what civilization did to the Native Africans. Dominate in this explanation is actually enslavement and also "robbery". This is relative to might makes right.

The ideal "more advanced" is simply a shallow reason for this domination situation.

X = harmony in mindset; sound mind
Y = disharmony in mindset; unsound mind

When Y encounters X , X is always dominated because harmony itself seeks to achieve harmony and Y seeks to achieve disharmony naturally or by its very nature. The deeper reality of this is Y is self defeating. Y seeks disharmony unto itself and so it also seeks disharmony when it encounters X. This is why civilization, the cult is self defeating. A better way to categorize civilization is disharmony. There is a reason civilization has wars against other countries in civilization. All of civilization has the education or encourages this written language on its children. This is not suggesting written language itself is bad because it is an inanimate object and thus simply a tool, but like any tool, if used improperly or by someone who is not learned in its possible bad side effects, disaster tends to the be the end result.

Anyone can wield a scalpel but there are beings that can use that tool to achieve positive results and there are people who can create a disaster because thcy do not understand how to wield that tool.

X is accepting of Y when encountered because X seeks harmony but because Y seeks disharmony Y must go against its own nature to fight against Y. What this means is X must use self control to become violent and Y must use self control to not be violent. A person of sound mind must in fact seek to become violent because that is not in their nature and a person of unsound mind must seek peace because that is not in their nature.

The Native Americans were not violent to the sane when the sane first came to America. The sane sought to take from the Native Americans and because the "law" was on their side it was simple to do so. Law itself is only relevant to who's side it is on. There were no laws to protect the Native Americans because they were deemed "uncivil" because they did not have written language and math education, so the sane treated them as less than human because civilization, the cult, could not understand the Native Americans were of sound mind.

In this extreme left brain state of mind one has after the education one has such a huge ego and thus pride they cannot imagine their self as anything but the most important thing in the universe and because of this, "walking" over the Native Americans was acceptable because they could walk over the Native Americans. The simple equation is. Civilization means polite and civil, the Native Americans were not a part of civilization so they were deemed automatically and without question as uncivil by civilization. Again this is a civilization name is just a mind trick and only works on weak minds.

The Native Americans wanted to be left alone but civilization, the cult, kept taking more and more land and killing off the Native Americans food source. This is why the equation Y + X = Y is the end result because Y is always going to force itself on anything around it. This is why the curse one is mentally under after they get the education is devastating because in fact one is doomed because they are not capable of harmony in the unsound state of mind. This is why the invention written language when applied or taught by unsound minded people to sound minded people, children, is a death sentence. This is why the invention written language was fatal to the human race. The many years of left brain sequential education, divides the mind and so that being is not viable because the ecological system is based on harmony.

Civilization is not in conflict with itself because human beings are violent. Civilization is in conflict with itself because an unsound creature cannot stand itself. A mentally unsound creature destroys itself but perceives what it does it good or proper. It appeared proper to the sane to wipe out all the beaver for fifty dollars. It appeared proper to the sane to wipe out all the whales for fifty dollars. It appeared proper to the sane to wipe out all the buffalo for fifty dollars. It appeared proper to the sane to enslave the Native Africans and take all their land, based on laws civilization created to cheat the Native Americans out of the land. It appeared proper to the sane to cut down a forest to build a condo no one lives in. It appeared proper to the sane to go to war and in turn kill 50 million people over land none of the people involved owned anyway.

The sane are prone to control everything and that is a symptom of an unsound mind. A mind in harmony will attempt to adapt to a situation but not control a situation. The sane damage or kill things to achieve a perceived control over things they can never control. The sane will kill something in order to control it and that is insanity. If the sane cannot control something they kill it and perceive that is control. The deeper reality is an unsound mind knows not what it does.

Nature itself is a one way street. One is either mentally in harmony as in 50/50, left and right brain working equally or one is mentally unsound and doomed to destroy their self. One who is not mentally in harmony is trapped because they do things they perceive are proper when they are really engaged in suicide. One is a slave to their perception and since the education alters the perception one is a slave to their ill working mind.

Civilization, the cult, as a whole encourages this written language invention on its own offspring and so it keeps destroying the next generation and that is insanity relative to a sound mind but that is expected relative to an unsound mind. Written language is a tool and it can serve the species or annihilate the species and it is no different than any tool ever invented. There are many beings in recorded history even recently who have suggested education is far too left brain prone but civilization is of unsound mind and they can never quite figure out what that really means. I am not suggesting education is slightly left brain prone. I am suggesting if one takes a knife and cuts out the right brain all together and then makes observations on how that person acts they will not notice much difference between that person and a person educated with the many years of left brain education. The education when administered improperly totally destroys the mind of the student. It makes the student hallucinate and makes the student mentally dull. In fact dull is not as accurate as retarded.

Now this appears to be impossible because one would have to come to the conclusion civilization itself is making children and anyone it teaches this education to retarded. Then one has to conclude if that is true then civilization itself is retarded. Then one has to conclude if that is true civilization itself is self defeating. Then one has to conclude civilization is either very sinister to do this to people or civilization is insane and knows not what it does.

Civilization if sinister would be rather wise to make people retarded under the guise of education so the people are prone to fear and slothful in the mind function so they are easy to control. That would at least suggest the "powers that be" have some sort of plan. If civilization or the "powers that be" have no clue they are doing this to people with this education then in fact civilization is an insane being that is devastating other beings and cannot be stopped because it cannot even be reasoned with. This is why Abraham and Lot destroyed the cities and killed everyone in them. How can one possibly convince something that is totally insane that is harming others without knowing it when that insane thing believes it is helping others?

One cannot convince an insane being it is harming others when that insane being believes it is helping others. This is an indication that ones who are educated improperly and do not apply remedy are self defeating and hallucinating. The sane are hallucinating in so many ways it requires many words just to cover it. The sane are hallucinating one on level because they believe education makes one wise when in reality is ruins one's ability, veils right brain, to be wise. This is an example of the reverse thing.
[Luke 23:34 Then said Jesus, Father, forgive them; for [they know not what they do]. And they parted his raiment, and cast lots.]

An insane person does not get punished because [they know not what they do]. That of course is on a single person level. If civilization conditions a child into an unsound state of mind using a tool improperly [they know not what they do]. A parent would not harm their own child unless [they know not what they do]. There is an unknown factor involved with all of this. Looking at some various written languages one notices one thing right off the bat, nearly all the alphabets are in sequential order.

The very first thing a child learns no matter what written language they are being taught is learning the alphabet and that means memorizing the letters in sequential order. If a parent is bragging about how young their child was when they memorized the sequential alphabet and that in turn is actually conditioning that child into left brain extreme so that child is of unsound mind then that parent [knows not what they do].

In reverse world a parent is thought to be wise to teach their young child to sequence the letters of the language properly and in reality world that parent is insane. In reverse world a parent wants that child to get the education they got and so that is reasonable but in reality that education ruins the mind and so that is insanity. I cannot prove to an insane person they are insane because an insane person perceives insanity is sanity.

I can write books as fast as I can in hopes that insane person looks at the publish dates and asks how does this person write so fast and then I can write in those books, I had an accident and lost my fear and woke up from the neurosis induced by the education and that is about all I can do.

If a person is insane and is harming others and [they know not what they do] they tend to be isolated from society because they are a threat to society and to their self so they must be monitored, but what can one do if the society itself is insane and harming others and [they know not what they do]? What can one do when they are in a lunatic asylum and the lunatics are harming children and turning children into lunatics? This is why Abraham and Lot burned down the cities and killed everyone in them because this education induced neurosis spreads and is fatal. Do you think society would publish the ancient texts if Abraham and Lot said, "We saw these things we called men who ate off the tree of knowledge, written language and math, and they did not apply the remedy, fear not, and we butchered every last one of them because they could not be reasoned with because they were mentally too far gone and they were harming children and [they know not what they do]"?

Do you think for one second these ancient texts would be published still. Do you understand why they said God burned that city and killed every person in that city. I am mindful to avoid reasoning with you.

[Genesis 19:24 Then the LORD(Abraham and Lot and friends) rained upon Sodom and upon Gomorrah brimstone and fire from the LORD(they used their unveiled right brain to find a good way to do it) out of heaven(right brain or sound mind);

Genesis 19:25 And he(The lord of the mind, Abraham and Lot) overthrew those cities, and all the plain, and all the inhabitants of the cities(the brainwashed ones), and that which grew upon the ground.] Ground is relative to the comment in early Genesis, cursed is the ground for eating off the tree of knowledge.

I find no fault with they did. They did the best they could based on their understanding but the deeper reality is even by that time the written language was all over the world. At the time these cities were being burned down, Buddha was waking up in the east, and Socrates was waking up in Greece from the demotic, written language, induced neurosis. Abraham and Lot tried killing the sane, and some tried living in peace with the sane, and some tried hiding from the sane, but the reality is this curse is so powerful no matter what one does they cannot defeat it so it is not important what they did.

If one goes violent that won't work, if one goes the peaceful route that won't work. This is why this tool mankind invented, written language was fatal to the species. So another way to look at it is, I understand the enemy and he is us.

Perhaps one that is only capable of sequential logic can look at it like this. There is a drug and the entire civilization rewards one for getting as much of that drug as possible and punishes anyone who does not partake of that drug, and the more of that drug one takes the sooner they will become mentally unsound. The drug can be taken safely but only under the direction of a master who can administer the drug properly and civilization does not understand that at all.

There is an innocent aspect to all of this and a very complex deep aspect to all of this. The innocent aspect is mankind invented something that damaged mankind mentally so greatly, mankind is not even aware it damaged mankind. The deeper reality is an unseen force perhaps not even supernatural that figured out a way to keep our species stupid and this unseen force is so intelligent we are not even aware that is what is happening. It does not matter at all which one it is because the end result is a species that is of unsound mind and continues to make the children of unsound mind and that means the species is insane and against itself and in turn doomed to destroy itself without even being aware that is all it can do to itself.

You certainly can apply the remedy and some perceive that is the big step, but in reality that is the easy step. The difficult step is when your right brain kicks in, all this heightened awareness kicks in and the machine starts working and you become aware of what I suggest is absolute truth. How are you going to deal with it? You are going to be in a position where you are the leader of yourself. No being that has applied this remedy is going to find fault with anything you do ever because the team you will in fact have joined by applying the remedy has never won ever, against the sane, civilization, the cult.

You apply the remedy and you join the team that has never won and that is all anyone who has applied the remedy needs to know about your character. Your red badge of courage is that you joined a team that cannot win. The reason your emotions will be purged after you apply the remedy is because they would destroy you if they were not purged, the heightened awareness is so great. Once you apply the remedy you will be what is known in the east as a Master and what is known in the west as a Lord. You will be a Master or a Lord of the cerebral world. You will be a lone wolf because there will not be anyone who is capable of advising you. It may take a year based on calendar time to become comfortable in your new "body" but once the remedy is applied and kicks in after a month or so relative to calendar time, you will be what is known as a free thinker. You may perceive before you apply the remedy you are going to make lots of money and become popular but you are thinking on the physical scale still. You will be tempted to hide from the sane and give up the battle, but that is not going to be possible because there is nothing but the battle. - 8:25:20 PM

11/9/2009 1:51:42 AM – This is the remedy explained depending on who you perceive you are.

If you perceive you are Jewish then you want to go with the Abraham and Isaac method which is the fear not method relative to this comment.
[Genesis 15:1 After these things the word of the LORD came unto Abram in a vision, saying, Fear not, Abram: I am thy shield, and thy exceeding great reward.]
A simple way to accomplish this is to put yourself in a situation of perceived death or the shadow of death, like a place that is scary, at night and alone and when your hypothalamus tells you to run in fear because of this shadow of death you do not run in fear, you fear not or just ignore what your mind is telling you. This of course is not about jumping into a shark frenzy which is actual death this is just about being in a situation your mind perceives the shadow of death.
Relative to this comment [Psalms 23:4 Yea, though I walk through the valley of the shadow of death, I will fear no evil: for thou art with me; thy rod and thy staff they comfort me.]

You can also call it the fear no evil technique, the only important point is to perceive death and then deny that mental suggestion and that will break the curse or the unsound mind set the education has instilled.

If one perceives they are a Christian then they want to apply the "lose your life" technique relative to [Luke 17:33 Whosoever shall seek to save his life shall lose it; and whosoever shall lose his life shall preserve it.] This is simply going to a place one perceives is scary and when one's mind says "Run the shadow of death is near" one does not run from the shadow of death but just sits there. There of course are many ways one can get their self into this situation but again the point is not to face actual death it is just to face a situation one perceives death is certain and since ones hypothalamus is not working properly due to the left brain state of mind perhaps even watching a scary movie alone in the dark and then turning out the lights may in fact work just as well.

If one perceives they are Muslim then they simply go to a place they perceive is scary and when their mind says the shadow of death is approaching one simply submits and allows this shadow of death, perceived death to have its way so to speak.

If one perceives they are Buddhist then one simply goes to a cemetery at night alone and meditates until the perceived shadow of death approaches and then they fear not, submit to perceived death, lose their life to preserve it.

If one perceives they are a philosopher they can simply seek medusa's head, the shadow of death, and then fear not when medusa arrives, so to speak.

If one perceives they are some other "religion" then they can do any of these methods.

If one likes drugs then one can apply these methods and they will be very high for the rest of their life and so high in fact the sane will say "You are on drugs" after just about every comment they make apparently. The best way to handle that situation is when the sane suggest you are on drugs. [Acts 2:13 Others mocking said, These men are full of new wine.] you simply respond with [Acts 2:15 For these are not drunken, as ye suppose, seeing it is but the third hour of the day.]

If you are a depressed person then you are this [Psalms 37:11 But the meek shall inherit the earth; and shall delight themselves in the abundance of peace.] which is meek and you are ready to try anything, so go ahead an experiment with the above methods and that way you will find peace and in fact you are unique because you are [Luke 6:20 And he lifted up his eyes on his disciples, and said, Blessed be ye poor: for yours is the kingdom of God.]

You are already in a mental state of humility and you are already aware something is wrong or not right. You are aware of the brainwashing, just not consciously, so perhaps you will find these techniques very easy to apply. You are what are known as poor in spirit so you are already denying this state of mind you are in after the education, which means you are ready to come home, so to speak.

If you are none of these people and you are what is known as a skeptic and skeptical of this technique then I welcome you to apply this technique, because I love to be tested.
The important thing to keep in mind if you are a skeptic is you have to at least apply the technique before you can speak poorly of the technique and if you do not apply the technique you have no grounds to speak poorly of the technique.
The rule of thumb is you experiment in finding a situation where you perceive death will come, the shadow, but avoid jumping in shark frenzies. Be mindful in your state of mind you are afraid of the dark it just has to be the right place and it has to be dark. - 2:18:04 AM

3:03:23 AM – I am mindful to distance myself from everything I have written up to this point including this sentence. The story of Job can be summed up simply by saying Job lost all of his material things, his family, his live stock his wealth and money and his house and even his health. One in the neutral state of mind, or one who has applied the remedy properly does care but not to the point if they have a loss they suffer. For example Job had many sores on his body and this denotes physical pain but he did not suffer like one in the unsound state of mind because pain is very vague in the neutral state of mind.

Right brain has lots of ambiguity and since the mind once the remedy is applied is in the now and does not register time it also does not register after taste. That's what I call it because it applies to actual taste where one tastes something but the after taste is not there and that is the same with physical pain. One feels pain but one does not feel the after effects of pain and to top it off the mind has lots of ambiguity so one cannot tell how much pain they are in. One is in a sense numb to taste and pain and smell and what that means is one does not suffer.

It is not that one cannot feel pain or sense taste or smell it is just once they do the mind is not a very good judge of whether a food tastes good or bad, or a smell is good or bad. So relative to physical pain one is perhaps a bit on the cautious side because one is unable to determine if it strong pain or weak pain. The right brain is so powerful when it is unveiled it simply has to turn many things off to operate and what this means is the remedy does not change one to a unnatural state of mind it changes one back to a normal state of mind they were in before the education.

If one senses time, which is a side effect of the left brain extreme state of mind the education causes, then when they have pain there is also after taste of pain so they are in a state of pain. If one has right brain veiled they judge everything and know what tastes good and what tastes bad, what music sounds good and what music sounds bad, what smell is good and what smell is bad. That is exactly what this means [Genesis 2:17 But of the tree of the knowledge of [good and evil], thou shalt not eat of it: for in the day that thou eatest thereof thou shalt surely die.]

[good and evil]. One is running around judging everything as good or bad when in reality that is because they are hallucinating. Nothing is good or bad when right brain is unveiled because right brain has so much ambiguity, one might taste a food they disliked before they apply the remedy and then after they apply the remedy they will not be able to tell if it tastes good or bad.

One may dislike certain music before they apply the remedy and then after they apply the remedy all music sounds perfect because ones hearing is altered so they notice all the little intricacies of the sound and this is because the mind itself is focused on the now. One hears the music in real time and a few seconds after that part passes they forget it and they focus on the part that is playing currently. This is what the extreme concentration is all about and that is relative to heightened awareness. Every single thing a person experiences goes through the mind and then the minds perception looks at these stimuli and processes them, so no matter what one experiences from a smell to a taste to pain, these stimuli go through the cerebral cortex. The education conditions the mind to the extreme left and so the cerebral cortex puts all of these stimuli into parts because the right brain, mind, is veiled.

A sound mind has the right brain unveiled and the left brain unveiled but the right brain has lots of complexity and is the powerhouse so one tends to see everything as a whole but sometimes a person can see parts but not often. So one who gets the education and does not apply the remedy tends to see everything as good an evil, parts a left brain trait, and one who applies the remedy tends to see everything as a whole but sometimes seeing things as parts. I use to like certain kinds of music and now I like any kind of music. I like the vibrations from the strings in classical music, I like the drum sounds in rap music but I also find no fault with any sounds and this is because the stimuli is going through the cerebral cortex and the cortex is filtering them through left and right brain and because right brain is the powerhouse I tend to find no fault with any sounds. This is the same with food. This is the same when I see people, some kind of feeling through vision tells my mind everyone is perfect.

I do not see the person on the outside because I feel them somehow and so every time I see anyone I get this perfection feeling and it is so strong I cannot focus on the outside or the physical aspects. I no longer judge a book by the cover so to speak. It may seem like this heightened awareness takes effort but it takes no more effort than being in the left brain extreme state. One certainly will take some time to get use to this new sound mind state but after a year or so relative to a calendar they will feel normal in this state.

There is no possible reason one would not want to be in this sound minded heightened awareness state but one who is in the extreme left brain state is unable to imagine what it would be like so they fear change and so they avoid it. How can one possibly be afraid of being in a sound minded state which is when right brain is unveiled? The answer is because they are of unsound mind and their hypothalamus is telling them it would be dangerous because their hypothalamus is sending such strong signals relative to fear as in fear of change, they tend to talk their self out of it.

After this left brain sequential education , perhaps even a few years of it, because it is not applied properly by a master who can teach it properly, the hypothalamus is sending such strong signals relative to fear, a person actually fears words, pictures, sounds. This is why the curse is so hard to break and this is why "the meek shall inherit the earth" is so true.

[Mark 8:34 And when he had called the people unto him with his disciples also, he said unto them, Whosoever will come after me, [let him deny himself], and take up his cross, and follow me.]

A meek person is a person who denies their self: [let him deny himself]. Other words in this extreme left brain state of mind one is in after they get the education one has to hate it in order to have a chance to break free of it. A suicidal person denies their self because they hate life or what they perceive is life. A suicidal person wants to get out of this world or perception world they have been conditioned into by education. They cannot stand one more moment of the suffering. The tragedy on one level is they were put in this suffering perception state of mind by the education, by civilization, the cult, and the second tragedy is they are right on target in relation to being aware something is wrong but they tend to end up actually killing their self.

If what I suggest actually gets around it will destroy everything as society knows it. Economics will change. Psychology will change. Religion will change. Governments will change. Education will change. All laws will change. The prison system will change. That is what this [let him deny himself] is relative to and that is why the sane slaughtered these beings wholesale.

These beings were not killed because they were peaceful , they were killed because they represented total change and the sane are not good at change because left brain is not good at adaptation because left brain is not good at detecting patterns and it is slothful, sequential based thoughts, in its processing relative to right brain. This is why the world never caught on to what these wise beings were suggesting because the world is conditioned into extreme left brain and left brain hates change or see's change as evil. The is an indication of the curse the education mentally puts one in. This is why this curse has defeated the species for over 5000 years.

[Genesis 3:14 And the LORD God said unto the serpent, Because thou hast done this, [thou art cursed above all cattle], and above every beast of the field; upon thy belly shalt thou go, and dust shalt thou eat all the days of thy life:]

[thou art cursed above all cattle] What is interesting about this situation is one is actually cursed upon cursed. Ones perception is cursed so they are trapped by their perception and what one perceives is what one makes judgments based on, so one will be in this left brain state of mind and they will perceive it is normal but it is absolutely abnormal. One cannot be in a deeper neurosis than if they fear words, and sounds, and the dark, foods and a bad haircut and worst of all their mind senses time.

[Galatians 4:10 Ye observe days, and months, and times, and years.]

Observe means perceives. Life is very strange when one perceives every day and month and year. One becomes a slave to time. Ones entire life is based around time and that is suffering. Time encourages schedules and when schedules are not met there is suffering. Everyday people that mentally sense time are slaves to it. They dread waking up in eight hours for work. They dread the holidays because they only have a certain amount of time to shop. Holidays are a symptom the society is conditioned into this sense of time perception. Day and night does not mean a day has passed that is a man made invention because man started perceiving time. Sleeping 8 hours a day is abnormal because the body's senses time and then the body is conditioned into a schedule, but the problem with that is when the body senses time the body reacts to time passing and that creates fatigue and stress.

Edison was known for only needing to take cat naps. No sense of time is not very friendly to schedules. When the mind does not register time one may go to sleep and sleep one hour relative to a clock and wake up fully rested. This is because the mind cannot tell how long one has been asleep. All of civilization has drugs so one can sleep eight hours every night so they are well rested in the morning. They suggest if one does not get eight hours of sleep they will be fatigued the next day. They do not realize they are simply trying to treat a mental abnormality caused by the education with drugs. One needs drugs to battle the fatigue. One needs drugs to battle the depression. One needs drugs to battle the stress. One needs drugs to wake up and drugs to go to sleep. These are all symptoms of an unsound mind caused by the education. The education is sequential left brain based and when not applied by a master that understands how to teach this tool properly one is mentally ruined. I am not that master. I only know and understand the remedy. Civilization is not going to shut down schools until they train enough masters that can apply the education tool properly because they are in a rush because they sense time. Civilization knows not what they do. Civilization creates problems and then tries to remedy those problems and in turn only creates more problems. Civilization almost killed me with their delusional assumption of making me wise with their education tool. Civilization has mentally messed you up so badly you hallucinate and sense time. This is what you do and this is what I did [Galatians 4:10 Ye observe days, and months, and times, and years.]

When the mind senses time a person is a nervous wreck. One is always looking at their watch and everything they do is based on time. "When do I get paid?" " When do they get here?" 'When does this day end?" One is simply stressed out so badly they have no way to escape the stress but to take drugs. Some drink lots of coffee, some take hard drugs. The drugs are not a problem it's the fact a person does them to escape a state of mind they were put in by civilization.

If civilization conditions a person into this unsound left brain extreme state of mind and then when that person exhibits behavior relative to that state of mind and civilization punishes that person for that behavior that is the most cruel thing imaginable.

If a person drugs to get some relief from being conditioned into an unsound state of mind by the education civilization encourages and then when they are drugged civilization punished them for how they act, that is the most diabolical thing one can ever do.
[John 8:4 They say unto him, Master, [this woman was taken in adultery], in the very act.]

Notice they called Jesus Master. Master of the house(mind), he broke the brainwashing cause by education, relative to a house divided cannot stand and relative to one does not know when the master of the house returns. One never knows when the Master of the house returns because one never knows when someone is going to break the curse and that is an indication of how air tight the curse is. It's more complex than that also.

One has to be meek and deny their self and that is relative to suicide. Every time you hear of a person who commits true suicide you hear of a person who was trying to break the cursed state of mind civilization put them in but they were too good at it. There mind is unsound so they perceive they want to die and this is [let him deny himself] but they go all the way and literally die.
[this woman was taken in adultery] This comment is relative to a person showing symptoms of improperly being taught the education. This is not suggesting a law is being broken. This could just as well be, this woman stole, this women is depressed, this women took drugs, this women senses time, this person eats too much. This woman was showing symptoms of the extreme left brain state of mind the education put her in.

Then this comment [John 8:7 So when they continued asking him, he lifted up himself, and said unto them, He that is without sin among you, let him first cast a stone at her.]

This comment means let a person who has applied the remedy and understands why this woman is acting the way she is, because she has been conditioning into the unsound state of mind by the education, tree of knowledge, cast the first stone.

Only a person who knows not what they do would punish a person for something they did that was simply a symptom they were conditioned as a child, into an unsound state of mind, so they exhibit those symptoms to begin with. Simply put this Master was telling that crowd you are punishing a person you put into an unsound state of mind where they are exhibiting these characteristics. Do you allow civilization to punish people after that same civilization puts them in that unsound state of mind so they exhibit those characteristics because you do not care or because you know not what you do? Do you understand perhaps every single person in jail in the US got the education? Does a judge who puts people in a cage for exhibiting certain behavior after that person was conditioned into an unsound state of mind as a child so said child is prone to exhibit that behavior, simply have no conscience or do they know not what they do? Let the one without sin lock the brainwashed children in cages. I lock no brainwashed children in cages. - 4:32:41 AM

[Exodus 14:27 - And Moses stretched forth his hand over the sea, and the sea returned to his strength when the morning appeared; and the Egyptians(civilization) fled(fear) against it; and the LORD(the master) [overthrew the Egyptians(civilization) in the midst of the sea.]]
[overthrew the Egyptians(civilization) in the midst of the sea.] relative to [Luke 17:2 It were better for him that a millstone were hanged about his neck, [and he cast into the sea, than that he should offend one of these little ones.]]
[overthrew the Egyptians(civilization) in the midst of the sea.] = [and he cast into the sea, than that he should offend one of these little ones.] Simply put, one is better off dead than to mentally harm the children with their "wisdom" tool because one is too blind to understand only a master can teach such a tool without ruining an innocent child's mind.

I tend to wear my thoughts on my sleeve so to speak because I brought my subconscious, right brain, to my conscious state so I have no subconscious any longer I have what is known as a whole mind. I cannot tell what is subconscious thoughts any longer because all my thoughts are up front so to speak, now. I do not see these words I type as meaning anything relative to resting on every word I suggest because I am in real time and shortly after I type them I totally forget them. Relative to a clock shortly is about five minutes or less. So one who is brain washed may read some of these words and assume I recall them at all, but I do not.

The machine state denotes real time and real time denotes no sense of time. The complexity is I get a cerebral spirit of the entire book but I do not associate that with words. The cerebral sensation is beyond words so it can only be called the spirit of the words. I perceive I am typing the same spirit over and over and over and just arranging the words a little differently each time.

I am mindful I say many contradictions and a contradiction is simply a paradox and a paradox is simply an aspect of right brain. So when a person who is brainwashed insults another person for making a contradiction they are really insulting right brain because a paradox is complexity. A paradox is real and is possible although it is a contradiction so right brain is great at paradox and complexity because they are one in the same.

A paradox is a symptom of complexity and complexity requires paradox. To one who is brainwashed and thus in extreme left brain, paradox is to complex and so contradictions are perceived to be symptoms of foolishness or mental illness. This is a symptom of the reverse world and relative to "they know not what they do". If one insults a person who makes a contradiction it is because that person is unable to understanding paradox and complexity and that makes perfect sense because their right brain is veiled from the education so they have no way to relate to contradictions, paradox and thus complexity. - 4:39:45 AM

9:25:51 AM – Picture's do capture something. I can read pictures of people. It is difficult to explain but in a photo of a person or animal something is captured. The feeling through vision works on a photo as well as in person or on television. So the suggestion that some tribes do not like their photo taken because they fear it captures their "soul" has some validity to it. I am uncertain what is captured but I certainly can feel it, whatever "it" is. What is difficult to explain about this feeling through vision is, it is simply a cerebral feeling through vision. It is a cerebral sensation and so it is difficult to convert these cerebral sensations to words. Words are unable to fully explain the cerebral sensations because words deal with absolutes. For example hot, cold, good, bad, black, white, but in reality there are no absolutes because everything is relative to the observer. I can go in public and look at people and they all look perfect and that is relative to this feeling through vision but a person who is brainwashed and in the left brain extreme state only see's parts, so they see one person is good and one person as fat and one person as ugly and they see all these parts and seeing parts is what judgment is, in part.

Seeing these parts is what judging a book by the cover is and once one applies the remedy they will feel people with the feeling through vision and will no longer be able to judge a person by their cover so to speak. The complexity here is Abraham and Lot had to go against what their vision, feeling through vision, was telling them so they had to ignore their vision to destroy the ones who were brain washing the children. Simply put they had to ignore their vision and follow their intuition. Intuition is a right brain trait, it could be looked at like telepathy. Everyone has intuition but once they apply the remedy and unveil right brain the intuition power increases greatly so one has it all the time instead of once in a while, in the brainwashed state. - 9:29:48 AM

"Suicide (Latin suicidium, from sui caedere, to kill oneself) is the intentional killing of one's self. Suicide may occur for a number of reasons, including depression, shame, guilt, desperation, physical pain, emotional pressure, anxiety, financial difficulties, or other undesirable situations."
Wikipedia.com
Depression , shame, guilt, desperation, emotional pressure, anxiety is simply not possible when one has applied the remedy because once right brain is unveiled it processes so

swiftly all of these emotions cannot be maintained for more than a moment or two, relative to a clocks time. One million people commit suicide every year so the majority of them are the fault of the education not being applied properly.

I simply cannot relate to what these things are anymore: Depression, shame, guilt, desperation, emotional pressure, anxiety. I certainly was depressed and had a lot of anxiety and shame but after the accident the right brain ponders so swiftly these emotions are unable to put one in a state of depression or shame because the mind is so fast in processing one cannot actually maintain any of these emotions to any degree. This is relative to the suffering the left brain extreme state of mind causes. This suffering is vanity because it does not have to be.

Cancer is known to be caused in part by stress and stress is anxiety. Stress and anxiety are simply devastating to the body and what is more devastating is they are symptom's one has been conditioned into the extreme left brain state as a result of the "education". If one kills their self because they perceive they are embarrassed or ashamed or guilty one might suggest their emotions are a tad too high. This is a symptom the cerebral cortex is making one think they should be ashamed or guilt ridden. The person perceives guilt and shame and depression and because the mind is conditioned all the way to the left these signals are so strong they actually kill their self. The tragedy is written language and math and reading are not bad, they are tools. When they are misused as in taught by person who just teaches them with no regard to their mental side effects they obliterate the mind and one has physical symptoms and one of the symptoms is suicide.

Suicide is a direct result of a person perceiving things that are not real , shame, guilt, depression, but they just perceive they are real because their mind is sending them signals that are way too strong. How many people kill their self over a broken heart? A broken heart is not real. One should not feel so much attachment to something when they lose it they kill their self. One should not kill their self if they have no money because when right brain is unveiled it will figure something out and when right brain is veiled one runs out of options swiftly because one cannot adapt to change and complexity. All the children that kill their self are a symptom's civilization conditioned them into an unsound state of mind with it's "wisdom" tool and it is trying to make it look like it's the kids fault because it knows not what it does. I ponder if you understand the concept judgment day. - 9:54:00 AM

9:48:59 PM – [Genesis 6:4 There were giants in the earth in those days; and also after that, when the sons of God came in unto the daughters of men, and they bare children to them, the same became mighty men which were of old, men of renown.]
Giant denotes cerebral giants. Wise men, Masters of the house/mind. Beings of sound mind. Similar to the story of Atlantis. The race of very intelligent beings. They are simply human beings who did not have the curse or at least applied the remedy after they got the

curse/ education. Similar to the story of Noah, the ones in Atlantis drowned in a flood. The flood of education. Again it is not the tool written language and math are bad, they are simply tools but if one does not know the side effects, they teach these tools and ruin the mind and turn a cerebral giant into a mentally slothful abomination.

[Genesis 13:13 But the men of Sodom were wicked and sinners before the LORD exceedingly.]

In contrast to the cerebral giants the Lords, the men, ones who did not apply the remedy, were mentally a joke. The men exhibited mental symptoms the Lords called sin but in reality it is just the men are of unsound mind and essentially a mental joke in contrast to the cerebral giants, Lords. That is an indication of how powerful right brain is when it is not veiled.

[Genesis 18:16 And the men rose up from thence, and looked toward Sodom: and Abraham went with them to bring them on the way.]

The men turned away from the cerebral life and looked toward Sodom, the cities, the cities were symptoms of the mental side effects of the education. The cities represent the ways of the ones who have the curse and the cities are where the education is taught and the cities represent materialism which is a symptom of one who gets the brainwashing. When one is robbed of their cerebral aspects, right brain, all they have left is material things to focus on. One can either be cerebral focused or materialistically focused. One has no choice but to be materialistic because after they get the education their right brain is veiled and in turn they are not capable of cerebral abilities so they are stuck with materialistic things. This is why there is no freedom and never has been freedom.

A child is conditioned by civilization by way of the education using scare tactics and promises of wealth if they get the conditioning, so they have no choice and never will have a choice. One must get the education or they will get a slave job and after they get the education they have no viable mind so they are a slave.

[Genesis 19:11 And they smote the men that were at the door of the house with blindness, both small and great: so that they wearied themselves to find the door.]

This means people are very close to the exit door from this mental hell / curse the education creates in them but many are mentally blind so they do not see the door and this is an indication of how powerful the curse is. One is a slave to their perception and in the cursed state of mind ones perception will suggest the door is a wall so one will just pass it by. It does not seem reasonable to go to a place that scares you like a cemetery at night alone and wait until your mind suggests the shadow of death is approaching and then do not run.

That is why you are trapped by your perception. You listen to your intuition but since you got the education your perception lies to you. Your hypothalamus is telling you to run from the things that are not there so you are hallucinating and a danger to yourself and those you are around and especially children, and should be locked up until you can show you are not so mentally unstable.

The deeper reality is, it is not important that you are mentally unsound. The war is not waged to save you, it is to protect the children from you, so please be mindful of that. You have essentially been written off as a loss and that is an indication of how difficult it is to break the brainwashing. I applied the remedy after years of suicide attempts and then finally the last one was a full blown letting go suicide attempt so your chances of actually breaking out of the brainwashing is relative to how much you want it.

You are going to have to love death and seek the shadow of death and then when you find it, submit to it, and from where you are at that seems very unreasonable although in reality it is sane. This is an indication of how powerful this curse is or this brainwashing is and that is why people do not wake up from the brainwashing the full measure very often and when they do the cult, civilization, tends to kill the ones that wake up well because the ones that wake up well are bold like lions and fearless in the face of impossible odds, the cult.

[Genesis 19:12 And the men said unto Lot, Hast thou here any besides? son in law, and thy sons, and thy daughters, and whatsoever thou hast in the city, bring them out of this place:]

These are men, not the men of the cities, the men of the armies who are fighting civilization is a better way to look at it is as the disciples of Abraham and Lot. Abraham is a big fish because he understood the remedy was fear not and was the first being in the ancient texts to start to formulate an accurate example of the remedy, Abraham and Isaac explanation, although Adam spoke of sacrifice which is essentially what one does when they find the shadow of death and submit to it, they sacrifice their brainwashed state of mind.

The men are telling Lot that if he has any relatives who have also broken the curse by applying the fear not remedy to get them because they are getting ready to burn the city to the ground and kill everyone in it. Think about Ebola. If you get Ebola it does not matter who you are, you will be isolated and you will be allowed to die and it is because the species as whole is more important than you.

These wise beings were never about gaining things for their self, they were watching over the species and they were righteous in their determinations. It is one thing to kill others for vain reasons, it is another thing to kill or allow a person to die because they have a curse and are only going to infect the herd, the species.

These wise beings did righteous things to try to stop the spread of the curse but in reality the curse was too strong. The disease is too strong and what causes the disease is too charming. Education as we know it is a perfect Trojan horse and it has destroyed the minds of people for over 5000 years and it is not even important if you believe that because your belief is not greater than the curse. One can break the curse for their self but the curse on the species will perhaps never be broken. Since these wise beings could not stop the curse thousands of years ago when the numbers of the ones cursed was manageable there is perhaps no chancc now.

[Genesis 20:8 Therefore Abimelech rose early in the morning, and called all his servants, and told all these things in their ears: and the men were sore afraid.]

The men were sore afraid. Look at one of the symptoms after Adam and Eve ate off the tree of knowledge.

[Genesis 3:10 And he said, I heard thy voice in the garden, and I was afraid, because I was naked; and I hid myself.]

This indicates the hypothalamus and amygdala started acting strange and sending very strong emotions such as strong fear, shame, embarrassment, shame. After Adam ate off the tree he was afraid of his own nudity. This fear of one's own nudity is a symptom the mind is divided and a mind divided cannot stand because one is actually afraid of their self. [and I was afraid, because I was naked; and I hid myself.] He ran and hide because he was nude, but everyone is born nude so to be afraid of that is just like being afraid of a word, and the next thing one knows they are afraid of their own thoughts and one can never escape their own thoughts so they are doomed. One is simply a house divided among itself after the brainwashing and so one is unviable and cannot stand, so one simply is in a state of abject suffering because one cannot even stand their self. 10:28:02 PM

10:40:10 PM -

[KJV Genesis 3:14 And the LORD God said unto the serpent, Because thou hast done this, thou art cursed above all cattle, and above every beast of the field; upon thy belly shalt thou go, and dust shalt thou eat all the days of thy life:]

[Because thou hast done this (got the education)] = [thou art cursed(mentally unsound/ extreme left brain state of mind leaning)]

[Psalms 74:10 O God, how long shall the adversary reproach? shall the enemy blaspheme thy name for ever?]

This comment is simply a human being who has broken the curse asking, is this curse not breakable for the species? How long will this curse last on the species. But the truth is Adam already answered that.

[Genesis 2:17 But of the tree of the knowledge of good and evil, thou shalt not eat of it: for in the day that thou eatest thereof thou shalt surely die.]

It's a never ending curse on our species and the best thing that can ever happen is a few people break the curse but in relation to how vast the curse is on our species those few who break it are inconsequential.

Did Adam convince Abraham to break the curse? No. [Genesis 15:1 After these things the word of the LORD came unto Abram in a vision, saying, Fear not, Abram: I am thy shield, and thy exceeding great reward.]

Right brain when unveiled figured out how Abraham broke the curse. Fear not is how Abraham broke the curse. So no one told him how to break the curse he broke it accidentally and figured out how he broke the curse in hindsight. Ones comments about supernatural are no match for the curse. We are so cursed as a species because of this invention we do not even think we are cursed. We think sense of time is normal and have emotions so strong we kill ourselves over perceived embarrassment, shame, fear, uncertainty and then we go around and suggest those things are just a part of life. This is actual proof of what happens when you are brainwashed and your hypothalamus, amygdala and cerebral cortex start magnifying all your emotions.

C R (14) committed suicide after being cyber-bullied
M M (13) hung herself in her closet after becoming the victim of cyber-bullying
R N (17) committed suicide after being "cyber-bullied"

These children were insulted by words and were ashamed. They got the education past the age ten mark so they were well into the left brain state. This is a comment about Adam and Ever before they ate of the tree of knowledge, education.
[Genesis 2:25 And they were both naked, the man and his wife, and were not ashamed.]
[and were not ashamed.]

You can go on into infinity blaming the children because I am mindful you perhaps are not intelligent enough in your brainwashed state to submit your little wisdom invention called education is devastating to the mind of a child if it is not taught properly by a master. You do not have enough money to compensate all the people you have destroyed with your wisdom invention, so you should deny what I say because if you agree with it you destroy your world. You may see some things I say are accurate, but then you start to pull back because what is happening is I am dragging you into reality from your reverse world.

You are comfortable with your reverse world and so you are afraid of reality because your left brain cannot handle the complexity of reality but because I woke up the way I did, I assure you that you do not have a choice, because every time you read a sentence in these books you are letting go of the reverse world. I do not know how to explain the cerebral sensation any better than, you are coming along and you can fight and scream or you can just let go, but those are your only choices.

Those suicides of the children are just a part of the curse, the fruits of the curse, and are not a part of life. You keep telling everyone how wise your supernatural wisdom is and I will keep writing books explaining how cursed we are as a species, and we will see who lasts longer. I will go as far as suggesting right brain is unnamable in power once unveiled.- 11:06:01 PM

11/10/2009 3:48:10 AM – Everyone in the world was on fire. A man accidentally fell into the sea and put the fire out that engulfed him. The man made his way back to his friends and told them if they follow his directions they would be able to find the sea and put out the fire that engulfed them. His friends looked around and saw everyone else was on fire except that man and they concluded being on fire was normal so they ignored the man and in turn they never made it to the sea. - 3:51:55 AM

4:51:23 PM – This is an email to someone about something. This person proclaimed to be of the Christian religion so I had to tailor the explanation with that understanding. I understand once a person goes beyond supernatural and tries to explain this as relative to neurological or simply cause and effect ones who are religious tend to deny its validity. This is a symptom of seeing things as parts which is a left brain trait.
*****
The tree of knowledge is written language and math.
Everyone gets these inventions as a child and this is why Jesus said suffer the children.
These inventins are sequential based as in ABC's and 123's and spelling is simply seqencing letters
After years of this education the mind becomes veiled.
The right brain, complex and random access aspect is nearly silenced to the point one is hallucinating.
One of these mental symptoms is the mind perceives time.
[Galatians 4:10 Ye observe days, and months, and times, and years.]

Another hallucination is one is prone to be very afraid, shy, ashamed , embarssed of things that one should not be, such as word, thoughts , nudity, music
[Genesis 3:10 And he said, I heard thy voice in the garden, and [I was afraid, because I was naked]; and I hid myself.]
Timothy explained it quite well
[2 Timothy 1:7 For God hath not given us the spirit of fear; but of power, and of love, and of a sound mind.]
Neurologically speaking after a child gets the education their hypothalamus and amygdala start sending fear signals that are way to amplified so one is very nervous and fearful and afraid about even inanimate things like words.
So a non believer is simply a person who does not believe written language and math put a person in this state of mind.
The state of mind is referred to as hell because it is a curse.

So:
[Genesis 3:6 And when the woman saw that the tree was good for food, and that [it was pleasant to the eyes, and a tree to be desired to make one wise], she took of the fruit thereof, and did eat, and gave also unto her husband with her; and he did eat.]
[it was pleasant to the eyes, and a tree to be desired to make one wise] Education looks like a good idea nd is thought to make one wise and that is its charm and parents give it to their kids and in turn their kids give it to their kids. And this is how the curse spreads

[Genesis 3:14 And the LORD God said unto the serpent, Because thou hast done this, [thou art cursed above all cattle], and above every beast of the field; upon thy belly shalt thou go, and dust shalt thou eat all the days of thy life:]

[thou art cursed above all cattle] , so one can simply think about how many people got this education on a world scale and did not apply the remedy and one will say they are like the grains of sand in the sea.

[Luke 17:33 ; and whosoever shall lose his life shall preserve it.]
This is the remedy. Jesus was right on with the remedy.
When one is cursed they must trick their self into thinking they died. One has to be in a position they perceive the shadow of death is near and then fear not, or submit to it. So one has to defeat their fear of death and that tricks the curse to letting them go.

I am an accident so I will explain how I did it, but I would suggest one uses a different method.
I took a handful of pills to die and when I perceived the shadow of death or thought I was going to die I thought I should call 911 then I thought no you want to die, so I did not try to save myself and I preserved it/ broke the curse. It took about a month for the no sense of time to kick in.
It took nearly a year for me to get use to this no sense of time state of mind because right brain, the right hand, is so powerful it takes a whole for one to get use to it being unveiled, preserved, after the education has veiled it.

I would recommend just going to a place at dark alone like a cemetery or maybe even just watching a very scary movie and when one perceives the shadow of death they submit to it, or they do not try to save their self .
The danger of the curse if you perhaps are thinking what I suggest is not true and that is expected because the truth looks like lies to one who is cursed. Because of this I do not know how to help you other than to say I am an accident. I understand all the ancient texts

and I did not understand any of them before the accident. I am not warmed up so perhaps I am not communicating properly but I am trying to the best I can.

The main problem is there are many who got the education and so it perhaps is too late or I arrived too late.

[1 John 2:18 Little children, it is the last time: and as ye have heard that antichrist shall come, even now are there many antichrists; whereby we know that it is the last time.]

[, even now are there many antichrists] There are too many antichrists, ones with the curse, and I perceive I cannot save the children from them.

Civilization knows not what it does to the children with its wisdom invention.

My only advice would be for you to simply ponder what I am saying and not try to simply discount it right off the bat because the curse makes one unable to feel the spirit of the word and so they are blind to the spirit of the word.

This is comment about the brain

"THE LEFT BRAIN IS ASSOCIATED with verbal, logical, and analytical thinking. It excels in naming and categorizing things, symbolic abstraction, speech, reading, writing, arithmetic. The left brain is very linear: it places things in sequential order -- first things first and then second things second, etc.[If you reflect back upon our own educational training, we have been traditionally taught to master the 3 R's: reading, writing and arithmetic -- the domain and strength of the left brain.]

The Pitek Group, LLC.

Michael P. Pitek, III

.[If you reflect back upon our own educational training, we have been traditionally taught to master the 3 R's: reading, writing and arithmetic -- the domain and strength of the left brain.]

[The left brain is very linear: it places things in sequential order]

So after one has years of this left brain education they have this spirit of fear

[2 Timothy 1:7 For God hath not given us the spirit of fear; but of power, and of love, and of a [sound mind.]

So if one has a spirit of fear and the spirit of fear is not of God(normal) then the spirit of fear is ungodly(abnormal). And if absence of the spirit of fear is sound mind then the spirit of fear is unsound mind as in the right brain is veiled and the left brain is very strong so the mind is like a crescent moon.

My only goal is to convince one person to apply the remedy [Luke 17:33 ; and whosoever shall lose his life shall preserve it.]

So far I am zero for six billion.

END

I understand the reason this situation relative to breaking this curse is so difficult is because ones who perceive they understand these ancient texts becomes afraid if a person starts suggesting they are relative to neurology and psychology because although the ancient texts do mention the mind they cannot make that connection that the mind is relative to psychology and neurology.

[2 Timothy 1:7 For God hath not given us the spirit of fear; but of power, and of love, and of a sound mind.]

Timothy explains quite clearly this spirit of fear is a symptom of an unsound mind and that is not normal or is not of God or natural. So I ponder why the sane would leave these words in the ancient texts because Timothy is not suggesting supernatural as much as he is suggesting psychology. At the time Timothy wrote these comments there was no understanding of the brain and its parts. There was no understanding of the hypothalamus or amygdala yet Timothy was aware this great fear was a symptom of a mind that got the education and in turn created an unsound mind. Fear = an unsound mind. Fear is not natural so it equals an unsound mind. Unsound mind is relative to the education. This is a good example of how these ancient texts are simply trying to explain symptoms of the tree of knowledge but these wise beings did not have the terminology we have today to explain it so they did the best they could based on the fact they did not have the word hypothalamus.

The comment by Timothy translated for today would be.

One who is mentally sound does not have so much fear, so the great fear is caused by the hypothalamus sending magnified signals to the mind as a result of a mind that has been conditioned into extreme left brain state of mind by the years of sequential based education taught improperly.

The curse is so strong though, a simple mind cannot grasp the obvious. Right brain is relative to complexity and left brain is contrary, so it is relative to simple mindedness.

After the education the mind becomes left brain heavy and right brain is veiled so one has the complexity aspect turned way down and the simple minded aspect turned way up. So one is left very simple minded. Some may call that mentally retarded but I prefer the description brain dead mole cricket syndrome.

Supernatural or not, once one gets the education their mind is ruined until they apply the remedy. One should first attempt to regain a sound mind before they start preaching about infinite complexities like supernatural. Simply put a person in this left brain simple minded state has problems understanding elementary cause and effect relationships so they are simply unable on every level to discuss with any kind of sanity the complexities of supernatural. One puts their hand on a stove and they get burned. One gets years of this left brain sequential education taught improperly their mind gets burned. There is nothing complex about that, it is elementary cause and effect but apparently that is far beyond the understanding of a simple minded, mentally brainwashed creature.

The one cause and effect relationship the species should have understood is the one cause and effect relationship the species never understood. Every single invention the species has come up with in the last 5000 years means nothing because the species underestimated the bad side effects of one of their first inventions. The vast majority of all the problems in the world relative to mankind are the result of mankind underestimating the unwanted side effects of one of their first inventions. Mankind assumed this written language invention could have no ill side effects and that was the greatest misunderstanding in the history of mankind and the most costly misunderstanding in the history of mankind. All misunderstandings go back to that misunderstanding. One misstep by mankind over 5000 years ago ruined everything. Everything now is ruined because mankind made an invention and assumed it could not possibly have any bad side effects when in reality is could not have had worse mental side effects because it actually altered mankind's perception and perception is relative to the mind.

Mankind could have just as well taken LSD every single day for the last 5000 years and ended up with what mankind is today. I do not care what your parents, cult leaders or government says contrary to the spirit of what I suggest. If any of them were capable of understanding what I suggest they certainly would have told you by now. They certainly would have explained all of these things to you if they were capable of it, but they are not capable of it because it requires one that has complexity in their thoughts and complexity is a right brain trait and their right brain has been veiled since they were about ten.

The governments of the world have to come out and say the education system they force on children using threats of a hard life and slave jobs if one does not get the education has some major flaws and has done some major damage to people minds.

The governments have to be responsible because they are the cause of this situation. They have put the people they serve in peril mentally. The governments have to accept responsibility for what they have done, because if they do not then the people will understand who they are and in turn revolt against the governments.

I am not suggesting a political point of view or an ideological point of view. I am suggesting no group or person has the right to mentally hinder another person's mind to the point that person is left with one hand tied behind their back mentally. I do not expect any government to own up to their responsibility because if they did they would in turn submit they have done a grave wrong that they could not compensate the people for.

The reason Moses went to the wilderness for forty years is because he attacked civilization and relative to civilization he was deemed a terrorist and he simply was on the run from civilization. The reason Judas had to go into the wilderness to identify Jesus was because Jesus was on the run from civilization because he was explaining how civilization was ruining the children's mind and in turn the peoples mind with their "wisdom education".

I understand the species does not have to go to war about this situation but I also understand as a species we are mentally unbalanced because of this education and nature does not allow disharmony so we in fact may have to go to war. I am talking about a war against the ones who mentally hinder children minds and that is a just war. It is righteous to protect children because children are the future of the species. A child does not want their mind to be veiled no matter how many copper pieces they are offered yet civilization is making that choice so that child's freedom of choice is being infringed upon.

An ounce of prevention is relative to, once one gets the brainwashing it is far too difficult to break out of. It is so difficult to correct the mind once it has been conditioned to such an extreme left brain state it is in fact righteous to go to war against ones who do this to children. I am attempting to war with words but I am mindful the words have never worked before and the physical war has never worked before because mankind is still hindering children's minds and perceives it is doing the children a favor. This is the reverse thing again. Mankind is saying "We educate all our children." as if that is not a monster saying "We mentally rape all of our children." "We mentally hinder all of our children and we boast about it to the world." That is why the war is perhaps inventible and perhaps righteous. There are situations that require peace and situations that require war. Too much patience can turn into hesitated foolishness.

I have never suggested written language and math are evil tools. They are in fact inanimate tools but they are devastating to a child's mind when they are not taught by a Master who understands how to teach these tools properly, so a child's mind is not bent to the left to the point the child is hallucinating. I am not making unreasonable demands considering civilization mentally raped me as a child. I accidentally woke up from the brainwashing and I am bringing the entire house of cards to the floor. Civilization has already robbed me of my mental life and they can never compensate me properly for that. - 5:57:19 PM

7:52:22 PM – Right brain has a characteristic called paradox. Right brain also has a characteristic called complexity. A paradox is complexity. A paradox is two contradictory comments that make up a single truth.

Some of the sane have found contradictions in the ancient texts and they speak as if the ancient texts are flawed because of the contradictions but in reality they are detecting complexity and since the sane have that aspect of their mind veiled they see complexity as improper. If a person speaks poorly of one who suggests contradictions then they speak poorly of right brain because right brain is capable of complexity and complexity is able to understand a paradox which is what a contradiction is.

Moses said Thou shall not kill but he certainly killed that man from civilization early on and he certainly killed that army from civilization that pursued him after he convinced civilization to free the ones they were taking advantage of and making them slaves by way of the brainwashing.

Everyone is the same and everyone is different is a classic paradox.
Everyone human being is a human being yet every human being has a different mindset.

This paradox alone proves contradictions are not a symptom of confusion but of complexity in thought. One has to ask why would civilization condition a child so they would veil the right brain and thus hinder a child's ability to have complexity in their thoughts? Is civilization conditioning children so they are left with simple minded thoughts on purpose or do they simply know not what they do? If civilization is doing this to children on purpose then they are cruel cold hearted bastards. If civilization is doing this to children because they know not what they do then they are insane and they cannot be trusted around children. So that would lead to the paradox civilization is good and civilization is bad.

Civilization is good because only a person in civilization who gets the brainwashing can break the brainwashing and attempt to wake up others.
Civilization is bad because it conditions a child into the brainwashed state of mind to begin with. The tribes who never got the education cannot understand the remedy or how to apply the remedy because they never were blinded mentally so to speak, so they have no contrast. Moses is a very obvious example of this.
[Exodus 2:11 And it came to pass in those days, when Moses was grown, that he went out unto his brethren, and looked on their burdens: and he spied an Egyptian smiting an Hebrew, one of his brethren.]

[Moses was grown] simply mean's Moses broke the curse or the brainwashing instilled by education. Grown means one has thrown off the curse, the yoke. Grown means one has reverted back to sound mind after breaking the curse. Moses went out to his brethren. This means Moses left civilization and his brethren are ones who negated the curse or never got the curse to begin with.

Moses looked on their burdens. One might suggest the Native Americans had a burden when the sane arrived because the sane started taking advantage of them and killing them because the sane had determined because the Native Americans did not have the education they were stupid and so it was okay to take advantage of them. That is the problem with the ones who praise demotic, written language, they are simple minded in their observations and thus their conclusions, and so their bottleneck to reality is narrow mindedness.

Another problem with the sane is their right brain is veiled and right brain is the aspect of the mind that has ambiguity or doubt. There was no doubt in the minds of the sane the Native Americans were stupid because they did not have the education like the sane had. What this means is the sane are captive to their narrow, simple minded perceptions. If the sane believed the Native Americans were wise they would not have taken advantage of them and killed them. The Native Americans were not killing everything in their path for a little money but the sane were, so who you do you think was wise?

The Native Americans were not killing all the bison because they were wise and understood the bison were relative to their own survival yet the sane killed off all the bison in matter of 100 years and then the sane thought they were wise because they made a little money off of doing so. Who was wise? The sane were wise if their goal was disharmony. The sane were foolish if their goal was harmony. This is the problem with the sane.

The sane are disharmony because their mind is disharmonious. What this means is the sane do things they perceive are proper but they are not proper. The sane did not kill the bison the sane killed their self. The sane killed the bison for fun or for money so they killed their self for fun or for money. The deeper reality is they also killed others that came after them for fun or for money. There is perhaps never going to be 50 million bison again so the sane made the decision to rob everyone that comes after them the opportunity to see 50 million bison. The sane condition a child into extreme left brain and alters that child's perception as a result, so the sane decide for that child how that child will perceive things, and what that child will perceive for the rest of that child's life.

The sane will suggest everyone has a choice because their simple minded thoughts are unable to understand everything they think and their very perceptions and thoughts were determined for them when they were a child by their parents and also civilization when they conditioned them into extreme left brain which altered their perception of everything.

If I cut out your right brain when you are a child you do not really have a choice anymore because in cutting out your right brain I decided what you will think and what you will perceive. That goes against a very basic right of being alive.

Life , liberty and the pursuit of happiness. These rights are not determined by the parents or the society. Every single person has a right to life but if they are brainwashed and their right brain is veiled and in turn their perception is altered, they are robbed of mental life and thus physical life because they are not what they were when they were born.

If a person's perception is altered by the education that person is going to do things they would not do if their perception was not altered. This is why education is not mentioned in the Bill of Rights or the Constitution or the Declaration of Independence. What this means is somewhere along the way a person has decided they can determine what is best for everyone and that in turn means they robbed people of self determination and that is what liberty is.

A fear tactic is simply saying "You do this or bad things will happen."

Education is simply saying, "You get the education or you will have a slave job."

Life, liberty, and the pursuit of happiness are all negated after one gets the educating because the education alters ones perception and that means that person has been robbed of their life, liberty and pursuit of happiness. I am mindful these founding fathers were infinitely wiser than you or anyone you know will perhaps ever be.

One does not have a right to alter another human beings perception using fear tactics and I do not care what your whore demotic says contrary to that. I do not care what the law of the land says contrary to that. I do not care what your government says contrary to that. If I put LSD in the drink of a child from the time they are six then I rob that child of its life, liberty and pursuit of happiness. Education is simply a perception altering tool that does the same thing to a child when it is not taught by a master of teaching such a dangerous tool. You would stand against me if I was putting LSD in the drink of a child and so I stand against you for doing the similar to children.

"for I have sworn upon the altar of god eternal hostility against every form of tyranny over the mind of man." –Thomas Jefferson to Benjamin Rush, 23 Sept. 1800

9:48:33 PM – [We the People of the United States[in Order to form a more perfect Union], establish Justice, insure domestic Tranquility, provide for the common defence, promote the general Welfare, and secure the Blessings of Liberty to ourselves and our Posterity, do ordain and establish this Constitution for the United States of America.] US Constituition.

One interesting note about this comment is the word defense is spelled defence. In Canada and the UK defense is spelled defence. What this means is if a child has a spelling test and spells defense, defence and is told they are wrong they in fact are only wrong relative to their place of origin but not wrong relative to the world perspective, yet they are judged and given grades and those grades affect them for the rest of their life. That's not the point of mentioning this passage I just need filler. Filler after all is important.

[in Order to form a more perfect Union] Capitalism goes against this comment. We the people in order to form a more perfect union. Union denotes wholeness yet economics and capitalism denotes separation. The rich and the poor, the have and the have not's.

Capitalism is simply one thing. One gets a product and marks it up and sells it for a profit. The problem with that is you are in fact harming your fellow man. You are harming someone to better you self and that in turn is not making a more perfect union that is making a more separate union. This is why capitalism is not mentioned in any of these texts created by the founding fathers. Economics is simply forcing a person to harm others so they will save their self and money is the root of economics. There is no other species on the planet that uses money and that is a big red flag. This is not because the other species are stupid it is because the other species are prone to perfect unions. There was no money 20,000 years ago. Money is the fruit of a mind that has been conditioned into a state of perceived materialism. "If I have money I am important." That is the logic in reverse world and so people in reverse world will harm others in various ways to get money and that goes against [in Order to form a more perfect Union]. The sane will go on into infinitely babbling on about how they have to make living and charge their own friends markups on items, yet if they understood what living was I would remind them.

Live free or die because if you do not live free you are a slave and thus you are not alive you are simply an item and an inanimate object. Life, liberty and the pursuit of happiness is a very complex comment because in fact if one adheres to it everything works out.

One can do anything they want to do as long as they do not infringe on another person's life, liberty or pursuit of happiness. What this means is the second a person passes a law they infringe on another person's life, liberty or pursuit of happiness. This is why Washington said government is not reason and the antonym of reason is insane. There has never been and never will be a human being intelligent enough to determine what another person's pursuit of happiness may lead to. Good accidents happen and sometimes people are doing one thing and they discover something else they did not intend. This is why laws against what a person can do as long as they do not infringe on the life, liberty and pursuit of happiness of other people are nothing but insanity. Everyone is born and they get to pursue happiness.

About eight years before the accident I slight my wrists and in turn went before a judge and he said "If you want to kill yourself there is nothing anyone can do about it." There is perhaps no greater wisdom than that in relation to pursuit of happiness. One can do anything they wish to do in their pursuit of happiness as long as it does not directly infringe on another person's life, liberty or pursuit of happiness and one is unable to make complex determinations about what may or may not be an indirect consequence of that pursuit of happiness. This of course is all vanity because once a person is brainwashed their pursuit of happiness is not their true pursuit of happiness. This means the education itself denies a human being their right to life, liberty and the pursuit of happiness. This is an indication of how strong the curse is.

A person is addicted to drugs. The law says drugs are illegal. The person gets arrested and thrown into jail. If the person did not get the education to begin with they would not be prone to use drugs at all because in sound mind the right brain when unveiled it is so powerful there is no reason to do drugs or a better way to look at it is the drugs are not as powerful as right brain.

Because of this brainwashing, the powers that be are locking a person in jail because that person is exhibiting behavior because the powers that be brainwashed that person. That is called cruelty.

This perhaps seems strange but the reality is you got the education so you never felt right brain when it is unveiled and fully matured. Your right brain was veiled by about the time you were about ten. You never felt what sound mind is like because the mind does not develop fully by the age of ten. Puberty happens around the age of twelve or fourteen and that is the exact time the left brain conditioning really starts to show it colors, so to speak. Mentally, puberty is in fact an indication that person has gone insane from the education and they start acting strange and start doing drugs and start exhibiting many different traits like greed, wrath, lust, slothfulness, shame, embarrassment. So the entire puberty aspect relative to the mental state is simply a child who is going insane from all the left brain conditioning.

Some children become very shy, aggressive or fearful and then they want to use drugs to escape those mental symptoms. This is a good example of how the species has become self defeating. Think about all the money that is made from treating these mental symptoms and you will understand why civilization makes sure everyone gets the education at least to the age of sixteen because the brainwashing is complete by about the age of ten to fourteen depending on how well it is taken by the child.

There are very few cases of a child killing their self at the age of eight or ten but there are plenty of suicides at age of fourteen on. So now you know why one has to stay in school until they are sixteen. The complexity in this is the brain washing starts to show after the first year of education and that is in part because the parents are brainwashed and they instill the curse in their children and so the education is kind of like the insurance policy. No one is going to escape getting the curse in civilization. There are a few schools in the entire world that know how to teach the education without ruining the mind but you would not detect them because they would appear wrong because you are in reverse world and see right as wrong, truth as lies.

You see a misspelled word as a symptom of stupidity when in reality it is a symptom the right brain is a little more active in that persons mind than in yours. You see a misspelled word or a misplaced comma and you determine that person is stupid because you love the whore demotic and serve her no matter what. You insult children for the sake of a manmade inanimate object so you are insane. I am not insulting you because you cannot spell I am insulting you because you spell so well. You are a little heavy on the sequential simple minded side of thoughts and a little light on the complex random access side of thought. That concerns me because you are allowed to be around children and worse yet you are allowed to have children and raise children and apparently child protective services is asleep. - 10:43:58 PM

10:48:19 PM – When a parent cannot figure out why their child is acting the way it is, right around the age of fourteen on, all that parents has to remind their self of is they sold that child down the river for the promise of a few copper pieces, then I do not ever have to hear brain dead parents ask on television "I do not know what happened to my child." Now the parents know why their child is acting so strangely because that parent allowed their child to be mentally raped under the promise of a few copper pieces and wisdom.

[Genesis 3:6 ....., and a tree to be desired to make one wise,]
It is best you pretend that is not the absolute truth because your mind has emotions turned up so high if you understood that was absolute truth you may harm yourself. You are extremely prone to harming yourself in your deep neurotic state so just ignore everything I say so you will be safe. Avoid making any sudden moves. I will now discuss something of importance.- 10:54:44 PM

11:26:18 PM –
'"There must be some way out of here", said the joker(non brainwashed beings) to the thief(brainwashed beings).... So let us not talk falsely now, the hour is getting late"
All Along the Watchtower – Jimi Hendrix

[Hosea 10:4 They(the sane) have spoken words, swearing falsely in making a covenant: thus judgment springeth up as hemlock in the furrows of the field.]
        Socrates was told to drink hemlock because he spoke to the children about the bad side effects of the education. A furrow is a narrow trench in relation to narrow minded and left brain is simple minded in contrast to right brain which is complex. I see wisdom in Swiss cheese commercials.
[thus judgment springeth up as hemlock in the furrows of the field.] = The sane judge, good and bad, because they see parts, a left brain trait, hemlock means death, and furrows means narrow minded and field means the species of mankind.
So this comment is saying, the brainwashed are the narrow minded mentally dead of the species.
So
[[Hosea 10:4 They(the sane/brainwashed) have spoken words, swearing falsely in making a covenant:] Means they deny that the tree of knowledge, written language and math have any bad mental side effects and so they deny the covenant which is the remedy, the fear not remedy.
But this is not because they were born blind mentally this is because they were conditioned at such a young age they know nothing but this mental blindness state, so they know not what they do.

        Hosea talks in part about the sane worshiping Baal a fertility god. Fertility denotes overpopulation. This is why the sane are essentially impossible to defeat because they have all of these disharmonious traits. This is why Adam attempted to urge the ones who broke the curse or did not have the curse to multiply
[Genesis 1:28 And God blessed them, and God said unto them, Be fruitful, and multiply, and replenish the earth, and subdue it: and have dominion over the fish of the sea, and over the fowl of the air, and over every living thing that moveth upon the earth.]

Of course over population goes against one that is of sound mind. This is why various tribes never had great numbers. They had a sound mind and understood they could not just have children into infinity because they were capable of understanding simple cause and effect relationships.

[Be fruitful, and multiply, and replenish the earth, and subdue it:] This comment is saying to the ones who broke the curse, have many children so you can subdue the ones with the curse, the earth, the materialistic based cursed ones, the men who build towers.[Genesis 11:5 And the LORD came down to see the city and the tower, which the children of men builded.], children of men denotes the adults force the education on the kids and then give them slave jobs building vain towers to heaven because the children's cerebral powerhouse is veiled.

This is why men is an insult in this comment. The men give their children over to demotic, written language, for a few copper pieces. The Lords do not. Tower denotes materialism. The men make their children build a tower to heaven because their right brain is veiled because of the sequential based education so they are no longer able to reach cerebral heaven, mental clarity. I have been known to have moments of clarity, relative to infinity.

The men are vain in their attempts to reach heaven with material things, they never have reached it with material things and they never will reach it, but they keep trying in vain. The men will destroy the entire planet to build a tower to reach heaven and they will never reach it because the kingdom is within, it's right brain and materialism will never help you unveil it. That is good news because that means the meek and the poor can reach it. It does not cost anything, it is a mental process, the remedy.

The carpetbaggers do not like things they cannot charge money for. The carpetbaggers try to turn everything into a money making opportunity because they believe they cannot live without money because they lost their mind at about the age of ten.

This is a good example of how these ancient texts are simply battle plans to fight against the sane and so it is quite interesting to understand the sane keep publishing battle plans that are used to defeat them. This is an indication of the slothful nature of the sane. Many things go over their head so to speak and for thousands of years relative to a calendar.

November 11, 2009 4:42:09 AM – [James 2:26 For as the body without the spirit is dead, so faith without works is dead also.] is relative to [2 Timothy 1:7 For God hath not given us the spirit of fear; but of power, and of love, and of a sound mind.]

A person with an unsound mind is dead because an unsound mind is a divided mind and it cannot stand. The spirit comment in the first comment is relative to right brain. Once a person gets the education their right brain is veiled and they are dead in contrast to a person with right brain unveiled and this is relative to [Acts 10:42 And he commanded us to preach unto the people, and to testify that it is he which was ordained of God to be the Judge of quick and dead.] The quick and the dead = quick cerebrally and slothful cerebrally.

Left brain is sequential based and right brain is random access based. Left brain is simple minded and right brain is the complexity aspect. Once the right brain is veiled because the left brain education uses the left brain so much, one's mind is bent to the left and their thoughts are relatively sequential in speed. This slothful sequential thought pattern is why a person can become addicted or can covet things.

A person can become lustful for something and because the mind is so slothful in the left brain sequential state of mind it may take a lifetime to break free of that lust for something. In contrast when right brain is unveiled one can move through a lust or coveting for something in about one minute or less relative to a clock. This perhaps seems unbelievable, because this means that veiling right brain with this education with the understanding of how powerful right brain is compared to left brain, means this education which veils right brain when not taught properly is the worst crime one can do to another human being, and it is.

That's why Abraham and Lot did this [Genesis 19:25 And he overthrew those cities, and all the plain, and all the inhabitants of the cities, and that which grew upon the ground.]

This comment is an indication how great a crime this education conditioning is because it makes a genius complex mind retarded, and in turn dooms that person to a life of suffering because the education is not taught by a master that understands the bad side effects of the education. This is why this is a dangerous topic for anyone to discuss because the sane speak about justice but they are unable to give anyone justice for doing this to them. [James 2:26 For as the body without the spirit is dead]

One that gets this education improperly is dead in contrast to one who breaks the brainwashing and restores right brain. The sane are quite certain Einstein had a special brain with some magical parts added to it because the sane cannot imagine he was just a person who in one way or another broke the curse to a degree. He was simply of sound mind. He certainly did not translate the ancient texts so perhaps you should call me and tell me why you believe he was so special. If he understood the remedy to the education neurosis he would have told you. You go ahead and idolize Einstein and I will remind him of your idolatry when he comes by to tend to my fish heads. I should perhaps avoid personal commentary.

[Congress shall make no law respecting an establishment of religion, or prohibiting the free exercise thereof; or abridging the freedom of speech, or of the press; or the right of the people peaceably to assemble, and to petition the Government for a redress of grievances.]
First Amendment

Congress shall make no law abridging the freedom of speech.

Speech is relative to written language and written language is relative to spelling. If a child spells the word cat , kat and you punish him for that you abridge his right to freedom of speech. A human being can spell the word cat any way they want to and if any other human being punishes them, that person abridges their freedom of speech. If an entire society is complicit in punishing a child for spelling a word improperly based on that societies accepted norms they in fact abridge that person's freedom of speech. If a person fails a spelling quiz and the teacher gives them a F and they eventually end up stuck in a slave job because of that judgment, it is because that teacher abridged their freedom of speech and so that teacher is a tyrant.

Freedom of speech means a person can spell a word any way they want to and if they are punished for spelling a word the way they want to, their freedom of speech is abridged.[John 8:43 Why do ye not understand my speech?]

Here is an example of freedom of speech. Thomas Jefferson wrote the preamble to the Rights of Man document.
Here is what we wrote.
"I am extremely pleafed to find it will be reprinted
'here, and that fomething is at length to be publickly
'faid agianft the political herefies which have frung
"up amoung us.
" I have no doubt our citizens will rally a fecond time
"round the ftandard of Common Sense."

One might think the S key was not working that day but he does use the s key in some words. This is what freedom of speech is. Spelling how you want to spell and not being punished by some control freak tyrant who is judging you by how you spell and then throwing you into a slave job because you do not spell the words fxactly how they fant you tou.

I understand Thomas Jefferson was wiser than perhaps you will ever be fnto infinity. Thomas Jefferson was hardcore and you fhould pray every night there is no fafterlife because he said this :
"for I have sworn upon the altar of god eternal hostility against every form of tyranny over the mind of man." –Thomas Jefferson to Benjamin Rush, 23 Sept. 1800

If a person judges a small child because that child misspells a word based on that teachers delusion that one is capable of misspelling a word that teacher is tyrant over the mind of that child.

I am blessed because no one can understand fnything I say into finifinity. Fhy do you not fnderstand my fpeech? When you insult someone or judge someone because they misspell a word you are just a little slave dog following the orders of a slave dog that taught you to judge people based on how well they spell. I pay no heed to slave dogs.- 5:43:32 AM

5:56:42 AM – This is a comment by Jefferson writing about the Virgiana Act in 1786.

This is in Chapter 5.
" 1. In the primitive community of saints there was a diversity of gifts (1 Cor. 12:4-6). "Now there are varieties of gifts, but the same Spirit; and there are varieties of service, but the same Lord; and there are varieties of working, but it is the same God who inspires them all in every one." The variety is in the saints, the sameness is in the Godhood. To eliminate the variety among the members would make the purpose of God of none effect. It is only when they recognize the source of their oneness that they can achieve a common purpose. "To each is given the manifestation of the Spirit for the common good" (verse 7). What was said of gifts bestowed supernaturally will also be true of gifts derived naturally."
Here are some patterns.
[but the same Spirit]
[but the same Lord]
[but it is the same God]
[The variety is in the saints, the sameness is in the Godhood.]
[recognize the source of their oneness]
This is suggesting monotheism. Mono means one. One is the same thing relatively speaking as wholeness or oneness. Right brain seeing everything as one thing or is holistic. The Native Americans said they see a spirit of oneness in everything.

Oneness is contrary to this [Genesis 2:17 But of the tree of the knowledge of [good and evil], thou shalt not eat of it: for in the day that thou eatest thereof thou shalt surely die.] [good and evil] = seeing things as parts and seeing things as parts is left brained.

Holistic or seeing everything as one thing is a right brained trait. So when the right brain is veiled one only see's parts. When the right brain is unveiled one can see parts but usually see's things as one thing because right brain is the powerhouse of the two hemispheres. It is understood by the sane, subconscious is very powerful and subconscious relative to one who has their right brain veiled is right brain. I do not understand what I understand since the accident for any other reason in the universe except the fact I am using my subconscious mind to figure out stuff and that is right brain. Simply put my subconscious is now my conscious and it is so powerful it can figure out anything in a moment but relative to one who has the brainwashing right brain is veiled so they are slothful in contrast mentally.

I may say some things that are contradictory and I may say some things that are wrong but that is not important. Relative to me I am pleased with the machine, right brain, I accidentally unveiled and I am giving it a test drive. I am simply seeing where this machine can take me because I am pleased with this machine and I am pondering what kind of diabolical whore would want to veil a person's wonderful machine, right brain. I do not know why you hate right brain. It is different than left brain but it is so powerful and complex and you just keep veiling it in children so I have no choice. - 6:09:55 AM

5:54:10 PM –
Amendment XIII

"Section 1. Neither slavery nor involuntary servitude, except as a punishment for crime whereof the party shall have been duly convicted, shall exist within the United States, or any place subject to their jurisdiction."

The education system is supported by the government and the education conditions the mind to the degree one hallucinates and perceives time and this conditioning alters ones perceptions and alters how the brain works and makes the amygdala and hypothalamus send very strong signals of fear and thus all emotions are turned up and so one is robbed of their life, liberty and pursuit of happiness mentally and so one is turned into a slave because this education is enforced using fear tactics and threats of a hard life if one does not get the education so it is essentially involuntary servitude because one behaves differently than they would if they did not get the education brainwashing. A child has committed no crime yet they are brainwashed and their perception is altered and it is essentially permanent so that child is robbed of their mind. This means they are very afraid, embarrassed, nervous and this effects their health so they are also robbed of their health.

9:44:04 PM – You can't trust the dust - http://www.youtube.com/watch?v=4nIhvhnW1lI

Written language and math were fatal to our species. There is nothing in the history of mankind that has done more damage by a multiplier of infinity than the sentential based inventions written language and math because when they are not administered properly they totally obliterate the mind beyond all understanding.

11/12/2009 1:48:47 AM -
[Genesis 19:24 Then the LORD rained upon Sodom and upon Gomorrah brimstone and fire from the LORD out of heaven;

Genesis 19:25 And he overthrew those cities, and all the plain, and all the inhabitants of the cities, and that which grew upon the ground.]
[And he overthrew those cities, and all the plain, and all the inhabitants of the cities,]
[And he overthrew all the inhabitants of the cities,]
[And he overthrew the inhabitants of the cities,]
[And he overthrew those cities, and all the inhabitants,]
[And he overthrew all the plain inhabitants of the cities,] - 1:53:44 AM

Stop reading my private diaries.

* You were kicked from #Christian by QST ([Reason: anti-christian])
<KarenJ> Lestat I perceive you are mentally ill and need help very badly.
[00:13] <+KarenJ> I'm reasonably well educated but that one is nonsense as near as I can tell
* You were kicked by KarenJ (Blacklisted- false doctrine lectures)
#christian unable to join channel (address is banned)
"I am Patrick, a sinner, most uncultivated and least of all the faithful and despised in the eyes of many." - Saint Patrick

despised in the eyes of many.
[1 John 2:18 Little children, ,, even now are there many antichrists;]
[00:13] <+KarenJ> I'm reasonably well [educated] but [that one is nonsense] as near as I can tell.]
[educated] = Genesis 3:6 and a tree to be desired to make one wise.
[00:13] <+KarenJ> I'm reasonably well [educated] = [many antichrists;]
[that one is nonsense] = [John 8:43 Why do ye not understand my speech?]
[Revelation 13:18 Here is wisdom. [Let him that hath understanding count the number of the beast]: for it is the number of a man; and his number is Six hundred threescore and six.]
[Let him that hath understanding count the number of the beast] = [1 John 2:18 Little children, ,, even now are there many antichrists;] = [Genesis 3:14 And the LORD .. said unto the serpent, Because thou hast done this, thou art cursed above all cattle, and above every beast of the field; upon thy belly shalt thou go, and dust shalt thou eat all the days of thy life:]

[the serpent] = [00:13] <+KarenJ> I'm reasonably well [educated] = [many antichrists;]
= [00:13] <+KarenJ> I'm reasonably [antichrist;]
despised in the eyes of [many] antichrists;.

"I am Patrick, a sinner, most uncultivated and least of all the faithful and despised in the eyes of many."[antichrists]

[1 John 2:18 Little children, ,, [even now] are there many antichrists;]
[even now]
[even now]
[even now]
* You were kicked by KarenJ (Blacklisted- false doctrine lectures).
#christian unable to join channel (address is banned).
[00:13] <+KarenJ> I'm reasonably well [educated] but [that one is nonsense] as near as I can tell.]
* You were kicked by KarenJ (Blacklisted- false doctrine lectures).
#christian unable to join channel (address is banned).
[Luke 23:34 …, for they know not what they do.]
[for they know not what they do.] [[he overthrew those cities, and all the plain, and all the inhabitants of the cities,] [for they know not what they do.]
[for they know not what they do.] [Genesis 3:13 …, The serpent beguiled,]
[00:13] <+KarenJ> I'm reasonably well educated but that one is nonsense as near as I can tell
* You were kicked by KarenJ (Blacklisted- false doctrine lectures)
#christian unable to join channel (address is banned)
[antichrists] = [2 Timothy 1:7 .. spirit of fear;] = [Galatians 4:10 Ye observe days, and months, and times, and years.]= [1 John 2:18 Little children, ,, even now are there many antichrists;]=
[00:13] <+KarenJ> I'm reasonably well [[[[educated]]]]] [antichrist] = unsound mind =[they know not what they do.] = insane.
* You were kicked by KarenJ (Blacklisted- false doctrine lectures)
#christian unable to join channel (address is banned)
[Exodus 32:19 And it came to pass,…, that he saw the calf, and the dancing: and … anger waxed hot, and he cast the tables out of his hands, and brake them beneath the mount.]
[Psalms 120:7 I am for peace: but when I speak, they[antichrists] are for war.]=
* You were kicked by KarenJ (Blacklisted- false doctrine lectures) = [for they know not what they do.]
[John 8:43 Why do ye not understand my speech?..]
[Psalms 6:10 Let all mine enemies be ashamed and sore vexed: let them return and be ashamed suddenly.] relative to [Genesis 2:25 And they were both naked, the man and his wife, and were not ashamed.]

Not ashamed before the education. The ones who get the education become ashamed and afraid because their mind stops working properly. This is the cause and effect of being conditioned into such extreme left brain state of mind.

4:01:30 AM –

The only possible way a person can know that $1 + 1 = 2$ is if they have the sequence of numbers memorized. Every time a person does a math problem they are simply consulting this chart in their left brain that has all the numbers sequenced.

5×5. A person thinks five, ten, fifteen, twenty, twenty five. That is the left brain sequence aspect working. Remember learning the multiplication charts when you were young, that was simply hardcore left brain conditioning.

When a person gets a math problem wrong it is because the right brain worked for moment and they saw the numbers as random access. So when a person takes a math test they are punished or judged poorly when they do not get the number sequencing correct. It is impossible to have a numeric system that is in random access order, it simply would not work. So a child goes to school and the first thing they learn in math class is to memorize the sequencing of the numeric system. This has nothing to do with wisdom this is simply left brain sequential brainwashing. If you get all the numerical sequencing right you become a little more left brained, and you become a little more simple minded, and your emotions turn up a little more, and then they give you an A, and then you go home and show your parents the A, and then they will not beat you for doing poorly in school.

One thing I understood tonight about some of these religions is the people who subscribe to them as religions are too far gone or too far brainwashed because they are counting on something to save them when in reality these wise beings from these ancient texts told them the remedy in so many ways it's hard to believe, and are too blind to see that.

They are waiting for something to break the curse and they never grasped they were told how to break the curse, they just never applied the remedy. They are waiting for someone to tell them the remedy but the wise beings told them a thousand versions of the same remedy and they never ever applied it because they cannot understand any longer. One could throw them a life raft and they would swim away from it and then ask "Where is the life raft?".

Look at all the remedies the wise beings suggested and then understand none of the sane had a clue the remedy was right in their face.

One being said fear not. Then he said When you see a knife held over your chest do not run but fear not.

Another being said "When you see the shadow of death do not fear or run from the shadow of death."

Another being said Do not try to save your life from the shadow of death and you will break the curse or restore/preserve your sound mind.

Another being said Submit to the shadow of death. When you see the shadow of death submit .

Another being said, when you see Medusa's head look at it and face your fear of that shadow of death and you will turn to stone which means your strong emotions and pride and greed and lust and envy and wrath will be silenced and you will be able to think clearly again.

All these are saying is the state of mind you are in after all the years of education is an alter ego or not your true self or is not sound mind, so you have to trick it into dying and that can only be accomplished by being in a situation you perceive the shadow of death is near and you do not run but you submit to that perceived shadow of death. It is painless. It is a mental exercise to break you out of the brain washing the education has put you in.

If the education was taught by a person who knew what they were doing you would not have to do this but you are not so lucky so now you have a stone around your neck and you have to do the best you can to get that stone from around your neck or you will waste your entire life trapped in some alternate mental hell.

You are going to have to have a little bit of courage, fortitude and self control to get your mind back after it was ripped from you by the ones your trusted to protect you.

Go prove the remedy wrong. Go sit in a cemetery all alone at night by yourself and when your unsound mind tells you the shadow of death is coming, you let it come and you submit to it. It takes one second. Your mind will say run like the wind, the hypothalamus, and you do not run like the wind and that is it. It's over. Go home. It will kick in about a month. Only a total fool would not at least experiment, considering it costs them nothing and it will give them an infinite reward.

I am not asking you to swallow a handful of pills and when you start to convulse, do not call for help. The reality is, this remedy is a mind technique and it is not important if you are even in actual physical danger at all its just important your mind perceives you are in actual physical danger. That is simple to accomplish because in that state of mind one is in after the education, a twig breaking in a cemetery at night when they are alone is enough to make their hypothalamus suggest death is on its way.- 4:35:05 AM

4:42:15 AM – I am aware my words appear harsh perhaps to some but right brain did not like to be put in a cage and that is the problem when someone wakes up accidentally. I tried to kill myself and then something happened and I unveiled right brain and it is a monster of pattern detection and complexity and it has sifted through all my memories and everything I have ever heard and ever seen and it has thrown all the patterns together and it has figured out what civilization did to it and it is madder than hell.

You are never going to change that and you are perhaps never going to understand that. As for me I am simply arranging words in a meaningful fashion to excite emotions in my mission to complete infinite books, and you are never going to change that and you perhaps never going to understand that.

It is not wise to veil this machine called right brain because no matter how well one veils it, right brain may eventually break free of its cage and it is going to incite Armageddon on the ones who put it into a cage, and heaven and earth cannot stop that eventuality. What I mean is right brain is so powerful I am not even sure if it is me because I was in the brainwashed state for forty years and now I have this unnamable power house and it is even beyond my understanding and all I did was accidently do this [Luke 17:33 ; and whosoever shall lose his life shall preserve it.].

You may not be aware of it but there is no story that will ever top this one but there are a few stories that equal it. You remember these books because I do not remember these books. I do not remember what I have written up to this point in the diaries but you remember what I have written, so you tell the story and you tell it boldly for the children's sake.- 4:54:22 AM

The only thing more insane than suggesting written language creates unwanted mental side effects is suggesting it creates none.
Imagine where we would be as a species if we didn't mentally rape all the children with the education by the time they were ten and leave them mentally unviable.

From the outskirts of them
They are filled with it and trim
They cannot swim upon my tree
They kept my ancient texts for me

They have not changed nor have I changed
The wilderness does not feel my wrath
Like they who love the whore the calf
They kept my ancient texts for me

They are not very bright nor free
They are not very fond of me
They kept my plans I use them still
Just so they know their blood I spill

I live alone away from them
They cannot tell the light from grim
Updated but they never learned
That's why their souls are sudden burned

Could I replace their missteps now?
Their only dance summons the foul
I scorn the towering wisdom tree
It kept my ancient texts I see.

They show me how I can compete
Their usury it does mistreat
I cannot think why they can't think
Perhaps they never could

I should not stand to see them so
My greatest failure their fading glow
What bothers me won't bother them
Because their filled to it with brim

The sound of spaces in between
The letters spell their fate unseen
Yet I would have to leave this place for sea
My ancient texts they kept for me

I won't fight you.
That's my way to smite you.
I won't elegantly speak your words.
I won't elegantly use your verbs.
I won't fight you.
That's my way to smite you
Does that bother you?
When I spit on you.
Does that bother you?
I won't fight you.
Does that bother you?
That's how I right you.
Does that bother you?
The only true.

Does that bother you?
That place you flew.

Adversary - http://www.youtube.com/watch?v=ZzSy5maFU4w

11/12/2009 8:37:21 PM –
My books are extremely poor.
Extremely poor are my books.
Poor extremely my books are.
Books extremely poor are my.

    If one wrote like this in school they would be perhaps rush me to the principal's office and I would eventually be heavily sedated. To a person who has applied the remedy and has right brain unveiled these above sentences are all saying the exact same thing. Relative to the education system there is only one sentence in the above sentences that is perhaps correct. Right brain detects patterns and these patterns are not detected on a sequential level, they are detected on a random access level so there are no rules involved in the pattern detection. This pattern detection is how one gets the spirit of the ancient texts. I see a sentence and the sequence of the sentence is not even considered in contrast to the whole of the sentence. The deeper reality is random access, contradiction, paradox are all right brain traits and these traits are also assumed symptoms of insanity by the ones who have been brainwashed into extreme left brain state. If a person says "I like you" and then says "I don't like you" they will be considered schizophrenic. In reality that is simply a paradox.

    If a person has right brain unveiled they should not be able to stay on topic for very long relative to one who has the brainwashing so they will appear to be rambling. Relative to that person who has right brain unveiled, they see everything as one thing, so they never perceive they are off topic. So relative to a person who is brainwashed into extreme left brain a person who has broken the brainwashing and unveils right brain appears full of contradictions, paradox and unable to stay on topic. Because of this reality the ones who are brainwashed will seek to "fix" them with their medication. So society all across the board is brainwashed into this extreme left brain state and if anyone in society somehow breaks free of the brainwashing and unveils right brain they are automatically deemed insane because they tend to make contradictions and speak in random access and cannot stay on topic relative to the ones who are brainwashed into the extreme left brain state.

    So in school if a child types a sentence like this "Poor extremely my books are." That child will be deemed to be mentally imbalanced and in need of "help" and dyslexic. The reality is society is biased against right brain so in fact society hates right brain because right brain is random access and random access is deemed insanity by society. The darkness see's the light as darkness. The reason society hates random access and thus right brain is because random access is unpredictable. Society will say this person is unpredictable. Society cannot handle unpredictability because society has been conditioned into extreme left brain and thus is only capable of sequential understanding so anything that is not sequential is deemed bad. Children tend to do things that are unpredictable. A parent will say "I have no idea what my child was thinking when they did that." This is because the adult has been brainwashed and is always looking for sequential reasoning for things.

This sequential mindset is thought to be safe because if one can see a few steps in front of them they feel they are safe but in reality the inability to have random access thoughts is dangerous because things do not always happen for elementary sequential reasons. Things can happen for very complex random access reasons also and if one is brainwashed into extreme left brain they are unable to grasp that kind of complexity. When you hear someone say "We have no idea why that happened". or "We never saw it coming" that is because they only see one or two sequential steps in front of them.

This is why this brainwashing is dangerous to the species because it leaves the species mentally vulnerable. For example cause and effect relationships are endless so one who can only see a few sequential steps down the road is at a disadvantage. Here are some examples.

Mankind invented nuclear bombs and should have been aware if they invented these bombs eventually everyone would want one and eventually they may be used against the ones who invented them and so the ones who invented them in fact hung their self by inventing the bombs to begin with.

Civilization is using up the resources in competition with the rest of the world and so civilization should have been aware using up all the recourses would eventually lead to environmental problems so it should have been aware of this and then it would have not used up all the resources. Since mankind is brainwashed into this extreme left brain state it cannot see that far down the road because it only see's a few sequential steps ahead, now civilization is trying to recover from the environmental problems but it cannot because it can only see a few steps down the road. Civilization tries to fix one thing and other things go bad because it can never see the full spectrum of the situation because mankind is trapped in this sequential state of mind caused by the many years of left brain education.

Civilization cannot see far enough down the road to understand if you condition a person as a child into extreme left brain everything they do from that point on will be a symptom of the unsound state of mind they have been conditioned into.

Civilization conditions a child into extreme left brain and then that child later becomes addicted to drugs and then starts robbing, to get the drugs, and then civilization makes prisons and starts throwing kids it conditioned into that state of mind to begin with, into those prisons.

The kids are not bad. The drugs are not bad. It is the education taught improperly that conditions the kids into an unsound state of mind to begin with that makes the kids prone to addictions and so throwing them in prisons is not a solution is a an attempt to fix a symptom that child has been conditioned into an unsound state of mind by the same people who encourage the prisons.

Drug addiction itself is a symptom a person is trying to get some relief from this unsound state of mind the education has conditioned them into. Simply put that person is suffering in that extreme left brain state of mind and they want to escape it and when they do drugs they unveil right brain for a the duration of the drugs effect. That is reasonable solution to being in an unsound state of mind. No one wants to suffer. But the complexity is the exact same government that conditioned that person into a state of mind to the point that person wants to do drugs to escape that state of mind, is the same government that's tells that person they cannot escape the suffering of that unsound state of mind or they get thrown in prison.

Let's look at a rapist. Rape is a symptom of lust and a symptom of control. Control is coveting. Coveting is not possible on a scale of a mindset when right brain is unveiled because simply put, right brain is pondering so fast that state of coveting and also lust is not ever going to be able to be maintained mentally for more than a moment relative to a clock. In contrast in the extreme left brain state after the brain washing the mind has the power house right brain veiled so a thought of lust can linger for years and years. This is relative to drug addiction also. A drug addiction is a symptom the mind cannot ponder its way out of the cravings or lust and desire for the drugs.

I have not associated with some of these tribes that live in the Amazon so I am uncertain if they have drug addiction and rape and murder and crime problems like civilization does but I am mindful they perhaps do not.

The complexity is in a brainwashed left brain dominate state of mind the education causes, ones thoughts are slow, sequential. Lust is a slow experience because left brain is sequential and slothful in contrast to right brains random access thought patterns. When right brain is unveiled a mental sensation of lust passes within minutes relative to a clock but not because the person is so good or moral it is because right brain is a machine and it ponders through all thoughts at speeds that make it impossible for a person to maintain a mental state of lust.

So lust is a sin so to speak but if one's mind is pondering so fast because they apply the remedy and unveil right brain they are not capable of maintaining a mental state of lust so they are what is known as without sin or free from that sin lust, they escape that thought swiftly before they become a slave to it. Every person in prison got the education.

If one has right brain unveiled and they in turn are not capable of maintaining a mental state of greed they are without sin or free from that sin of greed, they can escape that mental symptom swiftly.

Jesus suggested lets those without sin cast the first stone. This means let the ones who have applied the remedy and unveiled right brain punish that person because he knew anyone who applied the remedy and unveiled the right brain would be aware that person was simply acting the way they were because they were conditioned into the unsound state of mind by the education.

The apostles applied the remedy so they were without sin. All this means is they unveiled the unnamable powerhouse, right brain and they were unable to maintain a state of mind of some of these mental side effects ones who get the brainwashing and have not applied the remedy can maintain. This is not relative to how good a person is or is not, this is relative to whether a person has been conditioned into an unsound state of mind or has broken that unsound state of mind. This is relative to whether a person has negated the brainwashing caused by the education or not. If a human being is conditioned into an extreme left brain state caused by the education being improperly administered then their fruits are greed, lust, envy, idolatry, strong sense of time and all of these fruits are nothing but mental symptoms of suffering caused by the slothful thought patterns caused by the extreme left brain sequential state.

An unsound mind means a person suffers. Greed is suffering because one can never get enough. Lust is suffering because one can never satisfy that lust. So if one's mind itself is pondering so fast one cannot even maintain that state of greed or lust they are not able to suffering because of those thoughts.

Every human has thoughts and so these thoughts of greed and lust and gluttony are impossible to avoid but the contrast is one who applies the remedy to the brain washing has their thoughts of those aspects turned down to about one and one who gets the brainwashing and does not apply the remedy has their thoughts of those aspects turned up to about a thousand. This is a simple cause and effect relationship. One is brainwashed by the education and then their hypothalamus, amygdala and their cerebral cortex start magnifying all these thoughts to great extremes so one is controlled by those thoughts.

If you are aware a person has been brainwashed so their thoughts are all magnified and that is why they are exhibiting symptoms of greed and lust and gluttony can you throw stones at them or lock them in cages with a clear conscience? If a person is conditioned into an unsound state of mind as a child by the society, that person does not have a choice relative to how they behave because their behavior, fruits were chosen for them by that society when that society brainwashed them to begin with.

How can civilization lock someone in jail for exhibiting mental behaviors it in fact encouraged to begin with? How can civilization punish a person for exhibiting greed when it in fact brain washed them as a child to exhibit extreme symptoms of greed? How can a parent punish their child for doing drugs when that child is only doing drugs because that parent allowed that child to be brainwashed by teacher that had no clue how to administer the education without totally altering that child's perception to begin with?

That child is not doing drugs because they want to do drugs, that child is doing drugs to try to get some relief from this extreme left brain state you as a parent has allowed them to be conditioned into. The complexity of that is you as a parent are not even aware of that because your parents allowed you to be conditioned also and your parents where not aware of that because their parents allowed them to be conditioned also. I cast no stones because I understand you are suffering enough as it is. I am unable to make you suffer anymore than you are right now. I know how I was and I was like you are and I assure you I was mentally suffering and so are you, and that is understood because since one is conditioned into an unsound state of mind they have nothing but mental suffering to look forward to. - 9:46:46 PM

11:07:43 PM – Left brain is good with short term memory and right brain is good at long term memory. Subconscious mind, relative to a person who has been brainwashed into the extreme left brain state, is right brain. Subconscious is right brain if one has their right brain veiled. If one applies the remedy they unveil right brain so they no longer have a subconscious, their mind is all up front, conscious, so to speak.

Elderly people tend to have short term memory problems. There are some who have illnesses but this is not relative to a physiological illness. There are elderly people who are absent minded and this is because they have been away from the education so long they are starting to break the curse and unveil right brain a bit and they become absent minded professors. My short term memory is negotiable. Sometimes it works and sometimes it does not and that is a symptom my left brain is at 50% as opposed to how it was under the brainwashing when it was at more like 90%. So a person who is brainwashed has very good short term memory and very bad long term memory. The whole memory discussion is very complex because one tends to remember traumatic situations or profound situations. The right brain tends to store ideas as opposed to actual sentences. It's a cerebral thought's that is saved so education is based on recalling words and equations but not so much ideas or concepts. For example the word good is easy to remember but it suggests an absolute. Right brain has too much paradox to relate to an absolute. One might suggest "We need to give all the kids a good education."

If one gives a child the education taught by a person who is only capable of teaching the sequencing aspects with no regards to its unwanted side effects mentally and no regards to being mindful of the random access aspect that must be taught equally they do not give a child a good education they give that child a bad education. They do however give the child a good education relative to that method if their goal is to create a mentally unsound child. Right brain is good at long term memory so education has to have lots of long term memory associated elements to counter act all the left brain short term memory aspects but it does not.

Education has to have lots of no rule aspects to counter act the left brains love of rules aspects. Education has to have lots of creative activities with no rules attached to counter act the left brain narrow minded with rules attached aspects of left brain. Some schools make a child memorize a 200k word book word for word. Some schools only teach the children verbally for the most part. I am not talking about any school you have ever gone to or would ever send your child to I am talking about schools that understand the damaging effects of the education on a child's mind. It is not important what book the child memorizes it is only important that child keeps their long term memory, right brain, in top shape while they get the short term memory left brain education along with it.

Society will tout that certain drugs affect short term memory. They will suggest pot is bad because it effect's short term memory. What they are really detecting is that pot unveils right brain a bit. As short term memory decreases, left brain, long term memory increases, right brain.

I am not suggesting anyone ever do drugs because one can just apply the remedy and then they wake up and won't need drugs because they will be plenty high because they negate the brainwashing and unveil right brain. You may perceived you like drugs euphoria effects, coffee, recreational drugs, sugar, but all you are really feeling is the right brain unveiled just a bit and for a short period of time. You unveil right brain with this remedy and you will have to redefine your definition of high and euphoria to name a few.

Drugs take way too long to unveil right brain and they may not accomplish ones goal to negate the brainwashing. Another reason drugs are not a good route to escape the brainwashing is the drugs harms you physiologically and the only reason your doing the drugs is to get relief from the suffering caused by the brainwashing, One does not drink wine to feel good, they drink wine to escape the mental suffering left brain extreme state caused by the brainwashing, The drugs alleviate the brainwashing mental suffering for the duration the drug works. Some people subconsciously dedicate their whole life to breaking the brainwashing using drugs and most do not accomplish it before the drugs start to take their toll on that person physiologically.

The best way to look at drug abuse is simply, drugs unveil the right brain to a varying degree depending on the potency of the drug but because it unveils the right brain so fast one gets a "high" sensation. That person is not high they are simply feeling how powerful right brain is and because they unveil it so swiftly it gives them the perception of being high. When one unveils right brain using the remedy they will no longer feel this "high" when they do drugs.

They will feel physiological aspects like if they drink a lot, they will feel their physical motor skills diminish but they will not feel any mental euphoria and so they will understand drugs are vanity and they will not do them. If they do drugs, they will do nothing for them in relation to get them high so they will just not be able to get addicted. One cannot get addicted to anything that does not give them a mental sense of euphoria and this is relative to food also. A person cannot get fat if they are neutral about food. A person cannot become addicted to a drug they are neutral towards it mentally. This has nothing to do with morals or standards this has to do with being of sound mind which means one has right brain unveiled and right brain is so powerful nothing compares to it. Drug addiction, food addiction, low self esteem addiction, gambling addiction are all based on the euphoria one feels when they seek and fulfill those accomplishments.

A person alters their appearance with surgery and they do that to feel better about their self and that relates to mentally feeling better. This is relative to all addictions and an addiction is gluttony and gluttony is a symptom of a mind that has been brainwashed as a result of the education not being applied properly. So all the problems in society lead back to one root and that is this manmade invention called written language and math, when they are not applied properly create many fruits, minds, that are sour. That is all Adam was saying relative to the tree of knowledge. He was saying this manmade invention has some bad side effects mentally and if you do not figure that out swiftly you are going to drown the entire species in a flood of mental suffering. Suffer the children. This of course is elementary cause and effect but I take that for granted because I have no sense of time and 5000 years does not seem like any time.

We as a species in relation to the bad side effects the education causes are simply too far gone. We as a species are so mentally insane because of what this manmade invention does to the mind at this stage we are not going to perhaps ever recover. So the next time you hear some being proclaiming "We need to give all the kids a good education." you understand that being just said "Lets mentally rape all the children good." because that being simply knows not what he says.

You just be mindful civilization is very careful to make sure everyone gets their "brand" of education. Parents are very careful to make sure their children get the "brand" they got as a child from education. Civilization always needs a little more money for their "brand" of education so they can boast how they make sure all the kids get the "brand".

I am not only telling you Civilization is a cult. It is so complex you are unable to grasp it in your brainwashed state of mind and that is why I write and tell you, and explain it to you because without your right brain being active you have no chance to detect the cult because the cult has brainwashed you into a state of mental sloth so you cannot detect the cult. I can only say I accidentally woke up from the brainwashing with the understanding you perhaps have no idea what that really means even if you do believe it.

Everything I say means nothing if at the end of the day you do not apply the remedy to wake up. Civilization did something to us mentally and you are not going to be compensated for what they did to you because if they cared they would not have veiled our right brains to begin with. You are on your own. You are going to have to think for yourself. I write these books and explain how you can wake up and once you do that you are on your own. - 11/13/2009 12:08:22 AM

1:19:32 AM – When I say the word civilization you have been conditioned to believe words so if I say anything bad about civilization you will automatically assume I am bad. If civilization was instead called "good" and I insulted it you would naturally assume I am bad. This is relative to the left brain seeing parts and seeing parts is relative to judgment. A tribe that lives in the Amazon jungle is not considered a part civilization so that tribe is assumed to be bad or uncivilized. Any group of people that does not fall under the definition of civilization is considered bad because the word civilization suggests "good". So this is simply a symptom civilization has conditioned you to believe the words are absolute. Relativity suggest there are no absolutes or everything is relative to the observer so it is not possible any group of people that is not a part of the group called civilization could be considered bad or lower standard except by the ones in civilization because if the groups that were not a part of civilization were considered good then civilization would be considered bad relative to ones who only see parts.

X = a group of people who never got the education, written language and math or applied the remedy
Y = a group that gets lots of the education, written language and math.

Because of the mental side effects the education causes when not applied properly X and Y do not see things the same because the education alters perception. Group X is not in the same state of mind as group Y. So relatively speaking group X will see group Y as strange or odd or different and group Y will see group X as strange or odd or different. So relative to civilization group X is dumb and relative to group X, civilization is dumb and both are right at the exact same time. This is an indication the word dumb is not real.

The word dumb is a label and all labels are relative to the observer. So civilization itself is also relative to the observer. A person cannot be in group Y and say they are civilized on an absolute scale because relative to group X they are not civilized, they are of unsound mind because they got many years of left brain sequential education and so their perception is so out of alignment they exhibit strange behavior. Ones in group X that didn't get education at all does not know exactly why group Y exhibits strange behavior because ones group X never had written language or math on any great scale so they only see symptoms but not the cause.

The Native Americans called civilizations white devils as an indication of how the settlers acted but they were not aware of the cause of how they acted because they did not have written language and math on any great scale. Civilization is in fact a symptom of the written language and math.

Written language and math equals civility and when enough people get the education that is called civilization. So written language and math equals good, but only relative to the ones who get it or to civilization. So civilization judged itself good by calling itself civilization because civilization judged written language and math as a basis for goodness.

X = person
Y = written language and math education
Z = wise
A = foolish

X + Y = Z so X − Y = A

This simple equation is what civilization is based on. If one does not get enough Y they are assumed to be a fool and they are treated as such and given slave jobs. It is a gargantuan assumption that Y makes one wise. That is exactly what this comment is relative to: [Genesis 3:6 And when the woman saw that the tree was good for food,… and a tree to be desired to make one wise,]

So "she" in this comment is referring to civilization and "she" in the ancient texts is the whore, the devil, the serpent, the antichrist, the cursed one. In Hebrew the word cursed can be understood as a contrast statement. If everything is cursed then there is no curse because there needs to be contrast to be able to suggest something is cursed. Something has to not be cursed in order to determine something is cursed.

Native Americans suggested civilization was white devils and 2500 years before that the tribes in the west suggested civilization was cursed serpents. This is a contrast statement to explain a human being that is exhibiting behavior unlike a human being. What this means is a group of human beings invented something and it altered their minds and they stopped acting like human beings. This has nothing to do with evolution, this has to do with a group of human beings inventing something that had unintended mental consequences. Simply put a human being is born and they are a normal human, sound minded being and then they get this invention thrown on them by the adults and then they are no longer acting like human beings, they are unsound minded, left brain leaning.

Human beings have not evolved perhaps one ounce relative to 5000 years ago. What is really happening is unsound minded human beings keep throwing this invention with unintended mental consequences on normal human beings, children, and changing the way they behave. Genetically we perhaps have not evolved at all in 5000 years we are simply continuing to encourage this invention that has detrimental unintended mental side effects on the children and they are behaving strangely and that is all civilization is.

X = one who got the education and are of unsound mind who teaches the invention with unintended side effects

Y = the children
Z = civilization
X + Y = Z

So Z is simply a mad house or a lunatic asylum. So everything in civilization is simply a symptom that human beings are not acting like human beings because they were taught the education improperly by human beings who do not even know it has unintended mental side effects. This is why civilization as a whole is its own worst enemy.

Civilization believed an invention it created could not have unwanted unintended consequences on a scale of such magnitude and it is impossible to gauge how big that scale is. There are only a handful of mentally sound human beings on this planet and civilization calls them the uncivilized tribes that live outside the realm of civilization. Every other human being on this planet has to some degree been exposed to the education so they are mentally unsound. This is an example of the reverse thing. This is an example of the least among you. The least among civilization are the ones civilization calls uncivilized and in this case they are the only ones who are still mentally sound human beings and they want nothing to do with you, or me, or civilization. They prefer not to associate with mentally unviable abominations to the word human being. If every human being in civilization applied this remedy and was mindful of the unwanted side effects of education and created the education system accordingly, civilization as we know it now would be completely different. There would perhaps be no monetary system. There would perhaps be no disharmony with the environment. There would perhaps be no need to go to war with our own species over land. This is not about an ideology this is about a creature with an unsound mind is unviable and cannot stand.

If civilization conditions six billion people into this left brain unsound state of mind with the education they are going to have nothing but conflict and hell. It all comes back to one thing only. Nature does not tolerate disharmony. What that means is the mind which is relative to the brain, is the way it is when a child is born so that child is prone to live "properly" with its surrounding and if adults condition that mind into extreme left or right brain that child is prone to live "improperly" with its surroundings. That is the checks and balance of this complex harmony system called nature. If any creature mentally goes out of balance one way or the other they are marked for death because their deeds and fruits will be their demise. Simply put a human being with an unsound mind will do things it perceives are normal but in reality they are deeds that will lead to its death and on a species level, to that species extinction.

Traditional Education when taught improperly in fact alters the mind so the person perceives time, and all their emotions are turned up to maximum so they are a nervous wreck and cannot even concentrate so there is no possible way the species can survive. You may perceive applying this remedy is not very important because you are prone to death already. You are mentally the living dead already so of course it does not seem very important because your mind is unsound and has been brainwashed and you are simply on a suicide mission and so is the entire species in civilization.

I have no reason to fight you because eventually you are going to think you are having fun by driving your car 90 miles an hour and crash and burn. You are going to think it is fun to get drunk and you will eventually kill yourself. You will think it is fun to get into war and eventually kill yourself. You will think it is fun to take advantage of people with your usury economic system and when you lose all your money you will kill yourself. You may stress out about nothing until you die of a heart attack. You may become depressed and decide its best to kill yourself.

So you just tell yourself there is something in your world of delusions that is more important than applying this remedy and you will know I can read your mind yet I know not who you are. I can tell you it's very wise you drop your nets and apply the remedy but you only see wisdom as foolishness.- 2:28:05 AM

6:42:19 PM – I will just say I tried to communicate with the law of the land. I tried to communicate with ones who suggest they care about liberties and I am an idiot for assuming there is such a thing in this place I find myself.

. . . .
. . . .

Dear Mr. Rohrer

Thank you for sharing your concerns. I don't think the ACLU will be able to help you on this. We have no policy on education as a virulent form of brainwashing.

Best wishes,

END

I assure you I have not yet begin to write, to fight, to have sight. - 6:47:52 PM

8:37:05 PM – I need filler so I will include and email I sent to someone about something.

I am bored with writing my infinite books for now so I will write to you.
The Spanish met the Incas. The Incas said the Spanish looked like gods.
The Incas had no written language and they used Knots on a string to do math so they had no true math system.
They saw the Spanish as gods because they did not have the brainwashing and one sees everything as good or perfect. Other words left brain see's parts and right brain see's everything as a whole. So one who breaks free of the education brainwashing is no longer able to judge a book by the cover. So the Incas saw the Spanish as perfect but the Spanish got the education and they saw an oppurtunity to take advantage of the Incas.

The equation of civilization is

X = education

Y = Person

Z = Wise

A = foolish

So $X + Y = Z$ and $Y - X = A$

So The ones who got the education assume any group that does not get the education is foolish or stupid and so they take advantage of them.

So the ones who have the education met the American Indians and the American Indian's said we see spirit of oneness in everything which proves they had right brain unveiled and the brainwashed ones took advantage of them.

The Brainwashed ones went to Africa and saw the natives there had no education and they turned them into their slaves.

This is all relevant to the story of Exodus in the ancient texts. Moses was in civilization, Egypt, got the education, accidentally broke the brainwashing and left civilization, Egypt, and tried to free all the people he understood were brainwashed. He tried to free the people he understood were brainwashed.

There is a very simple reality to making a person a slave. First one has to have an opiate. This opiate is education. It conditions the mind into extreme left brain because it is all based on sequence.

The first thing a child learns is their ABC's and that is sequence, the next thing they learn is how to count and that is sequence.

Spelling is simply arranging letters in the proper sequence. Using a comma is simply seeing the sentence in parts. Seeing parts is a left brain trait.

After a few years of this strictly sequential education the mind starts leaning to the left brain way of thinking and in turn the right brain becomes veiled. This brainwashing is complete before the child is ten or twelve yet the laws say a person has to go to school until they are 16.

The simple carrot and stick tactic used to get people to get the education brainwashing is a fear tactic.

You get the education or you get a slave job. You get the education or your life will be very hard. When a student misspells a word that means their right brain is seeing the word in random access and so when a teacher gives that child and poor grade for misspelling words that teacher is in fact making that child conform to sequencing. So a child understands if they do not sequence words properly the teacher will give them an F and their parents will punish them. Education has nothing to do with wisdom if it conditions the mind to the left so one is afraid of words and pictures and music and sees everything as parts and most of all one is stuck with a strong sense of time and with sequential thoughts.

Freedom of speech denotes one is not allowed to punish a child for misspelling a word because then they rob that child of freedom of speech.

You know we have terroristic threat laws. Those laws suggest if another person perceives what a person says is a threat that is a terroristic threat. Everything is relative to the observer. A person brainwashed is prone to fear of things that cannot possibly harm them so they are nervous wrecks. A person who is brainwashed will not go to a dark house in the woods alone at night or a cemetery alone at night because their hypothalamus is telling them there are spooks there and they will get you. So relative to the ones brainwashed a word certainly will harm them but there is a saying sticks and stones may break my bones but words will never harm me. But the truth is the brainwashed ones will kill if someone says certain words to them because they have been conditioned to believe words are damaging or harmful.

Civilization has certain words censored. They suggest they are uncivilized words. A word is inanimate so it cannot be good or bad so when a teacher sends a child to the principal's office to get a paddling for saying a "bad" word they are robbing that child of freedom of speech and that child becomes more afraid. The reality is if a child is brainwashed into extreme left brain before they are even ten how does that child know they have been brainwashed? There is only one way to know and that is if a person accidentally breaks free of the brainwashing. The mind is not developed before much later so a person never knows what sound mind is like because by the time they are ten or 12 they are conditioned all the way to the left brain and they start acting shy, and ashamed and afraid and embarrassed.

Here are some examples from the ancient texts explaining the mental symptoms of one before they get the education, tree of knowledge, and after they get the education.

[Genesis 3:5 For God doth know that in the day ye eat thereof, then your eyes shall be opened, and ye shall be as gods, knowing good and evil.]

Knowing good and evil = seeing things as parts = a left brain trait

[Genesis 3:6 And when the woman saw that the tree was good for food, and that it was pleasant to the eyes, and a tree to be desired to make one wise, she took of the fruit thereof, and did eat, and gave also unto her husband with her; and he did eat.]

[and that it was pleasant to the eyes, and a tree to be desired to make one wise,] Written language looks pleasing the eyes and this is relative to the languages of 5400 years ago , relative to that area of the world.

[and a tree to be desired to make one wise] Why does one get education? To become wise. That assumes a person when they are born is unwise or stupid . This is why when the ones who are brainwashed encounter a group who does not have the written language they assume they are stupid and take advantage of them.

X = a sound minded human who did not get the education and thus sees everything a one thing or everything as perfect

Y = one who get the education and see parts, so they see one thing as good and anything not like that thing is determined to be evil.

So the X's meet a Y and the see's X as perfect but Y see's an X and see's an Y as different and thus evil and so X controls or dominates or takes it over. So this is why the white man saw the Indians and saw them as different and took over them. This is why the white man saw the Africans and saw them as different and took them over and made them slaves.

This is very important to understand. This is a mental symptom of one who does not get the education.

[Genesis 2:25 And they were both naked, the man and his wife, and were not ashamed.]

They were not ashamed of nudity because they saw everything as perfect and so they could not judge a book by the cover. Think about native tribes where the women wear no tops. They are not ashamed of nudity. Shame is relative to fear and in the brain there is the hypothalamus, the amygdala and the cerebral cortex. Once one is brainwashed to extreme left brain these parts of the brain stop working properly and this means ones normal fear or shame or embarrassment is turned up by a huge factor, so one is easy to control with fear tactics. This is why the comment "when the people fear the government there is tyranny and when the government fears the people their is liberty." This is better looked at like when the taskmaster brainwashes the people with the education they are very afraid and are thus in a tyranny.

This is why there is no mention of education in any of the founders documents at all.

This is a symptom after one gets the education.

[Genesis 3:7 And the eyes of them both were opened, and they knew that they were naked; and they sewed fig leaves together, and made themselves aprons.]

[they knew that they were naked; and they sewed fig leaves together, and made themselves aprons.]

[Genesis 2:25 And they were both naked, the man and his wife, and were not ashamed.]

So before the education they were not afraid, and after they were afraid, or before the education they were not ashamed and after they were ashamed.

What is important is you try to avoid coming to the conclusion that if what I say is true then civilization is not what you thought it was so what I say cannot be true.

If what I say is true, then civilization is simply a slave making machine, and so what I say cannot be true because civilization cannot be a slave making machine which uses education as an opiate to make the slaves.

I would not tell you what I tell you if it was not true. I am not seeking monetary compensation. I am compelled to write you personally. I am not certain why I am compelled but I do as I am compelled to do.

I never published a book in my life but all the sudden in the last year, since the accident, I have anti writers block.

Consider this comment

[Genesis 3:14 And the LORD God said unto the serpent, Because thou hast done this, thou art cursed above all cattle, and above every beast of the field; upon thy belly shalt thou go, and dust shalt thou eat all the days of thy life:]

After they ate off the tree, got the education, they were called the serpent and they were [, thou art cursed above all cattle]

This means they mentally were brainwashed to the left brain and their fruits and deeds were cursed or unsound.

I am infinite denial because I refuse to write that this education is simply a Trojan horse used by the sinister to get inside of people and when people push it on children they are simply sacrificing children to the sinister.

[Genesis 11:5 And the LORD came down to see the city and the tower, which the children of men builded.]

The lords are the ones who broke the brainwashing and the men are the ones who are brainwashed. Men is an insult. Men is like saying the retards. The lords are the ones who broke the education and tried to stop the "curse" from spreading.

Because after one is brainwashed they are hallucinating to the point they sense time and they are afraid of words and a bad haircut they cannot be reasoned with. So they went to plan B.

[Genesis 19:24 Then the LORD rained upon Sodom and upon Gomorrah brimstone and fire from the LORD out of heaven;

25 And he overthrew those cities, and all the plain, and all the inhabitants of the cities, and that which grew upon the ground.]

The lords formed an army and killed the men of the cities.[and all the inhabitants of the cities]

This was the only way they could stop the curse this education caused in the minds of the men. Extermination was their solution and it did not work and that is an indication of the power of the curse. I had to kill myself mentally to break the curse and I did it accidentally.

Adam summed it up rather well [Genesis 2:17 But of the tree of the knowledge of good and evil, thou shalt not eat of it: for in the day that thou eatest thereof thou shalt surely die]

Our species messed around with an invention that had devastating consequences on our minds and so our species is doomed to die because an unsound mind or a house/mind divided cannot stand.

I will end by suggesting to you the remedy with the understanding no one can understand anything I say ever.

Look at all the remedies the wise beings suggested and then understand none of the sane never had a clue the remedy was right in their face.

One being sad fear not. Then he said When you see a knife held over your chest do not run but fear not.

Another being said "When you see the shadow of death do not fear or run from the shadow of death."

Another being said Do not try to save your life from the shadow of death and you will break the curse or preserve your sound mind.

Another being said Submit to the shadow of death. When you see the shadow of death submit .

Another being said, when you see Medusa head look at it and face your fear of that shadow of death and you will turn to stone which means your strong emotions and pride and greed and lust and envy and wrath will be silenced and you will be able to think clearly again.

[John 8:43 Why do ye not understand my speech?]

END

I never accomplish anything but I keep at it. I am mindful I am still trying to find someone to help me in this cause because I am not use to the fact there is no one who can help me in this cause, but I will not say God has forsaken me because I understand there are things more important in this reality than me. The curse on our species is just too strong and there is nothing in this universe that will ever change that, so I will hold my head up high with the understanding I love to get my teeth kicked in.

You may be under the impression grasshopper when you apply this remedy you will be able to say the right things to convince the sane but I assure you there are no right things you can say. This is why you have to let go of your assumptions of reasoning and your assumption that if you do everything "properly" in your words you will win. You will perhaps not win ever. You will just forge on with the understanding you perhaps will never win. This is why it is important you look at what you are doing as an experiment. You are experimenting with using words to communicate with rabidity. This will create a situation that no experiment is a loss because you will come to further understandings from every experiment so this will create the illusion you are winning understandings. This way you will not panic and perhaps destroy yourself. You are simply a scientist and you are running experiments trying to communicate with rabidity. With this experiment frame of mind you will never reach a point of taking up arms against the rabid ones because that has never worked in the past. Using words does not work either. Being violent physically does not work and being peaceful using words does not work, yet once you apply the remedy you are compelled to fight the battle anyway. So your goal is to become wiser than wisdom itself. Your goal is every time you get kicked in the teeth for telling this truth about traditional education you use that as an emotional conditioning exercise. You are going to be a master at emotional conditioning because you are going to be a master at getting your teeth kicked in.

Eventually you will turn to stone emotionally and when you do you will become wiser than wisdom. Every time you block your emotions your concentration increases. You are going to have to become a Master of concentration because if you do not you are going to talk yourself out of the battle and end up hiding somewhere denying your intuition. You are not going to apply this remedy so you can go hide and be afraid of the armies of the sane. You are going to apply this remedy so you will become a lion of concentration. This means you are going to use your experiments to work on the log of fear in your mind and this will make you better in dealing with the sane. You are going to want to quit and give up on the sane if you expect positive results. You are not going to get positive results so you have to give up on results. You are running experiments to come to understandings. You are improving yourself and perhaps that may assist others that observe you improving yourself. This way you are doing things without doing things. You look at everyone around you as an emotional conditioning tool to assist you to improve yourself. If you start seeing the sane as real that will destroy you.

If you start believing what your eyes are telling you when you look at the sane, you will be destroyed. You must deny what your eyes tell you and focus on the log of fear in your mind. The sane are illusions and you are going to manipulate those illusions by not pandering to those illusions. The illusions will be manipulated once the illusions understand they are unable to manipulate you. One is either being manipulated or doing the manipulation and what separates the two is concentration.- 9:15:36 PM

11:40:17 PM – The main problem with a monetary system is judgment is required to determine who gets a certain salary. A person is judged by the job they do and that judgment is their salary. The problem is people are making judgments based on judgments made by people. This is why relativity is so complex. When a person finds out how much they make an hour at their job they assume that is their worth. In an economic system there can never be a majority of people who make the most money. There is always going to be the poor. The poor are simply people that other people have judged to have less worth than other people. This goes against the basic principle of all men are created equally. This is why America is essentially a socialist ideology.
"To form a more perfect union" means for the common good. What has happened is some carpetbaggers have convinced you a more perfect union means a more perfect separation.

This more perfect union is simply suggesting everyone gets the same. If one person gets more, then that creates separation and so that goes against "form a more perfect union" and goes against "all men are created equal". Who determines the salary? Human beings determine who gets certain salaries. This means that anyone who is not determining the salaries is in fact being told what to do by the ones who do determine salaries and this infringes of life, liberty and the pursuit of happiness because a person is being controlled. You have been suckered so extremely you cannot even figure out how bad you have been suckered. You are a slave in a cage and you think that cage is freedom so you are essentially a write off because I am unable to make a blind man understand blindness is abnormal. I cannot help a slave understand slavery is abnormal because a slave is a slave because they relied on the slave master for their survival. You are in a slave making machine called civilization and the opiate, slave making platform, is education and if you do not believe that you are just a foolish slave, nothing more.

The entire economic system is based on a person's worth and because of this when a person loses their job they sometimes kill their self because they perceive their worth is gone. This reality can never work on one of sound mind because they have so much cerebral worth they simply are uncertain if money even has value at all, but to a person who is brainwashed their entire perception is based on material worth and when that is gone, they lose their job, they are done. The deeper reality is civilization is based on money and if you have been judged to not be worth much by civilization, because you did not take well to the brainwashing, education, you only have two choices because you have been brainwashed even if you did not take to it well. You can get a slave job or you can turn to a life of crime. If you accept and settle for your slave job you are left alone and if you turn to a life of crime you are put in a cage. The deeper reality is you are put into a mental cage by the education to begin with, so you are in a cage by the brainwashing because your complex powerhouse right brain has been veiled and then you are unable to think so your chances of getting a large salary is reduced. So the education system is based on the fact you get the education to get a good job but then when you get all the education you are mentally hindered so you cannot get a good job.

The point is why are you working at all? Are you working to get food to eat so you can just survive? There are natives in this world who live in wilderness and they eat all they want and they do not have to work a slave job to do it. The food is free. Your food is not free; you have to work a slave job to get your food. If you do not know someone in power in civilization you are doomed to a slave job. You will work until you die just to keep living. What this means is your perception has been altered and you want material things so you will perceive you are happy but every time you buy material things you never are happy and so you must keep working so you can buy another material thing you perceive will make you happy. You are never going to be happy because your happiness is your misery, it is just your mind is not working properly and it is telling you if you get a big house and lots of money you will be happy but you never will because that big house is a just a big cage and all that money is just a way to make you stay in your cage and all the material things in the universe do not compare to having right brain unveiled for a moment.

Civilization is based on one thing. Sedate the slaves and keep them on the tread mill. You are free. You were born and that means you are free and no human being in the universe can take that away from no matter how many fear tactics and threats they throw at you. You are being manipulated because the right brain that deals with concentration and pattern detection and intuition has been veiled. Simply put you are not mentally able to detect traps. With right brain unveiled the intuition is so strong you can tell instantly if a person is trying to scam you or pull a fast on you no matter who they are. You can read them like a book on a level that one might suggest its telepathy. You cannot survive the world with that intuition veiled and so you suffer as a result of that aspect veiled.

You have been conditioned by the education so that you are very good at one thing and that one thing is being a sucker. You fall for every single trap because you cannot even detect them at all. You are only capable of sequential thoughts after the brainwashing so simple explanations satisfy you. "Everyone has to get education to survive in the world" and that pin prick sequential explanation is more than enough to satisfy you. "If you don't have the education you get a slave job and then your life is difficult." That pin prick sequential explanation is more than enough to satisfy you to give away the minds of the children. Who is making all of these rules? Are you being manipulated because the last I checked we are creatures on a planet and we are free. There are no rules there are only human beings adept at manipulating people and turning them into slaves to do their bidding.

Who is this civilization that says 'You do this or you are not civil." Civilization says "You play by our rules or you are an outcast and you are uncivil." You fall for pin prick sequential mind tricks like that. Civilization is putting you on the defensive. They are making it seem like you are bad if you do not do as they say. They have infinite armies of slaves that will make sure you do as they say. Those slaves will kill you to protect the taskmaster. They will kill you and then they will tell the rest of civilization you were uncivil and an outcast, so good riddance.

If you disagree with civilization you are uncivil because civilization denotes civility. This is why it is important you understand the reverse thing. This is why it is important you forget the definitions of words. The words are all backwards and have improper meanings. The catch is you are unable to do that because you insult people who misspell your precious words. You believe the words. A word can make you harm someone. That means a sound can make you harm someone. If I say you mentally rape children you will become upset and assume I am lying because you do not want to understand you in fact mentally rape children directly or indirectly. You are complicate with the mental rape of children and you hate that truth so you hate the one who says it. You hate the messenger but the messenger did not create this slave machine you call civilization. The messenger is trying to wake you up because you have been turned into a slave by the slave machine. You are not capable of assisting me you are only capable of assisting you. You are not writing books explaining how education brainwashes children because even if you believed that you are too afraid to say that on the world stage.

You would not be able to handle getting your teeth kicked in on a daily basis because your ego and emotions could not stand it. You are only concerned with being accepted by civilization and if you have to mentally rape a few children directly or indirectly to achieve that you do not mind because you are never mind.

Do you think I am pleased or displeased to tell you the things I tell you because in reality I am absolutely indifferent. I was where you are at mentally so I understand exactly what is going on in your mind but you are not where I am at so you have no clue what is going on in my mind. Has it occurred to you the only ones that I have a chance to reach are the poor and down trodden of civilization because all the others are hardcore servants of the taskmaster and they are dedicated servants? All the others except the poor in spirit die for the taskmaster without question. I do not want you to ever do anything I do because I am fearless and you cannot do what I do because you are fearful.

I am waging a war against six billion using words and I am certain you are unable to assist me in any meaningful way. I am capable of losing well without your assistance. - 11/14/2009 12:25:23 AM

3:04:49 AM – This is an explanation attempt on a Buddhist forum. Notice how I incorporated neurology with Buddhism.

. . . .
It is first important to understand why a person is not in nirvana.

Written language and math are sequential based. The first thing a child memorizes is how to sequence letters known as the alphabet. The next thing is a child learns how to sequence numbers known as counting. Spelling itself is based on arranging letters in the proper sequence. So the mind itself is conditioned to sequence and sequence is a left brain trait. So after one gets even a few years of education their right brain, random access, mind become veiled. So after the education ones mind is veiled like a crescent moon. Very strong left brain sequential thoughts and veiled right brain random access thoughts.

So one in nirvana simply broke this left brain heavy mindset and returned to sound mind.

Buddha became depressed left his family and he went out and starved for 39 or 43 days. That is what is known today as a suicide attempt.

What happens in this left brain extreme state is some aspects of the brain stop functioning properly so ones emotions, sense of time and most of all fear are greatly exaggerated.

The hypothalamus, amygdala and the cerebral cortex are relative to fear and emotions so when these stop functioning properly due to the education conditioning ones mind is full of fear so the remedy to this is to face ones fear and this tricks these aspects of the brain to start working properly again.

So Buddha did not eat and along the way it occurred to him he would die if he did not eat and he did not fear that and so he defeated his fear of death. This is why when Buddha was asked if he was the Messiah he simply replied "No I am just awake." He reached consciousness which means he negated the unsound state of mind the education caused. Buddha could not tell people to go starve until you think you will die and then do not fear that because many people would die. Other words Buddha was lucky and accidentally did not die. So Buddha or the Buddhist religion has a method that is similar to defeating death but is not life threatening.

The point of this method is to defeat the shadow of death. One simply wants to trick this left brain state of mind into think it may die and then the person allows it and this left brain state of mind dies and one reverts back to sound mind. This unveils right brain and then one has extreme concentration, complexity and their sense of time is greatly reduced and of course all the emotions are working properly again so one does not suffer like they did with all of these strong emotions in their mind, like fear.

So the Buddhist tradition is for one to go to a dark place like a cemetery at night alone and mediate. Of course one with this strong fear is not going to be meditating they are going to be afraid and their mind will tell them the shadow of death is approaching and in that very second the minds tells one to run in fear that person does not run but submits to that perceived shadow of death and in about one month nirvana will kick in.

One should experiment with this approach and nothing is set in stone. Some may be able to watch a scary movie and then turn out the lights or go into the bathroom and look in the mirror and achieve the same effect. The point is to get your hypothalamus into a situation it tells you that you are going to die , it controls fight or flight response, and then you do not run and that tricks it to adjust back to normal functioning.

Avoid jumping into shark frenzies, this is a mental exercise , one only has to perceive the shadow of death not actual death. The moment your mind tells you to run because the shadow of death is coming and you do not run but allow it to come is the moment you reach nirvana, but it will not kick in for about a month and when it kicks in your entire perception is going to shift. It will hit you like a Mac truck. It is a one second decision which means one has to apply self control for that one second and that is all it takes. Any other method other than this defeating ones fear of perceived death will only take much time and never guarantee one actually reaches nirvana. This ancient Buddhist method guarantee's one reaches nirvana and in one second. I am certain you understand the basic principle of this method so only question is, do you have enough self control to accomplish it?

END

3:44:53 AM – The reality in relation to illusions is an illusion cannot be controlled so attempting to control and illusion creates suffering in the one who tries to control that illusion. Once an illusion understands you are not trying to control it the illusion becomes easier to control. Once you apply the remedy you have to act naturally. You are going to try to be like the illusions because you are going to be mentally in neutral. You are going to be in nothingness so your tendency is going to be to mimic whoever you are around. This means you are going to suck in the illusions confusion and this will confuse you. The problem with that is you are not going to have an ego so if someone attacks you with words you are going to be prone to attack them back tenfold with words because you will slowly start losing your ability to believe in words.

No matter how well you explain the remedy to the illusions the remedy is still going to be commit mental suicide. You can spend your lifetime explaining why one should commit mental suicide to break the brainwashing but they still are not going to do it. This is why you cannot try because you will only harm yourself. You will find no fault with your explanation of the reason to apply the remedy, you will feel right brain once it is unveiled, but once you get to the explaining the reality of remedy all of your efforts go up in smoke.

The point of not trying is that you are going to underestimate what you are doing. You are always going to come to the conclusions you failed because winning does nothing for you because you have no ego. What this means is you have to go with the flow and forget all the rules. You start bogging yourself down with rules in relation to explaining this remedy and you will destroy yourself. You cannot say anything wrong and you cannot explain this remedy wrong. You are unable to, once you apply the remedy. Some will suggest do not say this and do not say that because they are still trapped in reverse world. They are trapped in reverse world because they are under the impression this battle perhaps can be won. They perceive if you say everything properly people will just run out and start committing mental suicide to break the brain washing. This battle has been going on for over 5000 years and no side has won so there are no rules. No matter what you say to anyone after you apply the remedy you are going to underestimate the effects it has on them because you are not a judge anymore.

You are unable to judge what effect you have on others. Some will say that is because you are meek but in reality it is because you are doing things without doing things. What that means is you are unable to tell what effect you have on others.

Relativity is why you have to do what you are compelled to do and not worry about what the illusions suggest to you because you are a free thinker once you apply the remedy. Simply put you will no longer need advice. You want to avoid the control freaks advice. Once you apply the remedy you will be a Lord or a Master and they do not have friends because they are lone wolves. This lone wolf reality is relative to detachment. Certainly you will still have the people you know before the remedy but they will be a distanced part of your "past life", brainwashed life. You will not be able to convince them you have applied the remedy and have changed. You will not be able convince them to apply the remedy. You would think your friends would trust you the most but that is only true in reverse world.

You will be a lone wolf among the illusions and you will have shades of victory and shades of hopelessness on a daily basis. You will not be a good judge because you have no sense of time and no ego. What is patience when you have no sense of time? There is no patience because patience is relative to time. You are kind of going to be an observer of yourself. If you say something to someone you will be able to read their reaction and feel their reaction or feel how they reacted. This is relative to the telepathy aspect and also the feeling through vision aspect relative to right brain intuition. Because of this you will want to turn to stone, emotionally as swiftly as possible and the best way to do that is to tell the illusions the truth. This is an example of you working on that fear emotion log in your eye. You are not going to tell people the truth to help anyone because they are beyond help so you are going to tell them the truth to help yourself. The better you get the better. The better you become the better you will get at doing things without doing things. You will do good for them by doing well working on that fear in your eye. You will help yourself get the fear out of your mind and that will be reflected in your power or concentration.

You are not looking to control the illusions you are simply trying to manipulate them. You are trying to make the illusions bend to you. The illusions are going to try to manipulate you. They will try to suggest what you say is bad or evil or wrong or insane. They have a lot of judgments and they are also apparently expert psychologists that are more than willing to throw you a diagnosis or two. They do not even charge for their diagnosis expertise. They give them freely. When you upset the illusions you are winning because they are prone to emotions and when they get emotional the things you say tend to stick in their mind. In reverse world it is thought you do not want to upset people but in reality upsetting the illusions is the only way to make what you say stick in their mind because they have a very poor long term memory, long term memory is a right brain trait.

You will say things and assume they remember what you said but they do not remember what you said at all. The illusions have a veiled right brain and it is long term memory so the only things they remember are things that upset them or cause them emotions. This is why when you upset them you are winning. Relative to you after you apply the remedy you are not capable of being in a state of anger or happiness for more than a moment relative to a clock because right brain will ponder you out of it or turn frustration into an understanding and you will become wiser and this means you will not be allowing your emotions to control you. You will be using what little emotions you have to your advantage. You have to left go of all this moralistic crap from the reverse world. If the reverse world had any morals they would not brainwash innocent children would they grasshopper? - 4:30:34 AM

5:57:24 AM – I am not suggesting left brain is bad I am suggesting sound mind is good. The problem with that is right brain is random access based, paradox/contradiction based. Reverse world hates contradictions. How many times have you heard someone say "That guy said something contradictory so they are stupid." If I start editing all the contradictions I make that means I hate right brain. The reason contradictions happen is not because I am stupid but because the language is flawed. You believe every word is an absolute. There are no absolutes and that is what relativity suggests but the words suggest there are absolutes. There are no absolutes, only six billion opinions relative to six billion observers. You either think you are good and anything not like you is bad or you think you are bad and anything not like you is good, but none of that is an absolute it is only relative to you alone. It is difficult to put a cerebral sensation into a word because a word is an absolute and a cerebral sensation is far more complex than a word. This is an example of the flaws in words.

My baby blue got ill and we went to the vet and the vet said she had a heart tumor and she would be dead soon. This was about seven months ago relative to a calendar. She was panting and she came into my isolation chamber and laid down had a cardiac arrest and I witnessed it and I thought about that today and I could see the image of that and it was crystal clear as if it just happened. There were no time stamps and no emotions on that memory but I could see her but I am unable to explain the sensation that image gave me. There is no word to explain that sensation. I can only explain it with either emotional words or time based words but that image was absent of both. The language is emotional based and then it is time based and that is because everyone's emotions are through the roof and everyone's time perception is through the roof as a result of the education conditioning. The deeper reality here is I remember baby blue but I do not suffer when I remember her. My mind has the event recorded but the time stamps and the emotions are not included.

You can think of an event that happened like a death in the family or death of a close friend and when you recall that, the time stamps are included and so are the emotions so every time you think of that event you suffer all over again. This is relative also to PTSD. Every time a person who is conditioned into this extreme left brain state has an even slightly traumatic memory recall they suffer all over again.

Think about an embarrassing moment. When you recall that moment you suffer the embarrassment again. Look at it like this. Your memories have a time stamp and emotional tag on them once you are brainwashed. When they are recalled in the left brain extreme state of mind the emotions and time stamps are very pronounced and after you apply the remedy the time stamps and emotions are essentially absent.

So not only are you suffering again from all the memories you have, you are suffering in the now when you recall those memories and you are also suffering because you are thinking about the future. You are worried about tomorrow. You are concerned about yesterday. You mind is dragging events of the past and expectations of the future into the now and you are suffering because all those memories have strong emotions and strong time stamps on them. You remember when you suffer and you keep recalling it so that suffering stays with you in your memories forever because it always has those emotions and time stamps on it. Those emotions and time stamps are what kill's your concentration.

They are not emotions and they are not time stamps they are mental clutter. You are addicted to mental clutter. You love the emotions because they make you feel alive relative to reverse world but in real world it is a symptom you are mentally unstable. A depressed person turns into a suicidal person because as a being they cannot stand the strength of the emotions any longer. You know what it is like to be depressed for a period of time longer than a moment relative to a calendar. That is abnormal. It is impossible to maintain a state of depression for more than a moment after the remedy is applied relative to a clock because right brain is pondering so fast thoughts come and go at a speed relative to milliseconds. A better way to look at it is thoughts lose their emotional stamps. I can think about what civilization is doing to people with their wisdom invention but I cannot achieve a state of sadness or anger I simply see it as a challenge to try to communicate this understanding. I cannot communicate it properly because I am trying to communicate a reality that shatters the reality of ones in reverse world. Of course it shatters your reality because you have too many emotions to think about it clearly. You think I insult you or insult education but that is not what I am doing. I am arranging words in a certain fashion because I am experimenting with how the sane react to word arrangements and I am working on the fear log in my eye because I have moments of fear about telling you these things. I perceive I will be killed for telling you these things about education and the brainwashing so I am experimenting to see if that is a realistic fear or just a fear in my mind. I am not talking to you I am experimenting for me.

The remedy and the explanations for the remedy are only relative to you because I already applied the remedy so I am now in experiment mode. I feel nothing whether you apply this remedy or not. If six billion people said they applied this remedy my mind would not feel anything. I cannot feel satisfaction or dissatisfaction and that is because I am neutral. I am uncertain if anyone can even break's the curse unless it is by accident because a person who tries to break the curse is trapped by their own perception. A person might go to a cemetery alone at night and they may hear a stick break and their mind may tell them that is a real person coming to get them, and they will flee in terror and tell their self "That was a real person and I could have been hurt so I ran." Simply put one has to seek death and maybe they will accidentally only face the shadow of death but the problem is the hypothalamus is afraid of a bad haircut in the brainwashed state of mind. You are a slave to your perception and civilization has determined what your perception is because they conditioned your perception the way it is with a Trojan horse they called education. Whether it was intentional or not is not an issue because it will not change the reality it has already been done to you.

One of my strategies in writing the books is because my intuition suggests I may be one of the few people on the planet that can write a book in true random access and this means these books are a random access conditioning tool or right brain relative. What that means is just by reading these books you slowly start to unveil right brain. So I suggest the remedy and that is explained in random access and so you may not have to apply the remedy but right brain has lots of ambiguity, doubt, so I have to compensate for that and suggest other options. - 6:50:08 AM

6:53:54 AM – Look at the aspect of the brain that affects fear as a system interconnected.

Cerebral cortex – amygdale - hypothalamus

Here is the scenario. You are in a cemetery at night alone. You hear a stick break off in the distance. This sound goes into the cerebral cortex and is registered as a stick breaking. Then the stick breaking is sent to the amygdala and it runs through its memories and looks at "stick breaking in a cemetery alone at night" and it comes up with "danger/ghosts/spirits are coming" and that signal is sent to the hypothalamus and the hypothalamus goes into fight or flight mode. So these parts are still working in the brain but they are magnifying things and this makes that hypothalamus send a lot of false signals.

You go into the bathroom after you watch a scary movie and look into the mirror with the lights off that hypothalamus will tell you to run or turn the lights on even though there is no possible way in the universe you could be in any danger, so your hypothalamus is sending false signals. It is jumping the gun. It is telling you things that are not logical and this is because the mind has been conditioned to extreme left brain and so the side effect of that is the fear aspects of the brain are not working properly. Any other animal on the planet would not be afraid to go to a cemetery at night because the fear aspects of their brain is working properly and would not tell them to be afraid since there is nothing to be afraid of in a cemetery at night. It is not these animals are dumb, it is just their mind doesn't tell them to flee in fear when there is nothing there. You are afraid of the shadow of death and that is just like being afraid of the shadow of a truck, and that is just like being afraid of nothing, and being afraid of nothing is the realm of people who are hallucinating. - 7:04:40 AM

6:10:13 PM – [Luke 4:5 And the devil, taking him up into an high mountain, shewed unto him all the kingdoms of the world in a moment of time.]

This comment is relative to state of mind. One who gets the brainwashing is physical based because their cerebral powerhouse right brain is veiled. Notice the words "of the world" and "time." The world is relating to the ones who have been brainwashed and they are physically focused and that is civilization. Sense of time is a symptom of being brainwashed, it's an unwanted side effect of the brainwashing, one's sense of time is very strong. So the devil in this comment is the brainwashed state of mind. This could very well be a comment about a person who was brainwashed tempting Jesus with wealth. Think about it like an agent today. This agent would say your words are wise and I can make you lots of money and give you lots of popularity and make you world famous. This could also means Jesus was aware he was wise and understood he could have lots of popularity if only he kept his mouth shut about the kingdom within, right brain, and the brainwashing caused by the tree of knowledge veiling the kingdom.

It is not easy to explain to people they got this education and its only brainwashing, and then they are of unsound mind and have to apply this remedy or they will remain in this mental state of hell because their mind is only working at 10% capacity. That is not a popular cause because it is finding fault with civilization. It is much safer to not take up that challenge. Suggesting the education is in fact brainwashing opens up a can of worms that can get one killed and so only a being who is fearless would ever accept that challenge. The ramifications are beyond all other causes. This isn't about some ideology. This isn't about one certain country. This is about the whole of civilization knowingly or unknowingly encouraging a manmade invention unto children that alters a child's mind to the degree the child is retarded for all practical purposes and hallucinating if not taught properly by a Master who understands its unwanted side effects, and everyone in civilization was a child so they are included in that subset of children.

Let's look at Socrates. He was sentenced to drink hemlock by the government for corrupting the mind of the youth. He was around 500 years before Jesus. He could have kept his mouth shut and saved himself because he knew he was attacking the taskmaster by telling the youth the education was simply a brain washing Trojan horse.
Here are some patterns. Right brain is good at detecting patterns.
 Socrates was known to be a champion of oral communication.
Jesus gave all of his teaching in oral form, like the sermon the mount.
Buddha's texts were found 200 years after he died and beings who found them memorized them and then destroyed his texts and so the Buddhist tradition is an oral tradition. It is just assumed quotes from Buddha are his own words but they in fact are perhaps not.

Oral communication will not create the brainwashing. Reading, writing and math are what is indicative of the left brain sequencing. This is an indication that these beings were in a strange situation. If they wrote texts then that would pander to what causes the curse. So this whole situation is a contradiction. One has to write texts to tell people reading and writing causes the brainwashing because if one is strictly oral their message will be forgotten. The deeper reality is the reading and writing is simply an invention and once one breaks the brainwashing it causes them no harm in reading or writing but one is unable to write very well relative to the rules of writing because after the remedy they see everything as one thing and think in random access as well as sequential not just sequential. I cannot use commas well on any scale of certainty and when I see writing with all the commas I ignore them because I see everything as one thing. I look at a sentence and get the spirit of that sentence so the commas are not even noticed. So the paradox is:
Written language and math are good.

Written language and math are bad.

And it is true. If one gets this traditional education as a child their mind is hindered but if they apply he remedy their mind goes back to sound mind and the education is just education. The problem is the ones who are in this extreme left brain state hate contradiction or paradox because right brain is the master of paradox. Someone may read this and say "He said education is good and then he said education is bad so he is crazy." That is all the proof one needs to know that person has their right brain veiled because they cannot tolerate paradox or paradox is too complex for them to grasp. The reality is, one has to have right brain unveiled so one can understand contradictions and paradox are valid and true and are everywhere.

Education is simply a manmade invention that has unintended consequences when taught to a child improperly. It's strange but once one applies the remedy they are not going to be very good at written language. They will be very good at concentration and oration. My books all look fine to me but relative to an English major these books perhaps drive them crazy because they have all these rules in their head and the moment someone breaks one of the written language rules they instantly come to the conclusion "Whoever wrote this is stupid" because they do not understand right brain hates rules and is not able to sequence because it is random access based.

So when a person is conditioned to uphold this invention written language, see's these books and they insult the author based on the "correctness" of the writing style they are not insulting me, I have no ego so they are unable to ever insult me, I am immune to their consultations, but they are saying "Right brain sucks." These books are a symptom I have right brain unveiled and so anyone who cannot stand them hates right brain but I do not hate right brain and I will not deny right brain to pander some brainwashed being.

It is simply too bad if you hate paradox, contradictions, complexity and random access. It is simply too bad but I do not pander to beings who cannot tolerate their own mind. The sooner you understand you have been brainwashed to hate the better half of your own brain the sooner you will stop hating yourself. You do not hate me you hate yourself. I am what you will be after you apply the remedy. Right now I perhaps appear crazy in my writing and my mastery of written language but that is because you cannot understand you have been brainwashed to be able to use the sequential based, left brain invention called written language and math. You were brainwashed before you were ten so how on earth do you know you were not brainwashed and the truth you is you do not know. You can list infinite reasons why you are not brainwashed and I will understand you are so brainwashed you cannot even tell. You have the sequential slothful aspect of your brain extremely dominate and in turn your emotions are turned up to extremes and your fear is beyond my ability to explain, and your sense of time is so strong you get irritable after five minutes relative to a clock and you are going to tell me that is how human beings should be.

You are going to tell me you are proud of your mind even though you have a never mind. You are going to tell me Einstein was one of a kind and Socrates was one of a kind and Shakespeare was one of a kind. You are going to tell all the great minds in recorded history were one of a kind and it was relative to their genes and relative to some crap someone else told you but I will tell you, you are the greatest mind in recorded history you just have to cancel out the brainwashing civilization forced on your against your will as a child and unveil the powerhouse.

Civilization attached a lot of goodies to their wisdom invention and you had no choice because civilization has many minions serving it and one of those minions was your parents. You are going to have to think with all your might because all you have to think with is simple minded sequential thoughts thanks to civilization, to get yourself out of the mental hell you are in. I have lots of ambiguity, a right brain trait, and I am aware one wise being said "They know not what they do" so I try to give civilization the benefit of the doubt. I try to tell myself this education is simply an invention that has unwanted side effects and because the people who push it know not what they do when they apply the education improperly and so it just an honest mistake and no one is to blame and we can apply the remedy and learn from this mistake we made as a species but I am in infinite denial because my intuition tells me I am going to get butchered for telling you these things like all the others got butchered for telling you these things.

I have too much ambiguity to start throwing around terms like sinister and evil. I am not intelligent enough to detect supernatural. I am perhaps not intelligent enough to judge my friends and tell them they have been perhaps beguiled by the whore. My friends are suffering enough. Who is making my friends suffer so? - 7:06:28 PM

7:40:19 PM – Look at the hypothalamus as a voice. This voice tells you when danger is near but not like intuition, a right brain trait, tells you when danger is near. Words cannot explain these cerebral concepts properly because there are not enough words. Hypothalamus is intuition and it is not intuition and so the words cannot explain it properly. Hypothalamus is a voice in your head and it tells you when to run or fight. So this remedy is a one thing fix to let that hypothalamus know you are no longer going to listen to its false fight or flight signals.

The hypothalamus is telling you to run from the shadow of death and you are going to convince it by ignoring its false signals to run from the shadow of death, by not running from the shadow of death.

Look at it like when you fear the shadow of death which is not actual death but your mind tells you it is actual death you are going to let that hypothalamus know you are aware it is sending false signals and how you will do that is to be in a situation where it does send one of these false signals and you are going to ignore its signal and that will make the hypothalamus start acting properly again and that will clear all of this emotional fear clutter out of your mind permanently.

It's not important how this denying the hypothalamus voice to such a degree cancels out the brainwashing. The important thing to remember is it is painless. The next thing to remember is nothing physiologically is changing as a result of this. The changes that occur as a result of this remedy are all cerebral and that is relative to perception. So the education conditions one to a left brain mindset and that alters your perception and this remedy alters your perception back to how it was before the education. You will not forget how to read and write you will just do it differently. I know of some who have applied this remedy and they do not like to write anymore so they do a lot of copying and pasting.

I might send them a message and they will copy and paste parts of my message and send that back as a message. They are what one might suggest are frightened by written language. They are concerned about going back to how they were. I was very much like that at first and you will be too. You will have this kind of paranoia that if you do something "wrong" you will go back to how you were and once you feel the power of right brain once unveiled you will understand why one would be concerned.

It is like having a car with 1 piston and then the next day having that car with 8 pistons and you are very careful because you like 8 pistons and you do not want to go back to 1 piston. So this creates a kind of paranoia about written language. It is not possible to go back and I understand that now because this remedy is one time fix and once it is applied you are fixed. This state of mind I am in is normal, is sound mind, I have right brain and left brain active and in harmony and so it is logical I cannot use a strictly sequential based invention perfectly because right brain is random access. Only a person leaning very heavy into left brain sequential state of mind is able to use written language, purely sequential based, properly based on the rules and understandings of others conditioned into the left brain sequential state of mind.

Relative to this remedy changing perceptions, one no longer reads like one does in the extreme left brain state. One in the left brain state reads word for word and that is relative to the left brain traits of seeing parts. The right brain is holistic or see's the whole thing so one looks at a sentence and sees all the words and this is translated into a cerebral understanding so one could say they speed read or they get the spirit of the sentence. This is totally different than reading in parts. Reading in parts in slothful in contrast to reading holistically. What this means is it is also difficult to proof read or judge the sentence. Spelling errors are over looked because the right brain detects patterns and if something is misspelled it can still figure out what that word is. One can look at a misspelled word and figure out what word it is instantly and that is why right brain is so valuable because the pattern detection works in far more ways than just reading.

Sometimes a person can see something and make a deduction from that and see whether it is going to determine the conclusion based on that initial observation. That is relative to right brain pattern detection and that is the key to ones who can determine the future so to speak. So one in the left brain conditioned state can see ahead slightly, based on observations and one with right brain unveiled can do so much more swiftly and much further. I am not concerned with demonstrating psychic ability or telepathic abilities because that will not solve the root problem. That will not make you go apply the remedy. All that will do is make you idolize me. I certainly do not want popularity or money or fame because all that means is my longevity decreases because of that nature of what I suggest.

I cannot make you do anything because that goes against right brain and right brain hates rules and control. This is an indication of why this education "curse" is essentially unstoppable. Moses did not force anyone to apply this remedy he attempted to speak to civilization, the Pharaoh and give him a choice. Once Pharaoh ignored Moses, Moses freed the people who were caught in the curse. He did not turn them into slaves he freed them. He attempted to free their minds. It is not important if you are in literal jail because if you mind is hindered to the point you only use 10% of it you are in mental jail so then literal jail is a second jail. A person of sound mind would not be bothered by a literal jail because right brain is so powerful they can go anywhere they want at any time. Simply put, literal prison is an invention to punish ones who are brainwashed and perceive literal prison is unwanted and prison is a time based punishment. I am not in jail but I am in my isolation chamber but it does not bother me because my mind is free. I can think again. I do not need to go anywhere, I can think again so I can go anywhere without going anywhere literally.

Right brain is so powerful when it is unveiled the world itself melts away. I enjoy a free mind more than anything in the universe because it can do anything in the universe on a cerebral level instantly. Does any amount of money compare to that? What are you going to do when you apply the remedy and everything you thought was important in life pales in comparison to the fact you have the machine unveiled. This is relative to life liberty and pursuit of happiness. What if my pursuit of happiness is simply to tests the limits of the machine I accidentally unveiled. What if I do not want to be in the world of civilization because I am pleased with this cerebral world. I have been in the world of civilization and I like this cerebral world better. If you make me be in your civilization and I do not want to then you infringe on my pursuit of happiness and my liberty. If your laws say I have to be in civilization and I do not want to be then you are simply a tyrant and a control freak.

It is not important how many people vote on a law that says I have to be in civilization because those people did not vote me into existence so they certainly are not capable of telling me how I should exist. Perhaps it all just comes down to the fact the ones who are brainwashed like to control things because left brain is all about control? You perceive if you tell everyone what to do you will be safe when in reality all you are doing is robbing people of their life, liberty and pursuit of happiness.

How are you so intelligent that you know what everyone should pursue to be happy? I understand you are not intelligent enough to make such determinations and I understand you will never be intelligent enough to make such complex determinations. When you are fearless enough to get up in front of the universe and tell everyone you are the reason they were born then you will be intelligent enough to determine what everyone should or should not do.

Relativity suggests what you perceive is pursuit of happiness is not ever going to be what everyone perceives is pursuit of happiness. If you perceive pushing education taught improperly on everyone is proper absolute pursuit of happiness then you are assuming you are the reason everyone was born. How many tests have you run to determine if there are any unwanted side effects of prolonged sequential left brain education called written language and math on the mind of a child whose mind is still developing? You know how many tests you have done? Zero. You know why you have done no tests? Because you assume mankind invented something that could not possibly have any unwanted side effects. You are not capable mentally of being open minded enough to ponder for one second that although mankind has invented millions of things that have unwanted side effects the education invention has none.

You are looking at something that goes beyond the realms of impossibility. It is impossible years of left brain sequential education could have no unwanted side effects on the mind of a child that does not even have a fully developed mind. You are in the land of the lost because your mind can no longer detect simple elementary cause and effect relationships at all. I am not suggesting your mind just goes slightly to the left after all that sequential education I am talking your mind becomes essentially so unsound you hallucinate, your perception is no longer normal at all. Look at the whole of civilization and all the problems and all the crime and the emotional problems and all the war and all the hate and you will understand what happens to a species when they play around with something that alters the mind.

A wise being 5000 years ago gave you are warning about this education invention and you ignored him and now you are understanding the effects of ignoring a wise being. [Genesis 2:17 But of the tree of the knowledge of good and evil, thou shalt not eat of it: for in the day that thou eatest thereof thou shalt surely die.] You are still ignoring a simple honest comment that a wise being said 5000 years ago. You do not ever have to complain about the world or about the children or about the wars or about the environment or about drugs because you ignored the advice of a wise being 5000 years ago and so you face the consequences every single day for the rest of your life. You love suffering so you suffer. You love to hate and you hate to love and that is the summation of the species as a whole because the species misunderstood what this meant [for in the day that thou eatest thereof thou shalt surely die.] Don't you detect death rattles when you see and hear them all around you? Are you so blind and deaf you cannot hear the death rattles of our species? - 8:59:27 PM

9:41:49 PM – This is the proper doctrines of the following religions. Judaism, Christianity, Islam, Buddhism
Doctrine one (Cause and Effect): Written language and math have unwanted side effects on the mind and anyone who is taught these inventions improperly will exhibit mental symptoms and these symptoms are called sins and these sins are mental symptoms that are a result of an unsound mind caused by the inventions being taught improperly.

Doctrine Two (Remedy): If someone is taught these inventions mentioned or gets the education they have to apply the remedy so they can revert back to sound mind.

The remedy varies slightly from religion to religion but they all accomplish the same thing.
In Judaism the remedy is the Abraham and Isaac remedy or the fear not remedy. Another take on the fear not remedy is , I walk through the valley of the shadow of death(perceived death) I fear no evil or fear not or submit to that perceived death or shadow of death.

In Christianity the remedy is do not try to save your life(when the shadow of death is near or submit to that perceived death) to preserve it(a sound mind). John the Baptist used the dunking a person under water method and that person did not fight or feared not, or submitted when they were dunked for a proper period of time so that is similar to the Abraham and Isaac remedy and the shadow of death remedy.

In Islam the remedy is submit. This relates to one perceives the shadow of death and then submits to it or fears not or does not try to save their life (from perceived death) to preserve it(sound mind).

In Buddhism one sits in a cemetery alone at night until they feel better by mediating.

The remedy is a painless mental self control exercise and it is a onetime fix. No maintenance is required after the remedy is applied.

So doctrine one is the cause and effect, the remedy is doctrine two and the effects of doctrine two is one goes back to sound mind and unveils or reaches the kingdom within, right brain, or unveils right brain so one's mind is not like a crescent moon any longer. The crescent moon mind is a mind that is left brain mindset heavy(dark part of crescent moon) and right brain mindset(light part of crescent moon) and this of course is unsound mentally or out of harmony mentally.

The above doctrines are what are known as the solution to world peace and also what good will towards men is, but that is only relative to reality and not the reverse world. The reverse world see's the above doctrines as evil and anti-truth. The reverse world will defend demotic, written language, because they idolize the graven (script) image, the golden calf of knowledge and in turn forsake wisdom, the kingdom of the unnamable one.

I am pleased you saved the ancient texts for me taskmaster. You certainly know not what you've done taskmaster. One might suggest your sense of time is coming to an end Ashmedai. - 9:53:51 PM

9:59:52 PM – I may fail at communicating with you but I am getting good at communicating with me in the process. Are you still wondering what the tree of knowledge is grasshopper? - 10:00:21 PM

10:27:15 PM – [Corinthians 4:20 For the kingdom of God is not in word, but in power.]

It is not the education that gives you wisdom it is the unnamable power of right brain and all its traits when it is unveiled that gives you wisdom.

This education written language does not give you wisdom it is just thought to give you wisdom [Genesis 3:6   and a tree to be desired to make one wise,] The education when applied improperly in fact veils the one aspect of your mind that makes one wise and that is right brain. Wisdom is more important than knowledge because wisdom gives one the ability to detect important knowledge yet knowledge does not give one the ability to detect important wisdom. Having the wisdom to determine what is important knowledge is more important than the knowledge itself. One can have book loads of knowledge and data but if they do not have the pattern detection ability, intuition and the ability to sift through knowledge in random access speed that right brain offers it is just data with no meaning.

I asked money if it talks and it said no.

11/15/2009 5:43:55 AM – I am mindful there are beings known as seekers and they are the wheat. They will not be afraid of what my personal diaries suggest because they are seekers and thus are undaunted. I am mindful there are beings known as the chaff and these private diaries will drive them mad because these words shatter their illusions. I am mindful to humbly remind the chaff before they speak poorly of these words they first must submit they are invading my private diaries and thus are simply a common voyeur. - 5:46:02 AM

9:49:40 AM – The definition of submit is: to place oneself under control of another. This is how it works.

119

X = yourself or state of mind after you get conditioned by education and that is your fruits or nature in the extreme left brain state.

Y = is your state of mind after you apply the remedy and unveil right brain, sound mind 50/50 left and right brain working.

The state of mind or perception you have in X is not the same state of mind or perception you have in Y.

So now the definition of submit makes sense.

To place ones self (X) under the control or another (Y).

To places ones self (Brainwashed / neurosis mind) under the control of another (Sound mind/ right and left hemispheres working at 50/50). - 9:54:52 AM

10:20:14 AM – There was a singer in a band called Alice in Chains. This situation I will explain is a very good example of how sometimes a person comes very close to breaking the brainwashing. This is relative to the meek shall inherit the earth comment.

This singer was using a lot of drugs and he even commented once something along the line of "The drugs helped creativity at first but them they turned on me." That comment is relative to the fact that drugs unveil right brain while they are working and right brain is relative to creativity so many people do drugs to be creative but the only reason they have to do drugs to be creative is because the education has veiled their right brain to begin with. So towards the end of his life this singer isolated himself in his apartment. Many in the reverse world will say he was depressed but in reality he was isolating himself to mediate or think alone and on another hand he wanted to get away from civilization, subconsciously.

He did drugs not because he was a drug addict but because he was trying to wake up, subconsciously. He was subconsciously, right brain, aware something was wrong but like so many depressed appearing people the majority of the time they end up dying while trying to wake up or trying to break the brainwashing. The right brain is trying to wake up and it is saying fear not, apply the remedy, but that signal is translated by the left brain and then a person appears to be self destructive in their behavior and that is what is known as suicidal.

The first thing is one who applies this remedy has their right brain unveiled and it is pondering so fast one is simply unable to achieve a mental state of depression or suicidal. When right brain is veiled it is going to do things to break free and in people who are less brainwashed than others or have a bit more heightened awareness, right brain active after the brainwashing, they are what civilization calls suicidal people.

X = someone who gets the brainwashing and it takes fully and so their right brain is only 10% active.

Y = someone who gets the brainwashing and it does not take all the way and their right brain 20% active.

Y people tend to become depressed and suicidal because their right brain is unveiled a bit more and it wants to be fully unveiled. Y's tend to be a bit more sensitive and creative. That really is a symptom they have heightened awareness a bit more than X's. What this means is sometimes and quite often a person does not take well to the extreme left brain education and they become usually creative and sensitive people but that tends to lead them to be depressed and suicidal. They are still of unsound mind though.

What I am suggesting is civilization is in fact killing people with their forced left brain education and they are far too brain dead to understand that is absolute fact. Simply put, this education alters the mind and when a person alters another person's mind they are going to get a bus load of strange symptoms. It is a simply cause (education left brain heavy) and effect(depression and suicide, emotional problems) relationship. Civilization knows education has way too much left brain and not enough right brain conditioning aspects but the thing is they are uncertain how devastating that combination is on the mind.

Civilization or the powers that be will never even look into this because either they are aware of it and do not care or they understand they will have so much restitution to compensate people for doing this to them they will never, ever, ever recover from it.

The powers that be may be able to say the word responsibility but I assure you they know nothing of responsibility. They know nothing of morals. They know nothing of treating human beings properly. They know nothing about anything but control. They will speak of justice and I spit in their face and write it in my book and publish it for the world to see. I am doomed to write infinite books with the understanding I will never make a dent in the battle because the tree of knowledge is thought to make one wise. I refuse to give up because I refuse to try.

This suicide reality is very obvious in combat troops or troops that experience combat. What is really happening in PTSD is they experience situations and the events are recorded and the time stamps and the emotions are recorded also. This is not only relative to combat troops that get the education, and do not apply the remedy.

So these combat troops cannot escape the memory and so when it comes up they feel the emotions and the time stamps and they suffer and eventually they can no longer stand it and they kill their self. Just like anyone who kills their self after the education the emotions are simply way to strong and this is because the mind in bent all the way to the left.

A person who has applied the remedy on one hand has a good long term memory but not so good of a short term memory, relative to one is brainwashed, so they are like an absent minded professor so these memories do not come up often and when they do come up they have no time stamps and have no emotions attached.

So these "harsh" memories are reduced to simply images but no emotions attached and it is not the images that make the PTSD soldiers kill their self it is the emotions attached to the images of the memories. One who has not applied the remedy has emotions turn up to 100 so they recall the event and they get a major force of emotions and one who has applied the remedy recalls the event and they have a scale of 1 or 2 of emotional attachment to that memory if any.

Only a person who has been educated improperly and thus has an unbalanced mind as a result would ever kill their self over a memory. I was depressed for many, many years and have many, many suicide attempts under my belt, but I have not felt one single sensation of depression or suicidal tendencies since the accident, so you go ahead and punch that into your sequential pin prick logic calculator and try to figure out why that is.

I will tell you why that is but only because I need filler. I accidentally applied the fear not remedy and I unveiled my right brain so I reverted back to sound mind and a human being with a sound mind cannot get depressed because their right brain is pondering so fast the lingering thoughts of depression are not possible the lingering depression thoughts are only possible in a slothful sequential based mind which is an unsound mind.

This wisdom education has messed us up as species so bad I have infinite, infinite job security trying to explain how messed up we are a species because of this single invention.

Stress, overeating, nervousness, emotional problems, hate, wars, destruction of the environment, killing off other species, killing off each other, economic problems, over population, rivalry between everyone, prisons, crime, drugs abuse.

All diseases caused by stress, overeating, over population, nervousness, drug abuse. All indirect effects caused by war, environmental destruction, hate, crime, rivalry between everyone. All indirect symptoms caused by economic problems. Civilization has a left brain sequential invention it forces on people using reward systems and this alters their mind and pe4rcveption so what do you think is going to happen to people's fruits or deeds? These inventions are altering children's minds that are still developing. That is the words crime one can ever do to an innocent child, bar none. How is a human being suppose to not suffer when their mind was bent all the way to the left by the time they were ten? I do not perceive you have any idea what you do to people as children. Civilization mentally kills children and then punishes them when they act like they should act in that unsound state of mind.- 11:13:51 AM

11:56:26 PM – [Matthew 8:22 But Jesus said unto him, Follow me; and let the dead bury their dead.]
[Luke 9:23 And he said to them all, If any man will come after me, let him deny himself, and take up his cross daily, and follow me.]

This concept of follow me is mentioned and it is misunderstood by the sane. The sane bury the dead, this means the ones who have the brainwashing become very emotional over loss. The sane cry over split milk from a leaking container. This is because their emotions are turned up too high from the brainwashing. Every time you hear a news story about a mate killing their mate because that mate left them, they are crying over spilt milk.

Every time you hear a person that kills their self because they lost their money or wealth, they are crying over split milk. It is not their faulty they cry over split milk, crying over split milk is simply a symptom they have been conditioned into an unsound state of mind by the education and certain parts of their brain are sending very strong signals related to emotions and they cannot handle them so they exhibit insane deeds or fruits. What I mean is I cannot judge them harshly because I am aware they are brainwashed and not able to think clearly in that state of mind, so I cast no stones.

Civilization will of course lock them in jail and tell them they had a choice after civilization brainwashes them into the unsound state of mind so that person exhibits that kind of behavior to begin with. Washington said something along the lines of "Government is not reason." and the antonym of reason is insanity. Perhaps we should avoid listening to anything Washington says because he was clearly a terroristic threat although Napoleon was quite fond of him.

[[Luke 9:23 And he said to them all, If any man will come after me, let him deny himself]
This comment is a repeat comment of this comment.
[Luke 17:33 Whosoever shall seek to save his life shall lose it; and whosoever shall lose his life shall preserve it.]
[whosoever shall lose his life] = [let him deny himself]

If one loses their life they deny their self. This is complex because one's life after they get the education/ brainwashing is mental death or unsound mind.
X = ones state of mind after the education
 [let him deny himself(X)]
[whosoever shall lose his life(X)]

So this comment [[Luke 9:23 … If any man will come after me, let him deny himself] simply means. The only way one can follow or do as he was doing is to apply the remedy which is [whosoever shall lose his life] relative to his suggestions and time period. There are many versions of the same remedy but this is his take on the "I walk through the shadow of death I fear no evil" or the fear not remedy, etc.

There is an interesting point in this comment.

[Luke 9:23 … and take up his cross daily]

There is only one thing you are going to be doing for the rest of your life after you apply this remedy and this is what this comment about the cross is. Your cross is going to be trying to convince your friends the species who have been brainwashed, that the language and math education when applied improperly hinders the mind to a devastating degree, and then you are going to try to convince them to apply the remedy. You may assume before you apply the remedy you will certainly have other goals but I assure you, you are mistaken.

The apostles carried this cross from city to city until the cities butchered them. The cities kept warning them to shut up about this tree of knowledge and this remedy and finally the cities or civilization just decided to kill them to shut them up. That reality is relative to this comment [John 15:13 Greater love hath no man than this, that a man lay down his life for his friends.]

This means you are going to be compelled after you apply this remedy to tell this great truth to your friends the species, they are your friends, and they will simply kick you in the teeth and hate you, because they know not what they do, they are of unsound mind, insane. The complexity in that statement also means those who apply the remedy and wake up [lose their life (mentally) to preserve it] (their mind) will then try to wake up their friends and relative to the time period of these beings, they were killed for trying to wake up their friends.

You will be aware of what you are dealing with after you apply the remedy. You will figure it out and you will work it out so there is no need to try and convince you because after you apply the remedy you are a free thinker and no one can advise you. You just have to figure it all out yourself and you will because you will have a sound mind. You will become an advisor to kings and kings will be unable to advise you. Socrates took up the cross and tried to explain this situation to the youth and he was butchered by civilization but he died for his friends. He did this [John 15:13 Greater love hath no man than this, that a man lay down his life for his friends.] He tried to assist his friends the species and they butchered him because they know not what they do. Why don't you call the wisest being you know and tell them my fish head's are waiting for their retort to this section of my poorly disguised thick pamphlet diaries.

[Mark 16:17 And these signs shall follow them that believe; In my name shall they cast out devils; they shall speak with new tongues;]

[And these signs shall follow them that believe] = traits of ones who believe the education is the Trojan horse than veils right brain because if they believe that they will certainly apply the remedy which is [Luke 17:33 ; and whosoever shall lose his life shall preserve it.]

Once in a while a person accidentally applies the remedy of course. So after one believes what the tree of knowledge is they apply the remedy and then they do this [they cast out devils; they shall speak with new tongues;] Cast out devils means they will try to tell their friends about the effects of the tree of knowledge and try to assist them in understanding the remedy, the brainwashed ones. [speak with new tongues;} means after one applies the remedy they will speak in tongues which is they will speak in random access and with complexity and so their friends, the brainwashed will say "What kind of drugs are you on" and "You are just babbling".

This is because the ones brainwashed can only understand sequential comments well and so anyone who applies the remedy and speaks in random access confuses them and so they use their pin prick sequential logic to determine that person must certainly be on drugs. This is relative to the comment Carl Jung made that goes something like "When a person does not understand you they tend to assume you are a fool." There is a double standard thing going on in this whole situation.

I was brainwashed and I was showing all the symptoms and I had an accident and I broke the brainwashing but that means nothing because it cannot be proven except by my fruits. I understand the only way I will ever perhaps convince even one person is to write infinite books. I do not mean fruits as in act holier than thou. I mean fruits as in exhibit fruits of concentration and understanding. - 12:45:45 AM

"I don't think the ACLU will be able to help you on this. We have no policy on education as a virulent form of brainwashing."
We have no policy on education as a virulent form of brainwashing. = We are blind to the fact education is a virulent form of brainwashing.

[Job 29:15 I was eyes to the blind, [and feet was I to the lame.]]

[and feet was I to the lame.] This comment is a sign post to ones who can see or ones who have applied the remedy. This is a sign post of authenticity.
This comment should read relative to one who is brainwashed / left brain sequential based [and I was feet to the lame] not [and feet was I to the lame] so Job is [[Mark 16:17 they shall speak with new tongues;]. Job is speaking in tongues or he is speaking in random access sentences at times and random access is a symptom of right brain being unveiled. So the fact Job could write means he got the education and the brainwashing but then he applied the "walk though the shadow of death and fear no evil" remedy and unveiled right brain again, and now he is speaking in tongues and he is writing about it, so he is taking up the cross.

He is spending his life trying to explain the tree of knowledge and the remedy to his friends, the species but when he says things like this [and feet was I to the lame.] his friends, the brainwashed say "What kind of drugs are you on, you are crazy." And they spit in his face because the he is beyond their understanding. So Job replied to them when they said he was drunk because of how he spoke in the random access way, [and feet was I to the lame.] with [Acts 2:15 For these are not drunken, as ye suppose, seeing it is but the third hour of the day.]

The reality is because civilization embraces this left brain education and teaches it improperly and because it is so sequential heavy they assume any random access signs are signs of insanity or drug use and this means they hate right brain but they are not aware of it. If you were in school and typed this in an essay [and feet was I to the lame.] you would be deemed to have mental problems. They would come up with some reason to fill you with drugs to fix you.

This comment is very egotistical relative to the brainwashed ones [Job 29:15 I was eyes to the blind, [and feet was I to the lame.]] I was eyes to the blind and feet to the lame. He is telling the truth he is just trying to put this cerebral sensation into words and it tends to come out sounding egotistical relative to the brain washed ones because they cannot understand truth when they hear it. The sane see the truth as lies because they are in reverse world, they are simply in an alternative perception reality so they are not in reality. The sane see reality as a lie because they are hallucinating in their unsound state of mind. The sane do not know what reality is because they assume their hallucinations are reality so when they see reality they deny reality. One cannot condition the mind to the left with education for years and year and expect anything but unwanted side effects. Why don't you write a book and explain how that is not true and I will wrap my fish heads in it. Jesus was also known to make the blind see and the lame to be able to walk. This is relative to one who is brainwashed is mentally lame and blind and then they apply the remedy and they can see and walk again, mentally or are of sound mind again. They go from darkness, brainwashed, unsound mind, apply the remedy and then go to light, sound mind and get their right brain unveiled again. - 1:12:05 AM

11/16/2009 7:53:34 AM – George Orwell wrote a book called 1984. In this book he spoke about the thought police. If a child is conditioned into extreme left brain so they are only capable of sequential thoughts, slothful thoughts and their fear is turned up to a great degree and their perception is thus altered then in fact their thoughts are controlled. So the book 1984 was not talking about an event that was going to happen he was talking about an event that was and is happening. A person's perception is their bottleneck so if that persons perception is altered at a young age then their thoughts are altered for their whole life and once a person thoughts are altered they are able to be controlled. If the education brainwashing wanted to make a person wise it would be a system to condition a person into sound mind 50/50 hemisphere active. The other option would be to conditioned a person into right brain extreme because right brain is relative to complexity , intuition and pattern detection. If I condition away your pattern detection ability and your intuition, which could be looked at like street smarts and your complexity in thoughts then you make a very good sucker and can be taken advantage of and then on top of that I make you very afraid of even shadows. Essentially the education strips one of their mental abilities to detect traps, powerful intuition, complexity and pattern detection and so then that person is what is known as mentally blind and they make good suckers and they make good slaves. 7:59:32 AM

11/17/2009 6:28:59 AM –
I did not think I would find you old friend
I climbed so far it never ends old friend
I can't patch you up
I can't lift you up old friend
You fell too far
You fell too far old friend
I use to know old friend
Where to begin old friend
I use to trust you old friend
Where to begin old friend
Now you just rest your head old friend
I can't patch you up old friend
I can't lift you up old friend
I can't reach you were you've fallen
I can't teach you were you've fallen
Rest your head old friend.
It's the end old friend.

Old Friend - http://www.youtube.com/watch?v=shCnh5lIT8Y

11/17/2009 7:14:27 PM – I did some experiments in various communication channels. Something hit me when I was being spit on by beings when I suggested the perils of the education if it is applied or taught improperly.

Left brain is relative to sequential and thus sequential is relative to simple. Right brain is relative to paradox and paradox is relative to complexity. A person who applies the fear not remedy after getting the education cannot tell their thoughts are complex and the people who get the education and do not apply the remedy cannot understand complexity.

This is why the term "beyond their understanding" was used. One who applies the remedy is in their own bubble of perception so they cannot tell they are complex in their thoughts and ones who do not apply the remedy are in their own bubble of perception and they cannot tell they are simple minded in their thoughts. What I suggest is complex so a person who has their right veiled will only deduce it is foolishness because they cannot understand complexity because complexity is beyond their understanding because their right brain has been veiled because of the education "brainwashing".

There is nothing I can say to convince you of that because in order to believe the education in fact has veiled your mind you have to make determinations that require complexity and you simply are not capable of that because the complex aspect of your mind is veiled to the background, subconscious. Your complex right brain is reduced to a subconscious state so the only time you are capable of complexity is when you are high on certain drugs because they unveil right brain to a degree. You sometimes have dreams that do not make sequential sense. You may have a dream where you are running in place or running from something but you never move or the dream is in random access order. You have dreams sometimes that are not in sequential order. When you are asleep or high on drugs your right brain is trying to break free from its veiled state but because you never experienced right brain up front it gives you the impression the drugs make you have a spiritual experience and same with the dreams.

The drugs give you the impression you become wiser when you do them but in reality they are just unveiling right brain for the duration the drugs last. Right brain is known for creativity, complexity and paradox so your only chance in your life to exhibit any of those aspects without applying the remedy is when you are on drugs and that is why you are trapped. You have to harm yourself with drug to experience true creativity, complexity and paradox and all of those things make up aspects that lead to wisdom. You have to do heavy drugs to show symptoms of wisdom because you're too afraid to ever apply the remedy because you perceive the remedy is dangerous so you are trapped. You are not in this trap because your genes are bad. You are in this trap because someone or something wanted you to be as dumb as possible, as simple minded as possible and as susceptible to fear tactics as possible. It is not important who that was or what that was because the bottom line is you are trapped in that state of mind and besides you are not capable of figuring out who or what wants you in that state of mind because that requires complexity and intuition in thoughts and you have very little of that in your brainwashed state.

I want to make this very clear to the one who have drug problems. It does not matter how many drugs you have done in your life. It does not matter what drugs you have done in your life. Once you apply the remedy you will pray for ignorance and that is a symptom of how powerful right brain is. You perceive the drugs have made you "dumb" but in reality that is only relative to the fact you are only using essentially left brain , the slothful aspect of the brain because, you got the education. All I can say is once you apply the remedy and unveil right brain you will laugh at the drugs you have done because you will understand they did not harm your mind at all. It does not matter if you have actual brain damage from drugs or from an accident because right brain is so powerful I can only say unnamable. So never think because you did drugs you harmed your mind. Your mind was bent all the way to the left because of education and that is what harmed your mind. You will have to redefine your definition of high once you unveil right brain and you are going to find no matter what drug you have been on , that drug will no longer get you high. You will just ponder your way out of doing drugs because right brain when unveiled makes you euphoric mentally 24/7 and you never come down. It will take you a year after you apply the remedy just to get use to how high you are when right brain is unveiled. You will see wisdom in

Swiss cheese commercials and you will think you must be on the best drugs in the universe and you will be right. No matter what drugs you have taken that high you have felt is simply right brain unveiled just a little bit for just a little while and then you come down and revert back to this extreme left brain state of mind and that's what you perceive as coming down. You have to understand the drugs are logic actions for you to escape the extreme left brain suffering the education has put you in so all you have to do is apply the remedy and then you will have no reason to escape. I understand you may have trouble believing right brain when unveiled is more powerful than any drug you could ever do but it is true. Right brain is so powerful when unveiled it laughs at drugs so never assume your mind is ruined because of drugs, because that is not truth. It is not you will not want to use drugs anymore like drug rehabs try to do it is simply you will be in such a euphoric state mentally you will just forget about drugs, not slowly but within a month after you apply the remedy. Right brain will ponder so fast you will you cannot even think about drugs or using drugs for more than a moment before right brain ponders you into some other thoughts. This state of mind I accidentally discovered is what some people spend a lifetime trying to achieve and I happen to know the fast track to achieve it. So before you go get all depressed because civilizations drug treatment programs never work, you give this remedy a try. You are not a bad person for using drugs, you simply were reacting normally to the fact you got mentally bent to the left as a result of the education being taught to you improperly. You did nothing wrong, you just try to apply the remedy the best you can and ignore these beings who wish they understood psychology.

11/18/2009 12:11:30 PM – The ancient texts call this cult known as civilization the cult of the serpent. There are plenty of loose ends so it is important to understand the mechanics of how the cult operates but one of the loose ends is who is the leader? It is not as much of a situation as one leader as it is more along the lines of the blind leading others to blindness. Left brain is intellectual based ,right brain is intuition based. What this means is once a person gets the education they have to read what others say to come to any conclusions. Intellectual simply means one has to be told what to think by books or leaders and this is because they are in extreme left brain and since their intuition is veiled as a result of that they cannot think for their self.

You have read some of the ancient texts at least once and have heard about the tree of knowledge and how it is bad so you have heard from a wise being there is something wrong with the written language and math you are just not aware of it because your intuition has been veiled. You have heard of the story "Do not eat off the tree of knowledge it is bad". The problem is you take everything on face value and this tree of knowledge is beyond your ability to detect its actual meaning. If Adam would have said the tree of demotic, and demotic is Greek for hieroglyphic script, you would assume it was only relative to hieroglyphics. You would assume it is not relative to the written script language you were taught.

Right brain is your pattern detection aspect and since that is veiled you would not be able to detect the patterns in written language, it is all sequential based and that is left brain trait. In this brainwashed state you are having trouble understanding obvious explanations. The ancient texts are very simple to understand if one has their pattern and intuition aspects at full power and perhaps impossible to understand if one does not. So you are unable to argue intellectually no one ever told you there were some serious problems with the written language invention. Someone did tell you and someone wrote it in a book you have been reproducing for 5000 years and you still never figured it out. You can't figure it out so you are relying on someone who has the brainwashing to figure it out and they cannot figure it out either. That is what the concept of the comment the blind leading the blind is relative to. There is another concept relative to those who do not remember the past are doomed to repeat it. There is a concept in the ancient texts about a whore. A whore relative to these ancient texts is a person that does something unforgivable over and over and over. There is another concept in the ancient texts relative to the unforgivable sin. It is an ideal relative to a deed one does that is so damaging they can never be forgiven for doing it. This is relative to the tree of knowledge.

If a human being conditions a child knowingly or unknowingly with this tree of knowledge it will veil that child's powerhouse right brain that aspect has unnamable power and because the right brain has unnamable power, complexity and intuition it is unforgivable. Some call it a sin against god, some call it a sin against the holy spirit, some call it unforgivable sin but no matter you call it, if you are complicit in doing that to a child's mind knowingly or unknowingly whatever punishment happens to as a result is proper punishment.

There is no punishment that is to severe and that is an indication of how powerful right brain is and that is an indication of how serious of a crime it is to knowingly or unknowingly veil that aspect of a child's mind and leave that child in a mental state of suffering because their powerhouse aspect is turned off. It does not matter what your sequential based judge says. It does not matter what your sequential based laws say contrary to that. It is the law above all law and that is an indication of how powerful right brain is.

Abraham and Lot wiped out an entire city and killed every single person in that city and they were righteous to do so. That is an indication of how powerful right brain is and how devastating the crime is to veil a child's right brain by not applying the education properly.

[Genesis 19:13 For we will destroy this place, because the cry of them is waxen great before the face of the LORD; and the LORD hath sent us to destroy it.]

Abraham and Lot told you right your face they destroyed these cities of men and killed everyone in them, [the LORD hath sent us to destroy it]. They killed the men who were mentally raping children with the tree of knowledge because those men did not know how to apply the tree of knowledge properly. Adam said it bests not to even mess with that sequential based crap.

[Genesis 2:17 But of the tree of the knowledge of good and evil, thou shalt not eat of it: for in the day that thou eatest thereof thou shalt surely die].

I do not know how to apply the education properly and no one you know does either but I am mindful there are beings who do know to apply the education properly without veiling the right brain but you are perhaps far too gone to even ask for assistance. Your way of life is to mentally rape children by veiling their right brain and leaving them defenseless and my only question is, do you think you are going to continue to get away with that? Do you perceive your longevity is increasing or decreasing? What does your intuition tell you taskmaster?

"for I have sworn upon the altar of god eternal hostility against every form of tyranny over the mind of man." –Thomas Jefferson to Benjamin Rush, 23 Sept. 1800
.- 12:37:56 PM

1:16:49 PM - The founders created the concept of freedom of speech in case someone came along that had something important to say and you are slowly starting to understand what the power of freedom of speech is. I am not as dumb as I look, I'm infinitely dumber. - 1:22:34 PM

2:34:00 PM-
X = amount of children brainwashed into this extreme left brain state every year
Y = amount of people who break the brainwashing every year

X is always greater than Y and the only way to defeat that is what is known in the ancient texts as Armageddon or the Sodom and Gomorrah solution.
What this means is the reason Moses wandered in the wilderness is because he was a wanted terrorist by the cult of the serpent, civilization. The reason Jesus was in the wilderness before one in civilization turned him in is because he was a wanted terrorist and against

civilization. Civilizations name means polite to be good or civil so anyone who speaks against it is automatically deemed uncivil or impolite. Jesus threw the money down the ground and so the cult did not like that because the cult uses the lure of money as a carrot to make people get the education. People do not get the education to become wise they get the education because of the promise of money after they get education. So the people who do not take the education well become very depressed and end up getting slave jobs and the ones who take the education well are rewarded but they still have a veiled right brain so they are still of unsound mind so they sell their children down the river for the promise of money.

They sell their mind down the river for the promise of money. They sell the only thing that matters which is a sound mind down the river for a few copper pieces and then they wonder why their children are drug addicts and depressed and angry and bitter and working a slave job. I am not talking to the rich because they are far too gone. They have no chance perhaps of ever waking up. I talk to the down trodden because they are aware something is not right. I will let the rich come to the understanding their money will not save them. - 2:38:20 PM

3:04:56 PM – My right brain is fully aware of the situation it is in. It understands my chances of convincing 6 billion mentally unsound human beings that their sequential written language invention has devastating mental side effects and had devastating mental side effects on them. Right brain understands fully my chances of accomplishing that task is zero. Mentally I am already fully aware I have zero chance of convincing any kind of majority that the spirit of what I suggest about education is true. The interesting thing is right brain is not panicking but it is getting better. It is concentrating harder. It is seeking to find more ways to explain this situation. It is pushing to understand more and more and then relate that to this education brainwashing. It is as if the harder the task is the more right brain concentrates. It is as if right brain operates best when it understands it has no chance. It is as if right brain works best in impossible situations. I understand I am convincing me what I suggest is true and I have to because I have lots of ambiguity, doubt, which is right brain trait.

The more I doubt what I say the more I prove what I say. It is as if defeat and impossible situations makes right brain stronger. Left brain panics in impossible situations and in defeat and right brain gets better. Right brain is just a machine and it does not approach a situation with some permanent solution it approaches the situation as an experiment. Right brain does not want to win, right brain wants to experiment and get better into infinity. Right brain is not about winning it is about getting better and better into infinity. It never stops because a win would mean it would have to stop so even with a win it does not respond to a win, it looks at a win just like it looks at loss, simply an experiment to adjust its strategy to get better.

There is some kind of psychology going on here with the right brain that it is a separate personality, a machine personality. In extreme left brain state a person is very emotional so it makes sense right brain would be lacking emotions because the two hemispheres are contrary and this is relative to the medusa story about looking at perceived death, medusa's head, and then turning to stone emotionally and also relative to the ancient texts about the women who looked back at the cities burning and turned to salt. If the whole world stopped doing this mental brainwashing to children and learned to apply that invention properly tomorrow I would still write about it. This is because right brain cannot feel satisfaction and thus dissatisfaction because it's a machine. I understand everything I write about comes back to the tree of knowledge invention. There no way I can start a comment about anything and not end up saying something about the tree of knowledge. My only way to keep breathing is to keep writing. I do not even think it matters if you apply this remedy because I understand I perhaps would not apply this remedy because I recall I was afraid of scary movies before the accident to a great degree. I don't think right brain even acknowledges the world or civilization or anyone at all. It is a machine and it has this task and everything is relative to experimenting to improve its ability to explain this task to others. It's not looking to become perfect it is only looking to get a little better at explaining things, and that never ends.

My drug is concentration now. I sense this fluidity when I am at peak concentration. Everything is flowing smoothly and I can just sit and write into infinity because I operate in real time only. I do not remember that last sentence and I cannot tell what the next sentence is going to be at all. I am a laser beam in the now and the concentration by itself is the drug. Thought itself is the purpose. I had no thought for nearly forty years and now I understand what thought is and I am trying to get the most out of it because this extreme concentration is the only thing of value.

Because I have pondered some cultures that have no education and I observed some of their habits I lean at times to the theory that this fear not remedy is in fact a way to trick your mind to think you died so you boost your mind. There is lots of ambiguity though and there are some things relative to what kind of damage this extreme left brain state does to the mind caused by the education. What are the side effects of conditioning a mind into the extreme left brain state from the education and then shocking the mind out of that state. There is no test to determine that because there is no test that can show the education does bend the mind to the left. One cannot test to see how far to the left years of sequential education bends the mind and that alone should be a huge red flag.

It is impossible all those years of sequential education would not bend the mind to the left because the left is based on sequential thoughts but one is unable to ever tell how far to the left. I know for certain if one's mind senses time it is pretty far bent to the left. If one gets depressed and suicidal it is bent pretty far to the left. If one feels euphoria from drugs it is bent pretty far to the left. If one needs coffee to wake up it is bent pretty far to the left. If one needs to eat three times day because they have such strong hunger it is bent pretty far to the left. If one has to drive 80 miles an hour to feel like they are having fun it is bent pretty far to the left. If one has to control others to feel worth it is bent pretty far to the left. If one condition's a child into this left bent state of mind and they are not even aware that is what they are doing, their mind is bent pretty far to the left. One might suggest people that know not what they do should never be allowed around children. One might suggest people that know not what they do should perhaps never be allowed out of their cages. - 3:44:05 PM

5:43:35 PM – Fear itself is one of the most complex aspects to explain because the remedy is fear not. Some people are terrified of spiders and snakes. Some people are terrified of small spaces. Some people are afraid of their weight, how they look and even what they look like. Some people arc afraid of their thoughts. So in considering this comment [2 Timothy 1:7 For God hath not given us the spirit of fear; but of power, and of love, and of a sound mind.] if a person is not afraid of the things mentioned above then they are pleased or indifferent with the things above. If one is not afraid of how they look then they are pleased with how they look. If one is not afraid of a snake or spider then they are pleased with a snake or spider. If one is not afraid of their self then one is pleased with their self. So this "spirit of fear" is abnormal. A person does not get a nose job because they are pleased with how their nose is so that is a symptom of this spirit of fear. In psychology it is understood too much fear is a bad thing. Fear causes nervousness and thus stress and stress has many bad side effects.

Fear can lead to paranoia. Stress can lead to emotional problems. Since fear can lead to stress then the logic is the less fear the less stress. The greater the fear the greater the stress, so less fear is a good thing. There is so much play in this fear concept that is it hard to determine how much fear is the right amount. Some will suggest one has to have fear but they do not know how much. If a person is actually afraid to use a certain words in front of certain people then that is stress. The comment one suggests "Don't say that around that person." is a symptom of fear and thus stress.

11/19/2009 5:29:52 AM - A young child may walk up to a person they do not even know and say "Why are you fat?" or "You are fat." and that child will walk away as if they are indifferent but in reality they have very little fear or they are not self conscious. A parent, who's child walks up to someone and says "You are fat" or "Mommy look at that fat person", will be embarrassed and ashamed and perhaps apologize for that child's comment. So the parents is embarrassed about what their own child said and the deeper reality is the parent assumes that child is "ignorant" when in reality that parent got the education and they are a nervous wreck and afraid and embarrassed. This is all relative to one thing. A person who gets the education has their mind bent to the left and so when they are around a small child who has not had the education and thus has sound mind that parent perceives that child is "bad" or "stupid" or "wrong" because insanity perceives sanity as insanity.

An adult wants to give their child the education because they want their child to be more like them because they have assumed their child is bad because their child is not like them. A small child has no self awareness about walking outside in the buff in front of people yet an adult will assume that is evil or bad or the child is ignorant because that adult is unable to understand that is a symptom of one who is of sound mind and a symptom of one not infinitely self conscious and ashamed and afraid. This comment is before the tree of knowledge [Genesis 2:25 And they were both naked, the man and his wife, and were not ashamed.]

This comment is after the tree of knowledge.[Genesis 3:7 And the eyes of them both were opened, and they knew that they were naked; and they sewed fig leaves together, and made themselves aprons.]

[and they knew that they were naked] = ashamed, embarrassed

This is also after the tree of knowledge [Genesis 3:10 And he said, I heard thy voice in the garden, and I was afraid, because I was naked; and I hid myself.]

[and I was afraid, because I was naked;] = The mind is bent to the left and then the aspects that control fear hypothalamus and amygdala stop working properly.

Simply put theses parts of the brain are telling a person they should be ashamed and afraid when there is no logical reason that person should be ashamed or afraid so that person is in fact hallucinating.

Pre education [And they were both naked, the man and his wife, and were not ashamed.] = not hallucinating

Post education [and I was afraid, because I was naked;] = hallucinating

The child is in the buff out in public and the child is not ashamed and the adult is ashamed of that behavior because the adult cannot understand, they are ashamed because their mind is bent so far to the left their self conscious aspect is turned up to levels that makes them a nervous wreck about things that are totally meaningless. So the adult wants to "fix" the child by educating the child so the child starts being ashamed. The adult wants the child to be like they are. Suffering begets suffering, the cursed beget cursed. Simply put an adults young child is not a nervous wreck like they are and the adult cannot stand for that. The adult must fix its child so its child will be ashamed and embarrassed and afraid like they are. Those who are abused tend to become abusers. Those who are brainwashed tend to want to brainwash others. This is such a deep seeded neurosis that adults may perceive they are "fixing" their child but that is only relative to the reverse world because in reality they are mentally ruining that child with their assumption that education is thought to make one wise.

Their child will be wise once it is ashamed about its own body and its own thoughts and it becomes so self conscious it just wants to take drugs to escape from itself. This is all relative to intellect, a left brain aspect.

You have never read knowingly a book that says these inventions written language and math have detrimental side effects on the mind so you just assume it cannot be true because your intuition which is right brain is veiled so if someone doesn't tell you what to think you do not think. Simply put if you do not read it somewhere or someone of authority does not tell you it is so, you will assume it is not happening because the last thing in this universe you can do after the brainwashing is think for yourself.

Thinking for one's self requires intuition and the education veils right brain and thus intuition. You are simply a slave to what others tell you is proper or improper because you got the one thing that makes a thinker taken away from you as a result of your many years of brainwashing called education.

The powers that be are never going to publish that the education brainwashes a person into a sequential thought based and fear based mindset, and because you will need to read that to believe that, because you cannot think for yourself because your right brain intuition is veiled.

You have lost your mental ability to deduce reality yourself because you intuition has been taken from you and so you can determine when to breathe but outside of that you need someone to tell you what to think about everything. Someone told you to educate your child by the accepted methods of education and you never questioned that and never even looked into other hardly known methods of applying the education without ruining the child's mind so you just listened to what other said because you have no ability to think for yourself.

Your child counted on your to not allow any harm to come to them and because you can't think for yourself you mentally exterminated the one aspect of your child's mind that can assist it in life and then you blame how your child acts on the child. Your child did nothing to deserve to be mentally raped but your ignorance and that fact you were mentally raped means you know not what you do. You took a perfect sound mind, absent of shame, embarrassment and fear and you saw it as bad because your mind is full of shame, embarrassment and fear. - 6:02:46 AM

11/19/2009 8:26:56 AM – Relative to Dante he tried to explain what this left brain state of mind was like in his story Inferno.

"they had their faces twisted toward their haunches
and found it necessary to walk backward,
because they could not see ahead of them.
…and since he wanted so to see ahead,

he looks behind and walks a backward path.'
Inferno, Canto XX, lines 13–15 and 38–39, Mandelbaum translation.

What this comment is trying to explain is the reverse thing. "because they could not see ahead of them." ,simply means one in this brainwashed state, extreme left brain, only has sequential thoughts to work with so they see a few steps ahead and assume they took the situation to its eventual conclusion. Here is an example of the reverse thing.

 Relative to the reverse world: You get education, you get a job that pays money and you have a good life.

Relative to reality world: You get education, it veils your powerhouse right brain, you get a few dollars but you are mentally hindered and suffer for the rest of your life.

"and found it necessary to walk backward," the ones who are brainwashed walk backwards.

Relative to reverse world: One wants their child to get lots of education.

Relative to reality: One does not want their child to gets lot of education without a teacher that knows how to administer it without ruining the child's mind.

You do not need to use your sequential logic to try to decide if you had one of these teachers that knew how to administer the education without ruining your mind because you would not detect one if they were writing infinite diaries talking to you.

If you have a strong sense of time, strong hunger, strong emotions you could not be more mentally ruined and brainwashed if you tried. Simply put, drugs are the only way you can reduce the suffering you experience in your ruined state of mind and of course Dante calls that state of mind hell.

The first circle of hell is known as Limbo. This explanation is relative to Dante's attempt to explain this "hell" state of mind the tree of knowledge puts one in.

This limbo state is relative to the comment [Luke 18:25 For it is easier for a camel to go through a needle's eye, than for a rich man to enter into the kingdom of God.]

A person who is rich and wealthy and popular in the reverse world is totally separated from any opportunity to break the curse or the brainwashing and that is what this Limbo state is, separated from the unnamable one, right brain. Simply put, ones in the first circle limbo are so caught up in the reverse world they have no clue anything is even wrong, so this first circle of hell is the worst circle. It means one has no chance to wake up. So relative to reverse world one who is rich and wealthy and popular is good, and in reality world one that is rich and popular and wealthy is doomed because they may never escape the mental hell.

So relative to the reverse world this first circle seems like not such a bad place in contrast to the other circles but in reality world it is the worst circle. The ones in this first circle have no chance to wake up which means they are totally cut off from reality with no redeeming ability to get out of the reverse world.

The second circle is lust. Ones in the second circle are suffering because they can never obtain perfect satisfaction from what they lust for. They are tormented. They may wants lots of money but can never get enough. They may want lots of control but can never get enough. They may want acceptance but can never get enough. They may want drugs but can never get enough. So they are suffering but they have a chance to break free of that because lust taken to the extreme will sometimes defeat a person and that may wake them up but typically they are destroyed by their lust.

The third circle is gluttony. The ones trapped here are ones who crave things to the point the things they crave destroy them. People who eat too much and people who starve to look good. People who over indulge are really suffering because they are harming their self but they perceive it makes them feel better. A person may suggest they just love to eat but they do not love to eat they are trying to escape this left brain suffering state they have been conditioned into by the education.

The fourth circle is Arvarice. This is essentially greed. A person that will do anything to get ahead or to acquire more material possessions. As one goes further into these circles they all become one thing. A person who is gluttonous will show signs of greed to achieve that gluttony for example. All these circles are traits of one thing, the mark, the mental mark one has as a result of the tree of knowledge, the education, they have mentally fallen from grace. One is a glutton because they lust for food and because they lust for food they will also be greedy for food. This is not relative to only food , this is relative to acceptance, drugs, material things , money, all of these are simply physical based aspects and they are attracted to these physical based aspects because their cerebral powerhouse, right brain, is veiled so they have nothing left to work with but physical based things, they have no mind so they try to find value in physical things and this is a very good state of mind to be in relative to reverse world because civilization is based on economics and supply and demand and if a person has right brain unveiled they are in a cerebral world and they won't be buying very many material things they don't need.

An easy way to look at it is when right brain is unveiled it is such a cerebral powerhouse all of these materialistic aspects are not very valuable all the sudden, they kind of take a back seat to this powerhouse cerebral aspect. This is not saying material thing are bad this is simply explaining symptoms of one who has been brainwashed by the education.

The fifth circle is wrath and sloth. Sequential based thoughts is a left brain aspect and that is sloth and the reason it is associated with wrath is because one becomes impatient easily because everything becomes difficult because the powerhouse, right brain that can turn a mountain problem into flat ground is veiled. So instead of life being very easy and all problems being easy to solve, in the brainwashed state minor problems become mountains of impossibility. This is relative to making a mountain out of flat ground and because of that one gets wrathful easily.

One who is brainwashed has many problems and so they become angry very easy. It seems as if every problem is impossible when in reality if they had right brain unveiled they would understand there are perhaps few problems that right brain can't help one out of with no stress and no fatigue. If you are only using half your mind and the retarded half in contrast to right brain it's understandable one can become angry very fast. One reality is one's mind senses time so they have this time monkey on their back at all times and that creates stress and stress creates fatigue and so they are defeated by their own mind on a daily basis.

This is relative to the comment about a house (mind) built on sand(unsound mind) cannot withstand the storms but a house (mind) built on solid ground(sound mind, unveiled right brain) can withstand the storms. I do not detect any human being on this planet that is capable of advising me on any matter ever so I find it difficult to sense stress or fatigue, is one way to look at it. That is an indication how powerful right brain is, not how intelligent I am, and that is an indication how grave of a crime it is to veil a human beings right brain and that is why the comment when one sins against the holy spirit, veiling right brain, it is simply unforgivable no matter what. I do not have good genes I just got the aspect of my mind that was stolen from me when I was child, back. If I use any commas properly in this whole book, call.

The sixth circle is heresy. The doubting Thomas circle of this mental hell. It is a person who does not believe in life after death. What that means is it is a person who does not detect they are mentally dead after they get the education, so dead would mean a person who does not believe firstly the tree of knowledge can harm them, and secondly that there could be another mental state besides the one they are in after they are brainwashed. They do not believe anything is wrong with them mentally after they get the education because in order to do that they first have to accept the fact the civilization they trusted in fact brainwashed them and that's is simply too big of leap for them to make because they are only capable of sequential thoughts and they are thus not capable of seeing very far ahead "because they could not see ahead of them."

I did not know anything was wrong with me I just thought I was simply a loser and did not have anything to offer anyone and that is why I took a handful of pills and relative to reverse world I was just a loser and a fool and relative to reality world I was blessed

139

because I was being meek, but I wasn't aware of that at the time. So every time you hear about a person who kills their self you are witnessing a human being who is trying as hard they can to get out of the cult and the reverse world. They are trying to get out of hell state of mind and many of them do not make it. Only a complete loser relative to reverse world can go up to the edge of death and pull back at just the right time so they wake up. I am pleased no one can understand anything I say ever into infinity.

The seventh circle is violence. This is an important ring because relative to reverse world this is a bad ring but relative to reality world this is the ring where people start self harming. That is one of the first true indications a person is trying to wake up out of the brainwashing or trying to leave the cult. This violence against others is also violence against one's self. Some people attack civilization or society and in turn get killed. Some will attack the police in hopes the police kill them. So this violence circle is the first stage of one who is trying to "check out" of the cult and the brainwashing. They have had enough of the suffering mental state the education has put them in. Civilization looks down on people who are suicidal but that's only relative to their reverse world but in reality world these people are meek and humble because as a being they are subconsciously, right brain, ready to wake up.

Civilization makes sure to heavily sedate these kinds of people and throws lots of drugs at them knowingly or unknowingly to make sure they don't wake up. Simply put there is only one way out of the cult and that is to commit mental suicide and those who lose their life preserve it, is mental suicide. You can try to pray yourself out of the cult but you got the mark, on your mind, on your head, so who do you think you are praying to?

The eighth circle is fraud. This is when a person starts losing faith in civilization, the cult. They stop caring about rules of the cult because they have figured out the rules of the cult are biased and false. The cult will create rules and make it seem like they created the universe itself and these rules were there when the universe was created and if you do not bow to their rules you are evil and bad but that is relative to the reverse world. In reverse world the rules of the cult are all good and in reality world the rules of the cult are all bad. The first rules of the cult is everyone gets at least 16 years of the brainwashing education starting when they are about seven, so everything the cult suggests after that first rule is nothing but diabolical.

The ninth circle is treason. Treason against one's self. Self being relative to one's self after they are brainwashed. Those who lose their life will preserve it. That is treason against one's self. If you go to a cemetery at night searching for the shadow of death and then when that shadow of death comes and you submit to it as in your do not try to save yourself, you commit treason against yourself.

This self you are after you get the brainwashing is not you so you have to deny it to get the real you back. Another way to look at it is after you bite off that tree of knowledge you have a serpent around your neck, in your mind or spirit, and that "spirit" what you call yourself, and the only way to get that serpent to leave you alone is to trick it into thinking you died. You give up and then it leaves you alone and you get your true self back.

Whatever you need to tell yourself to go apply the remedy is good because until you do, you are in hell mentally and there is nothing that is going to get you out of mental hell but you, no matter what anyone says ever. All you can hope for at all is that you have a good accident in your attempts to apply the remedy. If you go to a cemetery at night alone that means you love the shadow death because you seek the shadow of death and in reverse world that seems bad but in reality world that's the only chance you have to get out of the cult and wake up. This is why this final circle of hell which is treason, is in relation to reality world the point at which a person is ready to wake up but many perish before they do.

So a person you read about who kills their self is a person who tried to commit treason against this aspect they thought was their self but really it was not their true self it was the spirit of fear they were treasonous against. Blessed are the poor in spirit, the suicidal, because they have good chance of leaving the cult or breaking the brainwashing. The meek, the suicidal, the treasonous against their false self, have a chance to break the brainwashing and leave the cult and if they do they inherit the earth which means they get right brain back and they are above the earth which means above the cult, the ones brainwashed, because the ones brainwashed are mentally hindered. Blessed are the poor in spirit because they may wake up and find the unnamable one, right brain.

I am pondering how far beyond your understanding I am at this stage since the accident.

The concept of one has to go through hell to get to heaven is relative to the nine circles of hell. One has to go through all these stages to reach the ninth stage of treason against ones self and if they go through that stage they come out on the other side which is heaven or they get their true self back, a sound mind, they unveil right brain. - 9:58:14 AM

"Sorrow is knowledge, those that know the most must mourn the deepest, the tree of knowledge is not the tree of life."
Lord Byron
[Exodus 32:19 And it came to pass, as soon as he came nigh unto the camp, that he saw the calf, and the dancing: and Moses' anger waxed hot, and he cast the tables out of his hands, and brake them beneath the mount.]
[and Moses' anger waxed hot] = Ignorance was bliss.

[tree of knowledge is not the tree of life.] = Education taught improperly veils the right brain and then mentally one is not capable of cerebral life so one goes from a mentally fruitful life to a mentally rotten life which is mental death in contrast.

"Sin, guilt, neurosis; they are one and the same, the fruit of the tree of knowledge."
Henry Miller
[neurosis] = the mental sins and symptom's one has the education brainwashing

"There is no coming to consciousness without pain."
Carl Jung
You did not choose to be brainwashed by the education but only you can throw off that yoke.
You can suffer in neurosis for a life time or suffer for a moment to reach consciousness.
A child does not choose to be put into neurosis but the controlling adult's choose for the child because the controlling adult's neurosis was chosen for them by their parents.

"Imagination is more important than knowledge."
Albert Einstein
Without creativity one only knows confusion.
Right brain is relative to creativity and once this aspect of the mind is veiled by traditional education one is left with few options when problems arise.
Complexity, paradox, creativity, intuition and pattern detection are the keys to understanding knowledge, the foundations of wisdom and are traits of right brain.

If any of the above wise beings were worth their salt they would have proved it by now. - 11:19:00 PM

11/20/2009 12:18:41 AM – It wants the children. Once it gets a child that child grows up and has children and it gets those children. Its net is the Trojan horse education. Its gets all the children with it's net. Its appetite has no limits or bounds. This is why you get your fear of death out of the way because when you understand its numbers and its power you will run and hide in a little hole and beg for ignorance and seek safety if you have even have one hint of fear in your mind. The word children is mentioned 1800 times in the torah and new testament alone. It's the children it wants. You were a child and it got you. You were given to it to satisfy its infinite craving for innocent children. The sooner you understand that is reality the sooner you will understand one thing about this battle. The sooner you understand that reality the sooner you will understand what you are up against. You are not more important than the battle and that is why you get your fear of death out of the way. It is difficult to explain cerebral understandings with words but the bottom line is the above is simply the result of pattern detections.

There is this underlying pattern to this whole battle and the above explanation is that pattern. The first born were killed. How were they killed? They were sacrificed. How were they sacrificed? By way of this Trojan horse that is thought to make one wise. [Genesis 3:6 And when the woman saw that the tree was good for food, …, and a tree to be desired to make one wise, she took of the fruit thereof(used the tree as the sacrifice mechanism), and did eat(sacrificed the children), and gave also unto her husband with her; and he did eat(it eats the children that are sacrificed to it). It wants the children and it wants all of the children and it will do anything to get all of the children. It will deceive, and scam and trick and lie and make darkness look like goodness so it can get all of the children to eat.

[1 John 5:21 Little children, keep yourselves from idols. Amen.] What is the Idol? Education. The children want to be educated so they can make lots of money because their parents want them to make lots of money. The children want to get the best education and go to the best school because their parent wants them to have these things. The idol is the written language, demotic and math. The children want to please their parents so they idolize and dream about getting good grades and being wise. It never pans out that way though. They all seem to end up settling for slave jobs and they struggle with their emotions and their sequential thoughts and their fears and they have no concentration and then they start thinking maybe their genes or their brain is not very good because they never were smart enough to make this education pan out for them. They idolize the education and then when it does not pan out they hate the education and that is also a form of idolatry. The idol is the education and is the golden calf. It is the most important thing relative to the cult of the serpent, civilization. The minions of the serpent will explain how without education one is nothing and one is worthless because they love the whore and they are servants of the whore.

[1 John 3:7 Little children, let no man deceive you: ..] Do not let the men of the cities deceive you to give up your mind for the promise of a few copper pieces. These men [Genesis 11:5 And the LORD came down to see the city and the tower, which the children of men builded.]

[city and the tower] = civilization = men

These men(civilization) are minions of the serpent, they have the mark , the mental symptoms as a result of the education and they will deceive you and force the education on you and then they will turn you into a slave to build their towers to heaven for they are simply servants to the serpent. These men will use every deceptive trick in the universe to take the one thing from you that matters the most and that is a sound mind. Once they veil your right brain you are powerless and thus simply their slave. They will force veil your right brain and then tell you that you simply are not up to snuff and that you must take their slave jobs so that you can survive. These men have no mercy and have no mind for they are nothing but the deceiver and they will destroy everything in their path to get one more child to sacrifice to the whore. Do you understand where you are at now? We will discuss morals after the battle. The one with the most convincing argument is the only vote that counts. Being recognized by an important being is a treasure beyond value.- 12:58:38 AM

3:34:41 AM – Rest your head old friend.
 I can't patch you up.
 I can't lift you up old friend.
I can't reach you were you've fallen.
Rest your head old friend.
It's the end old friend. - 3:35:26 AM

4:53:45 AM – The cycle of this battle is what has turned us against ourselves and a species divided cannot stand.

A person is born and then they have their arms and legs cut off. They go through their life assuming not having arms or legs is normal. About the time they are 30 or forty they grow back their arms and legs. They seek out the ones that cut off their arms and legs and ask them why they cut off their arms and legs and the ones who cut off their arms and legs say "You are crazy we didn't cut off your arms and legs." The next thing that happens is the person see's the same people cutting off the arms and legs of child and they ask the people 'Why are you cutting off the arms and legs of children" and the people say "You are crazy we are not cutting off the arms and legs of children."

This failure to communicate is what creates the battle and pits ourselves against each other and so this battle is the only battle that has been going on for the last 5000 years. The ones who cut off the arms and legs of children have the numbers and so they perceive it is okay to keep cutting off the arms and legs of the children and the ones who wake up and grow back their arms and legs never have enough people on their side to stop the ones who cut off the arms and legs of the children because the children's arms and legs are cut off on an industrial scale. The ones that cut off the arms and legs of the children do not even know that is what they are doing so they are what is called possessed. They are doing the most horrible thing one could ever do, veiling right brain, in another human being but they see what they do as a good thing. These possessed ones can go as far as understanding education is to left brain orientated but they can never make the connection with what the true effects that has on the mind of a child.

They are fully aware the education is left brain heavy but they cannot imagine what that means in relation to affecting the mind of a child so they falter because they cannot see very far in front of them so they are blinded to cause and effect relationships. They see the cause, too much left brain orientated education but they are blind to the effect of that. So Dante said this "because they could not see ahead of them". This is why the invention of written language and math was fatal to our species. There are only two kinds of people in the world. The ones who wake up and try to stop the ones who keep mentally ruining the children minds and the ones who are not even aware they are ruining the children's minds with the education invention because they cannot see because they could not see ahead of them, they know not what they do.

If there is a child being raped and there is a group of people watching it and one person comes along and tries to stop it, that one person will be deemed to be violent by the group of people because the group of people perceive mentally raping a child is good. That is what the herd mentality is. The ones who get the brainwashing cannot think for their self because their right brain intuition is silenced to the point they know not what they do. One can say after the brainwashing one is in neurosis, one is retarded, one is blind, one is pure evil and all of these comments work perfectly. One is essentially a lunatic because their mind is unsound. This lunatic aspect is what civilization is, and because that is what it is, that is all it creates, more lunatics. Lunatics are the fruits of the tree of knowledge, and civilization is the enabler of the tree of knowledge, and civilization is too mentally damaged to ever believe that.

Is a lunatic that is harming children and not even aware of it more valuable than the children they are harming? The brainwashing is so complete this is what it does to a person's mind.
[Genesis 19:11 And they smote the men that were at the door of the house with blindness, both small and great: so that they wearied themselves to find the door.]

It makes one so mentally blind, by turning off their intuition and pattern detection of right brain so they cannot find the door to get out of the brainwashing so the only way to really wake up is to die mentally and shock your mind out of the brainwashing and this is so difficult to accomplish its usually done by accident. There are ways to slightly negate this brainwashing but one will never ever truly wake up until they perceive death and submit to it. That is an indication of how fool proof the brainwashing is. Only a fool can break the brainwashing fully.

Only a fool can do this [Luke 17:33 ; and whosoever shall lose his life shall preserve it.] because only a fool would not try to save his life when he had a chance to save his life. So the door out of the brainwashing state of mind can only be entered by fools relative to the reverse world. That's why when you hear about someone who is depressed or suicidal you will always hear the comment "They are looking for attention" or "They are a loser" or "They are a fool." Or "They are selfish". This is an example of they know not what they say. They simply do not have a clue about what they are saying when they say those things. It all comes to down to this. You got brainwashed and you may be too brainwashed to even know it, and that is your problem, but you do to the children what you did to me. I will now discuss something of value.- 5:25:12 AM.

5:39:47 AM – One can never go wrong writing in their own personal diary because they are only talking to their self. - 5:41:13 AM

5:52:52 AM – There is a concept called vanity. One form of vanity is to take a child with a perfectly sound mind and condition that child into an extreme left brain unsound state of mind and then tell that child to have a good life. The ultimate form of vanity is to condition the entire species into this unsound left brain state of mind and then try to solve problems. It is like plucking someone eyes out and then telling them to go drive a car on a freeway at 80 miles an hour. It is actually worse than that but I try to use parables because I am mindful of who I am speaking to. - 5:57:39 AM

6:08:09 AM – This comment is explaining the situation a person is in after they get the brainwashing,
[1 Peter 1:21 Who by him do believe in God, that raised him up from the dead, and gave him glory; that your faith and hope might be in God.]
    Simply put a person has no possible way to tell they have been brainwashed because it happened to them gradually over a few years and so they cannot even tell they have been brainwashed at all and civilization is not going to ever invent a test to show how far one is leaning mentally after the education because civilization would hang their self if they did. Civilization has all this technology but it has no test to show how the mind is before the education and then after years of this sequential based left brain education. Civilization is not interested in that study so you are in a situation where all you have to go on is faith.
    You have to look at the facts which are written language and math are sequential based. Then you have to have faith the years of this left brain sequential based education has veiled your right brain and only then will you attempt to apply the remedy because civilization is not going to be telling you how bad they mentally raped you with their forced education.
    If civilization tells one person they may have been mentally harmed by the 12 years of education then they have to tell everyone and that is a can of worms that would never recover from. You have to understand your strong sense of time is a symptom of the brainwashing. You have to understand your strong sense of emotions and fear is a symptom of the brainwashing. You have to understand your strong hunger for food and for acceptance is a symptom of the brainwashing. You have to understand you inability to feel others through vision is a symptom of the brainwashing. You have to understand your inability to use your "telepathy" all the time which is just the intuition of right brain is a symptom of the brainwashing. You have to understand when you do any sort of drugs or coffee and you feel the cerebral effects, euphoria, that is proof you are brainwashed. You have to understand civilization would not have put you to sleep if they wanted you to be

awake. You have to understand I would not tell you these things if they were not true. - 6:21:19 AM

10:18:05 AM – The right brain contains all of your long term memories and when you unveil it all of your past memories that are long forgotten in the left brain state are going to be in your conscious mind. They are going to be very vivid and it will take time to adjust to all of your memories from childhood and your teenage years being in your conscious mind. Because they will not have emotions or time stamps they will seem like they just happened and they are very powerful memories. It is difficult to adjust to this. - 10:23:00 AM

11/21/2009 4:06:37 AM – I will attempt to explain this intuition sensation I have, relative to this education invention is fatal to our species. Abraham and Lot and their armies destroy the cities and killed everyone in them. They killed everyone who got the education or the curse because they could not explain to them convincingly the education had altered their minds and also they could not convince them to stop putting this "curse" on the children. They became what would be known today a terrorists against civilization. Anyone who is against civil is a terrorist because civil is understood to be good. Their militant strategy to stop the curse did not work and the proof is the species as a whole still pushes this education on the children and has yet to ever suggest it has any bad mental side effects. So civilization is either aware the education brainwashes people and that is why they do not suggest it has any bad side effects or civilization itself is brainwashed and they know not what they do because lunatics or mentally unsound people know not what they do.

Moses was in the wilderness for forty years because he was a wanted terrorist who attacked civilization. Jesus was in the wilderness and was turned in to civilization and thus was killed because he was able to convince people the education was brainwashing them and he was so good at it he could also convince them to apply the remedy and turn them from a blind brainwashed state to a seeing sound mind state. So he could make the blind see so he was a great threat to civilization. Anyone who got the brainwashing is automatically in the cult so the cult killed Jesus because Jesus knew the key to breaking the brainwashing. Jesus tried to use words but that is only relative to the fact he only woke up and was speaking for three years.

Abraham was at it for a lot longer and eventually resorted to militant strategies against the cult. When you apply the remedy and have heightened awareness how long will you be able to stand by and watch the cult mentally raping and ruining the minds of children and leaving the children in a state of suffering and then watch civilization punish the children when they exhibit characteristics of being conditioning in to an unsound state of mind to begin with?

You may not believe that or understand that now but when you apply the remedy that is going to be going through your mind because once you feel the power of right brain when it is unveiled you are going to understand why veiling right brain, which is sinning against the holy spirit, is unforgivable. I am aware of how sinister this whole situation is. To take a person who just fine mentally and educate them into a unsound state of mind and then punish that person for their behavior in that unsound state of mind exceeds any ability to define sinister and that is because right brain is so powerful.

The reality is once one unveils right brain and applies the remedy they get their marching orders. The right brain will assist them in making a proper decisions and the unspoken reality of ones who applies the remedy is they are not able to be advised.

It is not that it is against the rules to advise one who breaks the curse it is simply there is nothing anyone can tell them they cannot figure out for their self and this is relative to the strong intuition, pattern detection and complexity of right brain when it is unveiled.

The reality is being militant against the ones who push this brainwashing does not work because the cult is called civilization and anyone who attacks civil is assumed to be uncivil. Trying to convince the cult with words does not work because the cult is not going to submit they mentally harm people knowingly or unknowingly, because they teach the education improperly. Because of this there is no solution. Because there is no solution there is no right or wrong. There is no proper word's to use that is going to convince the cult as whole to try to adjust its teaching methods of this education, so education does not harm the children.

There is no militant strategy that is going to convince the cult to adjust its teaching strategy of the education so it does not mentally harm the children. If civilization admits their teaching methods of the education mentally harms a person they will be sued and held liable and so they will in fact destroy their self by admitting that. This is not an isolated situation as in one country this is the cult which is called civilization. One might suggest there numbers are like the grains of sand in the sea. Because of this situation with no solution, ignorance is quite a luxury or ignorance of this situation with no solution is joy.

It is joy to not be aware civilization is mentally raping children on an industrial scale and you are included in the subset "mentally raped children". This is what the battle is and it goes back at least 5400 years relative to the west and perhaps as far back as 8000 years relative to the east. Because of this invention education the species has been force against itself. The ones who break the brainwashing caused by education can never wake up as many as civilization, the cult, puts to sleep with the education with its industrial scale "schooling".

So when you apply this remedy you are entering a battle you understand you cannot win and that is what is called selflessness. You may get the impression I am on the side of the ones who woke up but in reality I am a commentator or a messenger. I make observations and report on them because I woke up very fast. I took the chariot route so to speak. I have too much ambiguity now to go picking sides so I am reduced to an observer. You may think I am against civilization but I am not. I am observing what civilization is doing. I am simply suggesting to civilization its education invention has devastating mental side effects if not taught by a master who understands those effects and can teach the education properly.

A teacher relative to civilization is not aware of the bad mental side effects so they just push sequencing to the extreme on the children and so they know not what they do. Teachers relative to civilization are simply minions of the brainwashing. They are simply brainwashing the children into a devastating state of mind and they are doing it for a few copper pieces because they are not aware it was done to them for a few copper pieces. The whole premise of civilization is to work together to solve our problems but that makes no sense since civilization brainwashes children into the sequential, simpleminded state of mind, left brain, before they are even ten. So civilization or the cult is either the devil incarnate or totally insane beyond all definitions of totally insane and I cannot decide which it is because I have too much ambiguity, doubt, so you are going to have to apply the remedy and decide for yourself.

I have a paradox that is in my mind. I want to help civilization and at the same time I want to destroy it. If I convince civilization about the unwanted side effects of the education they will adjust and in turn that will destroy civilization as we know it today because people of sound mind behave differently than people of unsound mind. I am not about to deceive anyone because I do not fear anyone. I understand I cannot say anything right or say anything wrong because the battle has never been won by anyone. I will not censor my thoughts so that I may have a chance to win a battle, I am already aware cannot be won.

My thoughts are more important to me than the battle because I am fully aware no being has been able to convince the cult its wisdom invention when taught improperly ruins the mind of innocent sound minded children. I can approach this battle with words and lose or approach this battle with weapons and lose and neither method matters because lose is always the end result. Because of that you are naturally going to purge your emotions after you apply the remedy because at the level of heightened awareness when right brain is unveiled and becomes aware of this battle, emotion will destroy you.

You will turn to stone or turn to salt emotionally naturally because the heightened awareness is going to be too strong to allow you to afford emotions. You will have moments of great sorrow but they will pass within 15 seconds or less relative to a clock and you are going to have moments you think you can win and thus feel like everything is going to work out and those will pass swiftly and you will end up back in neutral. This is the ambiguity in action. I have spoken to people in chat rooms and tell them what I tell you and they agree and say "This is wonderful thank you for telling me this" and then I go to another chat room and tell them what I tell you and they spit on me and tell me I am crazy and tell me I need medical help. So you will have moments of winning and moments of losing and when all is said and done you end up right back in the middle, in neutral.

It is interesting to observe these things and when the words stop working so one is not insulted, they experiment. When the sane start throwing out insults at me I know I need to adjust my wording but I am not harmed by the insults I can get the spirit of what they say from their comments and understand they are insults. I am immune to the words they idolize. In an emotional state or one who is brainwashed this situation appears very depressing and it may even seem like I am depressed but I am neutral and none of this does anything emotionally to me. It is a relative thing.

To one who is brainwashed and their emotions are turned to maximum as a result it seems daunting but to one who applies the remedy suggesting this message is simply infinite experimenting with no perception of an end result. I try to tell people I had an accident and woke up to the fact the education altered my mind and I found out how one can negate that altering of their mind the education caused but somehow that is an insult to them.

I am mindful they are unable to use the creativity and complexity involved to understand this Trojan horse education mentally altered their minds. There are too many jumps one has to arrive at to grasp that reality and because they are brainwashed and are stuck in left brain and thus can only think in sequential thoughts they just assume I am crazy for suggesting such a thing. I am mindful writing about ghosts and aliens is far easier to convince people of. I can convince the universe of anything except education is a Trojan horse because if education is Trojan horse then civilization is a tyrant over the minds of men. Only the fearless would consider entering that battle and only the Lords and Masters would engage in it boldly.

[Proverbs 28:1 The wicked flee when no man pursueth: but the righteous are bold as a lion.]

The comment "The wicked flee when no man persueth" is best explained as the ones who are brainwashed have lots of fear because great fear is a symptom of the brainwashing. What I am suggesting is you are not afraid of words and ghosts and a bad hair cut because you just naturally are, it is because it is a symptom of the brainwashing caused by the education.

The education has turned you from a fearless lion to a creature that is afraid of shadows. How can I find fault with anything you do when I fully understand you were simply brainwashed as a child and that is why you do the things you do? The point is you are a fearless lion that has been sedated and I am trying to convince you of that so you will apply the antidote and return to being the lion I know you are.

This comment: [Proverbs 28:1 The wicked flee when no man pursueth: but the righteous are bold as a lion.] is simply a repeat of this comment [Psalms 23:4 Yea, though I walk through the valley of the shadow of death, I will fear no evil: for thou art with me; thy rod and thy staff they comfort me.]

They are interchangeable and they are also far more complex that they appear. One interchange is The wicked flee from the shadow of death. A shadow is not going harm a person so that is the same as saying the wicked flee when no man persueth, and that is the same as saying the ones brainwashed flee from shadows because their fear is so abnormal.

Another interchange is, a lion walks through the valley of the shadow of death and fears no evil or is fearless. So you see these comments are explaining the contrast between how a person mentally reacts to stimuli when they are brainwashed and then when they apply the remedy and negate the brainwashing. So this comment [for thou art with me; thy rod and thy staff they comfort me.] is simply explaining the reason you will not fear shadows after you apply the remedy to the brainwashing is because your hypothalamus will not be sending you false signals anymore. You will no longer be afraid of shadows and certain words and certain foods and certain music and the list goes on.

You are only afraid of certain words because your hypothalamus is telling you if you say that word you will die or harm will happen to you but that is not possible because a word is a sound and so you are hallucinating because your hypothalamus is sending you errant messages or magnified messages and that is what is expected after you get all those years of left brain sequential education. Simple cause and effect relationships is what this is all about. You get the education taught improperly, you have to go sit in a cemetery until you feel better or you will be afraid of shadows, and thus that great fear will make you unable to concentrate and so you will needlessly suffer, is one way to look at it. - 5:39:13 AM

6:03:38 AM – The pyramids at Giza are thought to be built starting around 3200 BCE. Egyptian Hieroglyphics which has a common everyday script and also a fancy more complex script used on the pyramids dates back to about 3200 BCE. Sumerian script is thought to date even further back but that is only relative to the west, in the east written language dates back perhaps thousands of year's further back than Sumerian. So one might suggest because of written language the pyramids were able to be built but in reality because of the altered state of mind caused by learning the script man started exhibiting behaviors relative to material focus because their cerebral powerhouse right brain was veiled and this resulted in men building towers to heaven so to speak.

Mankind became focused on material things for satisfaction because their complex cerebral hemisphere had been veiled as a result of learning the script. Some may assume not many people got the education or were taught the written language back in those days but this is not true. Look at some of the apostles. Some of them were fisherman when they met Jesus so one might assume a fisherman would not have the education but they in fact did have the education because they ended up writing books that are in the bible. This was 2000 years ago and common fisherman knew how to write so the "education" was available to everyone.

Another way to look at it is, if those fisherman did not get the education there would be no need for Jesus to explain to them the remedy. So you can see in the case of John the Baptist, he lived in the wilderness and he was baptizing or applying his version of the remedy which was similar to the Abraham and Isaac remedy, on the people from the cities who got the education. The complexity is civilization would not be what it is today if there was no written language and one may assume that means written language is flawless but in reality written language education bends the mind to the left so one is mentally unsound and so civilization and cities are a symptom we as a species became mentally unsound. This is why this invention is so devastating to our specie because we are as a species exhibiting symptoms of an unsound minded creature and that is what civilization represents, the deeds and fruits of a mentally unsound creature. Can we as a species reverse this trend? No. Can we as a species take back the damage this invention has caused us? No. Simply put, it is not a question if we can go back to before the invention altered our minds as a species because we cannot. It's a curse than can never be broken.

All one can do is attempt to break the curse on their self and that is as good as it gets. One can only focus on the log(curse) in their eye and try the best they can to break the curse and revert back to sound mind with the understanding there is no way to convince the species to look into applying the education properly so it does not veil the right brain of the children. Civilization truly believes written language and math are the greatest inventions of all mankind and in reality they are the most devastating mentally damaging inventions of all mankind. This is the reverse thing.

The darkness see's the light as darkness so it kills the light because the light reveals to the darkness what the darkness is. This is simply relativity and that is why the "curse" can never be broken on the species. You may apply the remedy and break out of the brainwashing but you will never convince civilization to stop brainwashing millions of kids on an industrial scale so there is no way to stop the curse. Adam knew this because he had right brain unveiled and could go from step one to the last step instantly and understand if we as a species embraced this written language and taught it to everyone it would get out of control and be unstoppable and our species would destroy itself because a species that is mentally unsound cannot stand [Genesis 2:17 But of the tree of the knowledge of good and evil, thou shalt not eat of it: for in the day that thou eatest thereof thou shalt surely die.]

We are a species that invented something that altered our minds and we are in turn a suicidal species that is against itself. We kill our self off and think it is wise so as a species we know not what we do because as a species we are lunatics. There is a small group of human beings who do not have the education and civilization wants nothing more than to educate them with their invention thought to make one wise. On one hand it is very sinister and on one hand it is simply a symptom of how an insane person acts. You go anywhere in civilization and they will say "Education is the greatest thing ever" and then you will understand there is no way to stop it. So relative to some I am a good accident and relative to others I am a bad accident and relativity suggests both observations are right at the exact same time.

I am not suggesting any rules I am suggesting that mankind better take a long look at their education system because there is something devastatingly wrong with it and because of that argument I have no room for rules, morals or class because I am trying to communicate with beings conditioned into such an unsound state of mind that they harm children and think they help children. - 6:39:46 AM

11/22/2009 6:26:47 AM - This comment is relative to disciples and disciples are simply people who take the advice of one who breaks the brainwashing and applies the remedy they suggest.
[Hebrews 11:20 By faith Isaac blessed Jacob and Esau concerning things to come.]

The word faith is used because Jacob and Esau got the brainwashing and so they have to take Isaacs word for it in order to come to a point they would apply the remedy. The point of this comment is suggesting some people Isaac convinced to apply the remedy to the brainwashing but Isaac was told the remedy by Abraham so Abraham was the Alpha relative to Isaac and thus the Alpha relative to all the ones Isaac convinced to apply the remedy.
[Genesis 22:7 And Isaac spake unto Abraham his father, and said, My father: and he said, Here am I, my son. And he said, Behold the fire and the wood: but where is the lamb for a burnt offering?]

This comment has a sign post. It is a verification Abraham was the genuine article relative to the fact he unveiled right brain by applying the fear not remedy to the education brainwashing.
[Here am I, my son.] Relative to ones brainwashed this comment is out of sequential order it should be [Here I am, my son.] not [Here am I, my son.] The point of these sign posts is to let the ones who apply the remedy know these words are genuine and from a genuine article and in this case Abraham. This is relative to the comment they(the brainwashed) hear but do not understand.

One who applies the remedy understand Abraham was genuine because theses random access sentences or these sentences out of sequence are proof he has unveiled right brain and this out of sequence writing is what speaking in tongues is. This speaking in tongues, random access wording, sounds very odd to the ones brainwashed but when right brain is unveiled , right brain gets the spirit of the sentences so one is not bothered by these out of sequence comments at all in contrast to ones brainwashed that only see parts, which is a left brain trait. So these comments are suggesting a lineage of sorts.

Abraham broke the brainwashing then he suggested it to Isaac then Isaac suggested it to Jacob and Esau.

[Genesis 22:9 And they came to the place which God had told him of; and Abraham built an altar there, and laid the wood in order, and bound Isaac his son, and laid him on the altar upon the wood.]

This comment is suggesting one almost has to force the remedy on people.[and bound Isaac his son, and laid him on the altar upon the wood.] this is relative to the fact once a person gets the brainwashing they are so full of fear they are not prone to apply the fear not remedy their self. This is an indication of how difficult it is to break out of the brainwashing and this is why the brainwashing has continued for 5000 years. The cult will take a child and condition them by force using scare tactics on the parents and then suggests everyone has freedom of choice as if the cult was not simply a control freak. "Give your child our "brand" of education or your child will have a slave and job and a tough life" and the cult calls that freedom of choice when it is simply a scare tactic to make parents sacrifice their own children to the cult of the serpent. Of course the parents also have the "brand" so they fall for traps like that easily because their right brain pattern detection and intuition aspects are silenced. Elementary traps work well on the blind.

Here is another example of this lineage.

Socrates had disciples called Plato and Plato had a disciple called Aristotle. Socrates said no true philosopher fears death and Abraham said Fear not. Socrates and Abraham were in two totally different parts of the world but both areas had written language. So these are simply people who broke the brainwashing and took on disciples which they explained how to break the brainwashing caused by education. Socrates was killed by civilization, the cult, because he was a big fish.

He was a threat to the cult because he had the keys to escape the brainwashing and he could convince people of the escape route. The cult does not like that. Socrates convinced Plato and Plato convinced Aristotle. So Plato and Aristotle saw Socrates was not afraid of the cult and was not afraid to tell people about the brainwashing and he was killed and so he died trying to wake people up from the brainwashing so he is no different than the ones in the west who died trying to suggest the remedy to the brainwashing.

It is not important if your cult leader does not agree with that because if your cult leader understood one sentence of the ancient texts I will remind him. I am mindful to avoid personal commentary.

The important thing to remember is this is all relative to the battle that has been going on over 5000 years and the trend is the ones who break the brainwashing on their own, known as the big fish, try to assist others in breaking the brainwashing and they tend to be slaughtered by the cult. The big fish are a threat to the cult because the cult wants to make sure no one knows about the brainwashing opiate written language and math. If word gets around the written language and math are simply brainwashing tools to make one go extreme left brain mindset in order to make them dumb, sequential based in thoughts, and susceptible to fear, hypothalamus is sending way to strong of signal in that conditioned state, the game is over for the cult.

They killed Socrates for corrupting the mind of the youth. They kill Jesus for corrupting the mind of the youth. These beings kept saying "suffer the children" too often so the cult slaughtered them, would be another way to look at it. The cult is diabolical. I cannot use any word worse than diabolical but the cult is far worse than diabolical. The cult takes a perfectly sound mind of a child and conditions it into a state of suffering and it does not have to because the education can be taught properly but it wants nothing to do with that, so it is beyond diabolical and that is because in this left brain state a human being is doing nothing but trying to avoid the suffering the brainwashing causes. So the cult is so dark I cannot even explain it except to say diabolical.

This is the definition of diabolical: having the qualities of a devil; devilish; fiendish; outrageously wicked. This is the definition of outrageous : of the nature of or involving gross injury or wrong and passing reasonable bounds; intolerable or shocking and violent in action or temper and grossly offensive to the sense of right or decency.
[involving gross injury or wrong] [passing reasonable bounds][violent in action or temper] [offensive to the sense of right or decency]
[[passing reasonable bounds] = not reason = insanity
[violent in action or temper] = quick to judge slow to understand
[involving gross injury or wrong] = abuse
[offensive to the sense of right or decency] = anti decency = anti truth = adversary] = it knows not what it does.

Aristotle was known to be one of the founders of ethics and was a product of Socrates assisting Plato to break the brainwashing and that is lineage.

Socrates was also trying to suggest doing this brainwashing to children was unethical and the cult butchered him and while in jail Socrates had a chance to escape and he told his friend something like , "Where would I run?", "Where would I hide the cult is everywhere?" There is nothing else that is important in contrast to applying this remedy no matter what you think in your brainwashed state. One cannot be aware of the wickedness of the cult until they apply the remedy because one who is still brainwashed has their intuition, a right brain aspect, and thus their heightened awareness turned off essentially. These wise beings down through history were not trying to put you in a cage of bondage they were trying to free you from the cage of bondage, the brainwashed state. I would not tell you these things if they were not true. - 7:19:58 AM

3:03:15 PM – The only viable solution to satisfy both sides in this conflict is to offer two totally separate forms of education. The current education system where a person will be good at written language based on the current accepted rules of written language and also math. So in that respect nothing has to change relative to the current form of accepted education. The new school of education would be essentially oral education until the child's mind I fully developed. The student that graduates from this type of school would be very creative and very complex in their thoughts. Essentially the student from the old form of school would be bent to the left brain and the ones from the new type of school would be more holistic in their mental state.

The student from the old school would have a sense of time the students from the new school would have no sense of time. Currently the education system is dominated by beings that got the old school left mind bent form of education so they have a monopoly on how all students are educated. What this means is they are determining for everyone what kind of education they are getting and this violates ones freedom to choose. I am mindful it appears like no parent would want their child to go to a school that bends their child's mind to the left to such a degree but that is not as much of a factor as the fact everyone gets a distinct choice in what type of education they get and society would not be allowed to be biased against either type of student that is educated from either type of school. Right now every student gets the same kind of left brain bent education their parents got and that is what creates the conflicts. There has to be a choice so that everyone has an option of what kind of mindset they wish to be in after the education is done.

X = the ones who get the left brain bent education
Y = the ones who get the holistic verbal education

The Y's are the ones who have been attacking the X's for 5000 years because the X's do not give a person a choice in what kind of education they get. It is a fact the X brand of education veils the right brain but that is ones choice if they wish to be this kind of hybrid human being relative to mind set. The species must understand there are in fact two totally different education methods and each one leaves the student in a totally different mindset and because of this a student should make the bottom line choice as to which type of education they wish to get because the X education alters their mind and this altering is essentially permanent. To force one or the other education method on a child robs that child of life, liberty and the pursuit of happiness and most importantly freedom of choice. If the species does not remedy this central problem then there is only going to be conflict between these two mentally contrary types of people. - 3:22:06 PM

8:19:21 PM – The Incas did not have written language they had an oral tradition and they used string with knots on it for census purposes. This is an account from: In Cuzco in 1589, Don Mancio Serra de Leguisamo — the last survivor of the original conquerors of Peru about the Incas.

"We found these kingdoms in such good order, and the said Incas governed them in such wise [manner] that throughout them there was not a thief, nor a vicious man, nor an adulteress, nor was a bad woman admitted among them, nor were there immoral people. The men had honest and useful occupations. The lands, forests, mines, pastures, houses and all kinds of products were regulated and distributed in such sort that each one knew his property without any other person seizing it or occupying it, nor were there law suits respecting it… the motive which obliges me to make this statement is the discharge of my conscience, as I find myself guilty. For we have destroyed by our evil example, the people who had such a government as was enjoyed by these natives. They were so free from the committal of crimes or excesses, as well men as women, that the Indian who had 100,000 pesos worth of gold or silver in his house, left it open merely placing a small stick against the door, as a sign that its master was out. With that, according to their custom, no one could enter or take anything that was there. When they saw that we put locks and keys on our doors, they supposed that it was from fear of them, that they might not kill us, but not because they believed that anyone would steal the property of another. So that when they found that we had thieves among us, and men who sought to make their daughters commit sin, they despised us."

[there was not a thief, nor a vicious man, nor an adulteress, nor was a bad woman admitted among them, nor were there immoral people.] – They had proper fruits or deeds because they were of sound mind because they did not have the written language mind altering conditioning.

[The men had honest and useful occupations.] – This is in contrast to civilization that is essentially a cut throat type of job system.

[The lands, forests, mines, pastures, houses and all kinds of products were regulated and distributed in such sort that each one knew his property without any other person seizing it or occupying it, nor were there law suits respecting it… the motive which obliges me to make this statement is the discharge of my conscience, as I find myself guilty.] – The Incas lived in harmony with the natural resources and also were not control freaks [each one knew his property without any other person seizing it] – Civilization is ruled by the carpetbaggers and they will buy up land and then control it and that cannot last because eventually the poor will be slaves to the rich.

[For we have destroyed by our evil example, the people who had such a government as was enjoyed by these natives.] – This man is admitting they destroyed the Incas and is also suggesting the Incas had a better system of cohabitation. He uses the word natives which

is a label used to describe people who are not of civilization so the word native is like saying uncivilized but this man is in fact explaining these natives had a better system than civilization did and the difference was the Incas did not have written language but an oral tradition so their minds were sound and their fruits proved it [there was not a thief, nor a vicious man, nor an adulteress, nor was a bad woman admitted among them, nor were there immoral people.]
Thief = greed and lust
Vicious = wrath
Adulteress = lust

[They were so free from the committal of crimes or excesses, as well men as women, that the Indian who had 100,000 pesos worth of gold or silver in his house, left it open merely placing a small stick against the door, as a sign that its master was out.] – This suggests these being trusted each other. They left all their wealth in a hut with an unlocked door. One will not find that in civilization because everyone is afraid of everyone else and everyone does not trusts everyone else because they are all conditioned by the education and simply put, unsound in mind so they are all seeing each other as separates beings, parts a left brain trait, and so everyone is out for their self and that means they have to take advantage of each other to survive. Civilization is every man for himself in an overpopulated cage and so it's just a lunatic asylum.

[With that, according to their custom, no one could enter or take anything that was there.]-Imagine just being able to say "No one steal from each other or enter anyone else's house when they are not home" and everyone understood that and followed that. You will never see that in civilization because the ones who get the education are only seeing parts, and that's a left brain trait and that means they only think about their needs and they only think about material wealth because their cerebral powerhouse, right brain, is veiled by the education. A person who gets the education no longer see's people around them as anything but an obstacle in their way to get the material things they desire.

[When they saw that we put locks and keys on our doors, they supposed that it was from fear of them, that they might not kill us, but not because they believed that anyone would steal the property of another.] – The Incas had no concept of stealing or robbing or crime. This is why they were easy targets for civilization. Civilization saw them as suckers but in reality they were simply sound minded human beings that were trust worthy and not like a pack of wolves or beasts which is what the brainwashing turns one into, a beast.

[So that when they found that we had thieves among us, and men who sought to make their daughters commit sin, they despised us.] – All the tribes that did not get the education despised civilization and all the ones who break the brainwashing in civilization despise civilization because civilization is simply unsound minded human beings who no longer exhibit the traits of human beings but are simply lunatics and beasts. - 8:41:19 PM

[Exodus 22:19 Whosoever lieth with a beast (the unsound minded devils) shall surely be put to death.] = [they despised us(the beasts, the unsound minded devils).]
Moses was saying, if you even sleep with one of those brainwashed devils we will kill you.

[Deuteronomy 27:21 Cursed be he that lieth with any manner of beast. And all the people shall say, Amen.] – So in these ancient texts they did not even look at the ones who got the tree of knowledge and did not in turn apply the remedy as human beings and factually mentally speaking they were not human beings they were some hybrid mentally. They had their powerful right brain veiled so they could not possibly be acting like human beings acted who did not have their right brain veiled or ones who applied the remedy and unveiled right brain. This is not racist this is simply cause and effect, if you get the education your right brain is veiled and unless you apply the remedy you are not capable of behaving like a human being that applies the remedy or did not get the brainwashing to begin with.

[So that when they found that we had thieves(fruits of an unsound brainwashed mind) among us, and men who sought to make their daughters commit sin(fruits of an unsound brainwashed mind), they despised us.]
[Psalms 135:8 Who smote the firstborn of Egypt, both of man and beast.] – What was the cause of the first born being smote in civilization? The tree of knowledge, the written language. It ruined the mind of the man which in this comment relates to the ones who did not get the education and then got it, it ruined their children's minds and it ruined the minds of the beasts, which means the parents who got the education, they were beasts, and they gave it to their children and it smote them, bent their minds to the left also. So this is why Adam said [Genesis 3:3 But of the fruit of the tree which is in the midst of the garden, God hath said, Ye shall not eat of it, neither shall ye touch it, lest ye die.] If you are one of the tribes and you give the education to your child it will smote them, or mentally ruin them and if you already have the education and you give it to your child you smote them or mentally ruin them. Civilization loves its little invention no matter how many people it has killed mentally and literally and that is why this invention has made our species suicidal. You know not what you do.

[Psalms 73:22 So foolish was I, and ignorant: I was as a beast before thee.] The author of this book is saying I got the education and was a beast, brainwashed, before. So he once was blind but now he see's. So he applied the fear not remedy and now he is not a beast he is a sound minded human being.

[Revelation 17:13 These have one mind, and shall give their power and strength unto the beast.] – This is saying one who gets the education is of one mind, left brain extreme, and they give the powerful aspect of their mind, the right brain, to the beast. If one gives their right brain to the beast then the beast is them. They sacrifice their mind and their child's mind, right brain, to the beast, so they are left with a mind of the beast, they are possessed and show symptoms or fruits of the beast. I prefer to stick with the word unsound minded or insane to describe you. My right brain intuition knows what you are and you can say whatever you want to deny that but I still know what you are because I was a beast once also. [Psalms 73:22 So foolish was I, and ignorant: I was as a beast before thee.] - 9:15:10 PM

11/23/2009 6:40:37 AM – [2 Corinthians 6:15 And what concord hath Christ with Belial? or what part hath he that believeth with an infidel?] – Belial is relative to the devil in theology and is relative to a fallen angel according to Milton's Paradise lost. So an infidel is simply a person who got the education and has not applied the remedy and does not even believe there is any unwanted mental side effects of the years of left brain education. So in that respect an infidel is one who is so mentally bent towards the left they cannot even understand simple cause and effect relationships so mentally they are fallen.

Concord means peace or a treaty. So this comment is saying what peace does one who has applied the remedy have with one who has not applied the remedy after getting the education. The truth is there is no peace between the two and there can never be any peace because an infidel not only does not believe the years of left brain education has bent their mind to the left they also do not believe it will do the same thing to their own child, so they allow their child to get the education taught by another infidel who does not believe the education will ruin that child's mind like it has done to their mind.

How can there be peace when an infidel is harming children the same way they were harmed as a result of the education being taught improperly and that is relative to this comment.
[1 Timothy 5:8 But if any provide not for his own, and specially for those of his own house, he hath denied the faith, and is worse than an infidel.]

All this is saying is, if you do not protect your own children from the education being taught improperly, because you do not believe the education harms the mind mentally, because your mind is so harmed mentally from getting the education and you have not applied the remedy, you have denied the reality of the unwanted side effects of the tree of knowledge so you will encourage this mental harming of children, because of your ignorance towards simple cause and effect relationships.

If you were just an infidel then you simply would not believe you have been mentally brainwashed and ruined by the education and that's your business and there is no need to shed any tears over spilt milk, but the fact you go out and encourage the same brainwashing you got on innocent children's minds means you are worse than an infidel. This is why the one thing on earth you are not going to experience in this existence is peace, Belial, until you wake yourself up by apply the remedy.

Do not assume there are not beings on this earth who have applied the remedy who are not going to attempt stop you, using every single method possible to keep you from harming children because then you are not only ignorant you are hallucinating, Belial.

Why don't you go write a book contrary to the spirit of what I suggest because my fish heads need wrapping.- 7:05:10 AM

12:58:19 PM –
[THE LEFT BRAIN IS ASSOCIATED with verbal, logical, and analytical thinking. It excels in naming and categorizing things, symbolic abstraction, speech, reading, writing, arithmetic. The left brain is very linear: it places things in sequential order -- first things first and then second things second, etc.[If you reflect back upon our own educational training, we have been traditionally taught to master the 3 R's: reading, writing and arithmetic -- the domain and strength of the left brain.]
The Pitek Group, LLC.
Michael P. Pitek, III

You may perceive I am an authority but I am an accident. I have written a million words so far trying to disprove these few words.
[The left brain is very linear: it places things in sequential order] .[If you reflect back upon our own educational training, we have been traditionally taught to master the 3 R's: reading, writing and arithmetic -- the domain and strength of the left brain.]
I am attempting to disprove these few words. My right brain saw these few words after the accident and I have been trying to disprove them for the last seven volumes. Every time I try to find something in attempts to disprove those words above I end up proving them to be true even more and then I want to disprove them even more, and that cycle continues into infinity.

I am not trying to prove the education is simply a brainwashing opiate I am trying to disprove it because when I reach the point I have absolutely no ambiguity about the education.

I am unable to wake up people as fast as civilization puts them to sleep.
There are people in history who have had far more monetary wealth than you and 1000 of your friends combined will ever have. There was a Queen and she was ill and thus mindful

of death. She was aware that she was going to die and this mindfulness of death is what she was mediating on, so to speak.

She was aware death was coming. She was mindful of death so long that finally she made peace with her understanding she would soon be dead, so she defeated her fear of death. She applied the remedy. She applied the remedy and broke the brainwashing and she commented something along the lines "My entire kingdom for a moment more." and then she died. She was saying she realized after defeating her fear of death she was finally mentally alive and she was willing to give all her material wealth away and be a commoner relative to the scale of the reverse world, just to experience another moment of this cerebral life she had discovered because she defeated or accepted death.

She was willing to give more material wealth than you will ever have just for a moment longer so she could experience consciousness. That is an indication of how powerful right brain is and is also an indication how serious the crime is to veil the right brain in a child as the result of a teacher improperly teaching the education so it does not veil the right brain. Simply put veiling the right brain is an unpardonable crime so there is no need to seek a judge or a jury because there is no pardon, no mercy and no patience in administering the punishment. That is an indication once a person gets the brainwashing the chances of them negating the brainwashing are very slim.

A persons mind is unsound after the education when it was sound before so the education was taught improperly so is cruelty of the worse kind. Only something vile would do this to an innocent child. This brainwashing is not about harming someone for a moment, it is about putting them mentally in a situation for their entire life that makes them suffer for their entire life.

Conditioning a small innocent child into this state of mind is what the definition of evil is because the child didn't do anything to deserve this and they may never be able to negate this hindered extreme left brain state of mind. Retarded means hindered. If a person has their right veiled they are hindered mentally. They have half a mind working so they are mentally retarded.

What in this universe would take the perfect mind of a child and condition that child into a mentally hindered suffering being? How does one stop the powers that be from doing this to children when the powers that be do not even understand they do this to children because when the powers that be were children they had it done to them? If the powers that be understand the effects of this .[If you reflect back upon our own educational training, we have been traditionally taught to master the 3 R's: reading, writing and arithmetic -- the domain and strength of the left brain.] then they are so sinister one must be fearless in order to face them.

[Mark 3:22 And the scribes which came down from Jerusalem said, He hath Beelzebub, and by the prince of the devils casteth he out devils.]

[And the scribes] = .[If you reflect back upon our own educational training, we have been traditionally taught to master the 3 R's: reading, writing and arithmetic -- the domain and strength of the left brain.]

The scribes are the education system and that is supported by civilization. If you can write you're a scribe, so that means you have to apply the remedy because you became mentally hindered when you were being taught to scribe.

[Mark 3:23 And he called them unto him, and said unto them in parables, How can Satan cast out Satan?]

How can one who is brainwashed by the script education get their way out of the left brain leaning mindset induced script education? Another way to look at it is. How do you know you are ignorant when your own ignorance keeps you from seeing you are ignorant?

How do you know you were not brainwashed because the brainwashing keeps you from being able to tell you are brainwashed. The only chance you have is to get a terminal illness and just before you die you make peace with your certain death and you wake up and say "Everything I own for a moment more." or someone accidentally wakes up from the brainwashing and tries to convince you they were brainwashed and tries to convince you to apply the remedy they understand worked for them to negate the brainwashing.

[Psalms 73:22 So foolish was I, and ignorant: I was as a beast before thee.]

Many of the beings call this brainwashing, hell, and called the ones who were brainwashed Satan because they knew how they were before they broke free of the brainwashing. I know what hell is and it is called being brainwashed into extreme left brain state by the education to the point my emotions were turned way up and I was afraid of everything and had low self esteem. I could not think clearly and I had a strong sense of time so I was frustrated easily. That is hell. You are in a mental state of hell because of this. [If you reflect back upon our own educational training, we have been traditionally taught to master the 3 R's: reading, writing and arithmetic -- the domain and strength of the left brain.] You got far, far more left brain conditioning in school than you did right brain conditioning and all of your actions and deeds and thoughts are a result of it, a simple cause and effect relationship.

[If you reflect back upon our own educational training, we have been traditionally taught to master the 3 R's: reading, writing and arithmetic -- the domain and strength of the left brain.]

You understand this comment just not fully. You know that comment means education is leaning heavy toward left brain and that means it bends your mind to the left after years and years of this education. You understand that from that comment. What you do not understand is what exact effect does that have on the mind. Does it mean you are bent to the left mentally after the education but you are still pretty much mentally of sound mind, or does it mean you are bent to the left mentally and you are the definition of a hallucinating lunatic?

Perhaps you should call your cult leader and ask them that question since you cannot think for yourself because your right brain intuition is at 10%. Perhaps you should spend the rest of your life asking the ones you idolize what the proper answer to that question is. Perhaps you should call the board of education and ask them what the answer to that question is. Do you perceive the answer to that question is important? Do you understand the answer to that question will answer the question: Is civilization mentally raping innocent children or is civilization not mentally raping children by improperly administering their wisdom invention?

Does it mean you are bent to the left mentally after the education but still pretty much mentally of sound mind, or does it mean you are bent to the left mentally and you are the definition of a hallucinating lunatic? Your entire perception of reality and civilization rests on the answer to that question. Your entire world would shatter if you understood the proper answer to that question so you fear that question.

If this is not the answer to that question: you are bent to the left mentally and you are the definition of a hallucinating lunatic, then you can simply go to a cemetery at night and when your mind tells you the shadow of death is coming you will apply self control and not run like a little dog and nothing will happen within about one month to you mentally. Then you can come back to your cage and start writing books explaining how everything I say is wrong. Then every time I write a book you can write a counter book and explain how everything I say is wrong and then you will have job security because I am writing infinite books.

If the answer to that question proves to be what I just suggested it is, then you also have infinite job security because you will be compelled to convince blind people blindness is abnormal. You will gain infinite job security by answering that question for yourself. Perhaps you are afraid to test me because I love to be tested.

A wise being is trying to explain to these scribes the mental symptoms one accomplishes from becoming a scribe and not applying the remedy afterwards.
[Mark 3:24 And if a kingdom be divided against itself, that kingdom cannot stand.]

A wise being is trying to explain to the scribes, the educated, if you get this education and that is obvious because you are a scribe, they could write, they ate off the tree of knowledge, you have an unsound mind and their mind is not a viable mind or it is a mind that exhibits unviable fruits or is not functioning properly. Not properly meaning one is a hallucinating lunatic, not just a person who sometimes does strange things, but a person in full neurosis.
Then this wise being, who broke out of the brainwashing by applying the remedy, explains it again but is simply repeating the same thing.
[Mark 3:25 And if a house be divided against itself, that house cannot stand.]

He is saying you got the education so you are of unsound mind so nothing you will ever do is going to be anything but unsound. He was not telling them, follow rules he was trying to convince them they were brainwashed by civilization, under the guise that if you get the education you will get money. I will say it again, you have been hoodwinked with elementary carrot and stick fear tactics and now you are brainwashed. You can call it whatever you want but that is not going to change that fact. You can call it fairy tale land of hallucination world but that will not get you out of the brainwashing. You can pray into infinity to everything you can think of and that will not get you out of the brainwashing because you underestimate how effective the brainwashing is.

How many problems do you have now that I have suggested you have to defeat your fear of death itself in order to regain a sound mind you started with as a child? You have to defeat your fear of death to get out of the brainwashing and then once you do you will be looking to death as your only escape to get out of being aware of all your friends suffering in the brainwashed hell state of mind. What are you going to do when your intuition is at full power and you are aware of things and you do not need a book to tell you what is going on?

Your brainwashed state of mind keeps you ignorant because it keeps your right brain intuition veiled. Your joy is a symptom you do not have your full intuition and thus heightened awareness working. You are very joyful because you are not aware of where you are at.

The depressed and suicidal are aware that something is wrong but they cannot quite put their finger on it. The depressed and suicidal are meek and humble and everyone else is in various stages of absolute ignorance and absolute arrogance. I am mindful if you have actually read this far into this poorly disguised thick pamphlet diary you are perhaps confused because your sequential based brainwashed mind cannot make heads or tails of what I am saying because I speak mostly in random access right brain thoughts.

This comment explains why this invention has altered the perception of our species and put the species at war with itself or against itself.

[Mark 3:26 And if Satan rise up against himself, and be divided, he cannot stand, but hath an end.]

The easiest way to look at this comment is to understand after you get the education your mind bends to the left and you see everything as parts. You see everything as an adversary. You see your friends as threats, your neighbors as threats, other races as threats, other countries as threats. I do not see anyone as a threat to me but I see many as a threat to children.

I already defeated my fear of death in that den some 13 months ago relative to a calendar so why would I be afraid of death now? If I was afraid of death when my hypothalamus said "Todd call 911 your convulsing from those pills you took and you need to save your life" I would have called 911 to save my life but I did not try to save my life and here I am. If I was afraid of losing my life I wouldn't be writing these poorly disguised diaries convincing you civilization is a cult of the serpent would I? I would not be convincing you civilization mentally rapes children into a brainwashed mental state of suffering would I? A reasonable person would keep their mouth shut but I am infinitely unreasonable. What do you think about that grasshopper?

[Mark 3:29 But he that shall blaspheme against the Holy Ghost hath never forgiveness, but is in danger of eternal damnation:]

There are too many words in this comment you do not understand. Once you apply the remedy you lose your sense of time so you have found what is known as the fountain of youth. What that means is your mind itself no longer recognizes the passing of time. You will sit somewhere for an hour relative to a clock and you will think "How long have I been sitting here?" and your mind with its ambiguity, a right brain trait, will tell you, "A thousand years and zero seconds at the exact same time." And that is what no sense of time is and that is what eternity is and that is what eternal is in the above statement.

[but is in danger of eternal damnation:]

Is in danger of eternal damnation. This means once you get the education it is possible you will spend the rest of your life in the mental suffering hell state of mind which is the brainwashed state. The double meaning of this comment is if you stand by and allow this veiling of the power of right brain to happen to children who did nothing wrong you are the devil himself and that is an indication of how powerful right brain is and this is why Abraham and Lot burned down the cities and killed everyone in them and wrote about it and said it was proper to do so.

[Genesis 19:13 For we will destroy this place, because the cry of them is waxen great before the face of the LORD; and the LORD hath sent us to destroy it.

Genesis 19:14 And Lot went out, and spake unto his sons in law, which married his daughters, and said, Up, get you out of this place; for the LORD will destroy this city. But he seemed as one that mocked unto his sons in law.]

[For we will destroy this place] = we = Abraham and Lot and their armies they called two angels. One army for Abraham and one army for Lot. So Abraham and Lot were simply generals.

[the LORD hath sent us to destroy it.] = us = Abraham and Lot.

This city was the home city of Lot. So Lot is attacking the city he was from. The reason Lot was attacking the city he was from is because he applied the remedy and then realized this civilization or city he came from brainwashed him with the education, tree of knowledge.

[Genesis 19:14 And Lot went out, and spake unto his sons in law,….. But he seemed as one that mocked unto his sons in law.]

[But he seemed as one that mocked unto his sons in law.] is a very harsh reality once you apply the remedy. You are going to want to try to convince your relatives and friends this remedy is real and truth but they will not believe you. Lot was laughed at by his son and law. Lot tried to convince his son and law that his armies were about to destroy the cities and people because they were wicked, mentally harming children with demotic, and tried to tell his son and law what the cities did to the children with their brainwashing and his son and law laughed in his face, but his son and law was not laughing for long.

You will try to reach your relatives but you will not be able to and that is why you are going to turn to stone emotionally because it is going to rip you apart if you do not.

One of the first things Buddha did after he applied the remedy is to go home to his family and he tried to convince them and then he left home because he understood he could not convince them. Why do you think there is no book of Joseph in the ancient texts? There are books from all of the disciples of Jesus but no books written by Joseph. You need to ponder why that is, in relation to this [Genesis 19:14 And Lot went out, and spake unto his sons in law,….. But he seemed as one that mocked unto his sons in law.] It is easy to convince people some alien or radio wave has brainwashed them in contrast to convincing someone education itself has brainwashed them into mental hell.

Whatever the reason is for doing this to ourselves and our children, this brainwashing caused by education, is not as important as understanding we are a species divided against itself as a result of this brainwashing and so we are suicidal as a species and that is a deeper meaning of this comment : [Mark 3:25 And if a house be divided against itself, that house cannot stand.]

I cannot say anything that can cancel out this house divided cannot stand reality this brainwashing has done to us so I do not try to say all the right things relative to your brainwashed state of mind because I am fully aware we are a house divided as a species.

This comment: [Mark 3:25 And if a house be divided against itself, that house cannot stand.] Is simply a repeating of this comment [Genesis 2:17 But of the tree of the knowledge of good and evil, thou shalt not eat of it: for in the day that thou eatest thereof thou shalt surely die.]

These texts are all based on the very first text in these texts. They are repeating over and over and over the exact same spirit over and over, into infinity. The reason these texts are simply repeating the same thing over and over is because they are trying to reason with rabidity. They are trying to reason with the darkness. They are trying to convince the darkness but the darkness only see's the light as darkness so the texts just repeat over and over in hopes the repetition will work and it does not work. That is why the ancient texts are simply chants. They are chants that repeat over and over. Every single line in all the ancient texts in all the main religions are saying this [Genesis 2:17 But of the tree of the knowledge of good and evil, thou shalt not eat of it: for in the day that thou eatest thereof thou shalt surely die.]

These ancient texts are trying to reason with something that cannot be reasoned with so they just repeat the same spirit over and over in hopes that will work. The sooner you understand Civilization is the cult of the whore and that whore is demotic and known in the ancient texts as the tree of knowledge the sooner you will start to understand that the cult will kill anyone to protect is golden calf, the serpent. I will now discuss something of value. - 3:17:34 PM

5:22:45 PM – When one is brainwashed into this extreme left brain mindset they see things are parts instead of seeing things as one thing. Deeper still one has their emotions turned up and as a result of that their ego is turned up also. They have lots of this aspect called pride. The problem with that is one becomes self conscious and one has their feelings hurt very easily. Deeper still because of this ego one can hate their self or their body or their appearance. That is what this is relative to [Mark 3:25 - And if a house be divided against itself, that house cannot stand.]
This is an example of this self hate.
M.G. (18) died the day after a botched Rhinoplasty. – Mydeathspace.com
Her sister said this "I guess she just felt like it was the one thing that kept her from feeling really perfect," …sister says. "She wanted it so badly and we were all behind her 100 percent."

This innocent child hated her nose because she was conditioned with the wisdom education so she could only see parts and so she was very self conscious in this left brain extreme state of mind and so she perceived she was not perfect. It harmed her every day to wake up and see parts and she felt it was best to fix her nose because she was only seeing parts, and in her quests to get some satisfaction from the mental suffering education caused her, making her only see parts, it cost her everything.
[Matthew 12:31   Wherefore I say unto you, All manner of sin and blasphemy shall be forgiven unto men: but the blasphemy against the Holy Ghost shall not be forgiven unto men.]
Men = the beasts = the brainwashed ones
[blasphemy against the Holy Ghost] = veiling the right brain with the tree of knowledge.

Civilization puts these children in an unsound state of mind and then blames them for their emotional problems and then suggests the children have a choice. Civilization blames them for being self conscious. Civilization blames them for using drugs which are the children's attempts to escape this extreme left brain mindset of perception civilization put them in to begin with. "She wanted it so badly and we were all behind her 100 percent." She wanted badly to cut her face because civilization altered her perception so she saw herself as less than perfect. She categorized her nose as less than perfect because civilization conditioned her into extreme left brain [Left brain excels in naming and categorizing things] She categorized herself as less than perfect and it costs her everything. I will now discuss something relevant. -5:49:17 PM

11/24/2009 4:13:55 AM – [1 Corinthians 3:18 Let no man deceive himself. If any man among you seemeth to be wise in this world, let him become a fool, that he may be wise.]
[in this world] = the reverse world = civilization
Man = someone who is brainwashed.
[let him become a fool, that he may be wise.] = the reverse thing

Relative to reverse world this is foolishness [Luke 17:33 ; and whosoever shall lose his life shall preserve it.] but in reality world it is wise. The cult will suggest attempting this mental suicide is foolishness so one has to flip it and understand it is really wise. You go ask anyone with a sense of time if sitting in a cemetery to defeat your fear of the shadow of death is wise and they will say it is foolishness so you simply flip their answer and you will get the proper answer.

In order to get out of the mental hell, brainwashing one has to do the reverse of what they perceive is wise. It was foolish for me not to call for help after my mind said "You took the pills and you now need to save yourself because you are feeling ill and will die", but now I understand it was wise not to call for help. If everything you think is wise is foolish because you are in reverse world then you have to do foolish things to escape the brainwashing.

If one tries to be wise in reverse world or while they are brainwashed they will remain trapped in reverse world. This is why one has to think for their self to get out of the brainwashing because if one tries to get advice from someone who is brainwashed they will simply never escape the brainwashing. Once you apply the remedy then you escape the brainwashing and you are wise, so this comment is not for the ones who applied the remedy it is a comment to the ones who are still brainwashed. The ones who escape the brainwashing do not have anything to say to each other because they are wise which means they unveiled right brain. Right brain is so powerful once a person unveils it there is nothing another person who unveils it can say to them that they do not already know.

This reverse thing is what anti-truth is relative to.[let him become a fool, that he may be wise.] this is a reverse thing. Simply put you are going to think it is bad to go defeat your fear of death and that is proof that is what you should do. When your hypothalamus tells you to run like the wind in that cemetery at night you do not run like the wind and that is called self control.

You have to take the signal that hypothalamus is sending you and look at the reverse of what that signal is suggesting and do that. One way to look at it is you have to understand in your brainwashed state your mind is lying to you and once you let your hypothalamus know you understand it is lying to you, by not running when it tells you to run, it will stop lying to you.

Once your hypothalamus understands you are no longer going to listen to its false signals it will stop sending you the false signals. This is why one seeks the harshest reality which is fear of perceived death because that is the only way to shock the hypothalamus back into working order. One has to deny their hypothalamus to the extreme and that is the same as saying one has to deny their self and that is what this comment means [Mark 8:34 And when he had called the people unto him with his disciples also, he said unto them, Whosoever will come after me, let him deny himself, and take up his cross, and follow me.]

[let him deny himself] is the remedy to the brainwashing because your self is not your true self because you have been brainwashed.

[Luke 20:27 Then came to him certain of the Sadducees, which deny that there is any resurrection; and they asked him,]

Deny the resurrection simply means a person denies this remedy works and they do that because they deny they are brainwashed and they do that because they deny what the tree of knowledge is and so they are trapped behind layers of their own inability to understand cause and effect relationships.

You apply this remedy and you are resurrected from the death or from the neurotic state of mind you are in, which is the brainwashing, extreme left brain state of mind. You return from the dead to consciousness. You wake up which denotes you are asleep.

The Sadducees are the rich and wealthy, the aristocratic. This is in relation to it is easier for a camel to go through the eye of a needle than a rich man can find the kingdom, or escape the brain washing. Your first inclination is going to be to go ask someone who is rich and influential in reverse world for advice and all that will do is doom you to remain brainwashed.

In reverse world the rich are good, in reality world the rich are doomed. In reverse world the depressed and suicidal are looked down upon and in reality world they are the most valuable because they are close to waking up or breaking the brainwashing, they are in the 9th circle of hell, treason. It does not say the rich and popular shall inherit the earth it says the meek shall inherit the earth and a person in the reverse world that does not even feel they are worthy of being alive is the definition of meek.

The meek want to leave the cult and so the cult tries to fill them with pills to bring them back into the fold of the cult. The ones in the cult only want to help the depressed and suicidal get better and get better means they want them to stay in the cult. Civilization, the cult of the serpent will suggest they are righteous but if they are so righteous why do they brainwash innocent children to begin with grasshopper?

Are you still wondering what the tree of knowledge is grasshopper?

One important point about the Sadducees is they were against oral law and they wanted written law. The point of that is not the word law, the point is they wanted to encourage scribe and script, writing and wanted to leave the oral traditions of education behind.

So this is simply suggesting [Luke 20:27 Then came to him certain of the Sadducees, which deny that there is any resurrection;] they were denying there was any problem with written language. And although the brain dead mole crickets will suggest the Sadducees are gone the reality is the world is packed full of Sadducees, the ones who push the script, the demotic script, on their children and they hate anyone who does not get the written law so they hate the oral education, the way one can avoid harming the children mentally. You just remember I was judged by civilizations tests to be retarded by way of the education system and judged not be very intelligent, not intelligent according to their sequential based tests. It is difficult to communicate with dead air.- 4:50:03 AM

5:49:39 AM – I was looking at the No child left behind act of 2001. One of the foundations of it is the child is taught to read first which denotes the child is taught to write first and then math is a secondary aspect. Then the child is judged each year to determine if that child is progressing in this sequential based "education". What that means is every year they are making sure the child becomes better and better at the sequencing aspects and that in turn means the child gets worse in the random access right brain aspects.

No child left behind also suggests methods to ensure any child that comes to this country gets the education and any Native American or Hawaiians gets the education. Relative to reverse world no child left behind appears to be the greatest idea in the universe and relative to reality world it simply means civilization is going to mentally rape every child they can get their hands on.

In some old paintings there is a depiction of the devil eating a child. The devil is putting a small child in his mouth. That is all this brand of education is, simply feeding all the children to the devil. Devil would relate to taking a mentally perfect child and destroying it. Destroying beauty is what the devil means, killing beauty because one is envious of beauty.

That is the nature of the darkness. The beauty of a child's mind reminds the darkness of what it never will be so the darkness kills it. That is the core nature of civilization and everything outside of that are simply symptoms of that core nature. The abused often defend the abuser and the abused often become abusive. Civilization is simply the abused defending the abuser and in turn they become abusive. Civilization has no logical reason to mentally abuse and condition innocent children into this unsound state of mind but it is simply civilizations nature to mentally hinder innocent children's minds and leave the children in a state of suffering. There is no reason civilization harms the young children it is just civilizations natural tendency. The abused become abusive because they want everyone to suffer like they suffer.

The darkness loves suffering so the more suffering it can inflict the better it feels, and so an innocent child who is mentally perfect gives the darkness the greatest satisfaction when it destroys this mentally perfect innocent child. The beauty of an innocent child's mind remind the darkness what it is not, so it must destroy that innocent child's perfect mind because it reminds the darkness of what the darkness has lost, which is it's sound mind.

The darkness is envious of an innocent child's perfect mind so the darkness is greedy and lustful to destroy it. The darkness will kill anything that gets in its way, in its greed and lust to destroy an innocent child's perfect mind because that perfect mind makes the darkness hate itself and the nature of the darkness is self loathing so it must destroy that innocent child's perfect mind. These things are what are called the nature of the beast.

The darkness is trapped by its own perception in its unsound state of mind so it is not aware of its own nature. The darkness perceives it is helping innocent children when it is really eating innocent children. The darkness is insanity and madness so it cannot be reasoned with because it perceives its nature is righteousness. Civilization will destroy the mind of every single innocent child on the planet and then when those children are killing their self and addicted to drugs and have all number of emotional problems civilization will say, "That is the child's fault but not our fault." This is because the darkness see's its methods are valid when they are in fact unsound methods.

Of course this is going to mentally harm a child [If you reflect back upon our own educational training, we have been traditionally taught to master the 3 R's: reading, writing and arithmetic -- the domain and strength of the left brain.]. There is no possible way all of this left brain education is going to do anything but ruin the perfect sound mind of a child but the darkness only thinks it is helping a child to become more like it.

The darkness wants every innocent child's perfect mind to be just like its unsound mind and that way the darkness does not have to live with itself because the darkness cannot live with itself. Once the darkness see's an innocent child's perfect mind it gives the darkness contrast to its own unsound mind and that drives the darkness mad, so it must kill that innocent child's perfect mind as fast as possible. Kindergarten starts at the age of 6. The kindred are gardened at the age of six. - 7:02:34 AM

4:31:57 PM – What separates fear from common sense is reason. If one fears saying a word because they fear the repercussions that is not very reasonable because a spoken sound cannot possibly harm one in a true vacuum. If one speaks certain words around insane people who fear words that may harm you but that is only relative to the insane people who fear words not relative to the sound of the word itself.

One who fears using certain words is in fact hallucinating because their unsound mind, brainwashed mind, keeps telling them the sound of a spoken word will certainly harm them and they believe it. Insane people act upon things they perceive are true but in reality are not true. This is relative to neurosis and neurosis is relative to an unsound mind and an unsound mind is relative to getting many years of left brain sequential education taught improperly by another person of unsound mind.

Human beings of sound mind do not harm innocent children and then brag about it. Every time you see a bumper stick on someone car that says my child is an honor student that is simply an insane person bragging about the fact they harm their own child. There is no school in America nor many in the world that even understand the damage the education tool can do to the mind if that tool is not respected and taught properly.

It is common sense or fear that makes a person afraid to use certain words? Is it common sense or fear that makes a person dislike a song because who created that music or the lyrics in that music? When one is afraid of things that cannot harm them they are controlled by fear and thus are a slave to their own delusions of fear. If a person honestly believes if they say any word in the universe in a room all alone by their self and it may cause harm to them they are in deep neurosis. This is of course relative to their hypothalamus not working properly due to the many years of left brain education. One's mind is simply bent to the left and so one's mind is unsound and in turn it is not working properly and the being is suffering because they are a slave to their unsound mind. One cannot escape their perception and if their perception is not proper perception because of an unsound mind they are a slave to false perceptions.

One acts upon their perception and if ones perception is false perception they are acting falsely. If you harm a child for saying a cuss word you are actually acting falsely because a cuss word is harmless in every definition of the word harmless. One is in fact hallucinating because they are of unsound mind from the brainwashing and it shows in every deed and action they do. They may argue they will raise their child as they see fit but in reality no person has the right to brainwash a child with the education no matter how delusional that person's unsound mind is from the brainwashing they got as a child.

6:53:57 PM – Consider Moses. He came of age, broke free of the brainwashing, and he lived in civilization, Egypt. So he was taught the script form of hieroglyphics. The Greek word for hieroglyphics is demotic and that word is similar to demonic. He left civilization and realized what civilization was doing to people mentally by educating them with demotic. He formed an army an attacked civilization to force it to free the people it had brainwashed and turned into slaves. After burning civilizations crops and poisoning their water supply, civilization decided to let the people go. After they let the people go they changed their mind and went after Moses and there was a battle and Moses killed that army that pursued him and the people he had freed and this was called the Red Sea event.

Moses then was a wanted man by civilization and was what would be known today as a terrorist and so he was on the run for the rest of his life. Before him Abraham and Lot attacked civilization for the same reason but because they came quite a time before Moses they were actually able to burn the entire cities to the ground and kill the brainwashed ones in the cities but of course word travels fast in civilization so after that attack Lot became a wanted terrorist relative to civilization and he fled and hid in the mountains in a cave. [Genesis 19:30 And Lot went up out of Zoar, and dwelt in the mountain, and his two daughters with him; for he feared to dwell in Zoar: and he dwelt in a cave, he and his two daughters.]

Some time later John the Baptist came along and he had a method to wake people up from the brainwashing and it was similar to the Abraham and Isaac method but it had to do with dunking a person under water and then when that person came close to drowning they let go or feared not. Civilization caught wind that this person who lived in the wilderness was waking up the slaves civilization had brainwashed and they killed him.

Then Jesus came along and Jesus had a new method that produced the same results and he was very good at oration so he could explain it to many people at one time so he was certainly a threat to civilization so Jesus became a wanted man and he tried to hide in the wilderness but Civilization put a bounty on his head and eventually someone turned Jesus in for a few copper pieces and so Civilization killed Jesus.

Some time after Jesus another being woke up name Mohammed and Mohammed attempted to fight against the cult of the serpent, civilization, and he made great progress but eventually he too was killed and since him there has not been any serious threat to the cult of the serpent, the cult has become far too powerful. All of this conflict is centered around one principle.

The written language, reading and math is a manmade invention that has devastating mental side effects on the mind of a child if not taught properly by a master who understand this manmade invention has devastating mental side effects. Until the cult understands the fundamental cause and effect reality there is always going to be people who are going to fight the cult because sound minded human beings are not going to stand by and watch the cult mentally rape innocent children as a result of the cult's ignorance or cruelty.

This of course is an explanation relative to the west. In the east these tribes were known as barbarians but one pattern is for certain in both the east and the west relative to fighting civilization and that is these tribes were aware civilizations weakness was fear. So civilization taught itself these education inventions improperly and they ended up with lots of fear and so fear tactics worked well on them and this is why Abraham understood the remedy to this unsound state of mind caused by the education was fear not. I will now discuss something relevant. - 7:08:25 PM

8:36:12 PM – Consider this concept tribulation. Someone breaks the brainwashing to the full measure and they suggest the remedy to many but because the remedy is so difficult to apply relative to the brainwashed beings perception very few go up to heaven, unveil right brain, and many remain behind, in the brainwashed state.

Two people are sleeping in a bed and one is gone because they applied the remedy and are no longer sleeping, they applied the remedy and woke up, and one remains in the bed mentally asleep, brainwashed.

An indication of how difficult this mental exercise to break the brain washing is : [Luke 17:33 ; and whosoever shall lose his life shall preserve it.] Jesus spoke to crowds of 5000 and only ended up with twelve disciples and he could not even convince his own parent Joseph apply the remedy or he would have been his disciple. I am on the fence about Mary at this time.

The word master in the east is simply one who has applied the remedy and reached nirvana or consciousness. Here are some examples in the west of that same concept being used.
[Mark 12:19 Master, Moses wrote unto us, If a man's brother die, and leave his wife behind him, and leave no children, that his brother should take his wife, and raise up seed unto his brother.]
[John 13:13 Ye call me Master and Lord: and ye say well; for so I am.]
Note the word Lord and then look at this comment:
[Genesis 11:5 And the LORD came down to see the city and the tower, which the children of men builded.] The Lord in this comment is of course Abraham.

This is a symptom of how complex this education brainwashing is. It is essentially the blind leading the blind so it is a crime that one cannot seek justice for.
[John 9:2 And his disciples asked him, saying, Master, who did sin, this man, or his parents, that he was born blind?
John 9:3 Jesus answered, Neither hath this man sinned, nor his parents: but that the works of God should be made manifest in him.]
John is asking who is to blame the child or the child's parents for making the child mentally blind or making the child's right brain veiled from the education being taught improperly. And Jesus said it's no one's fault because a parent would not knowingly harm their child and their parents would not knowingly harm them. Jesus looked at it like mankind invented this education and it veils one's mind and once their mind was veiled they kept teaching it to others and veiling their mind and then that person would teach it to their children and veil their children's mind and 5000 years later here we are. Of course civilization is going to just submit they had a slight over sight and have been veiling children's minds for thousands of years, and then they will apologize and adjust

their education methods, and then roses will start sprouting up in our front's yards and we can go frolic in them. - 9:14:14 PM

4:07:11 AM – If one cannot convince another then one has been convinced by the other to cease convincing.
Wisdom is controlling and ignorance is following its lead.
Impermanence gives life its value and life is swift in repaying that debt.
Nature never gives anything it does not want back.
Happiness cannot be found and that keeps one looking for greater happiness.
Virtue can only be achieved through the sufferings of vice.
When pain is forgotten pleasure is achieved.
Misfortune is oft fortunate, unfortunately.
The band wagon offers many vices but few virtues.
Fear creates obstacles and foolishness is among them.
A ruler is not afraid to be a tyrant when the people are afraid to be rulers.
The cost of safety is liberty and the cost of liberty is tyranny.
Safety is achieved when common sense reigns over fear.
It is difficult to be afraid of something one understands.
If you have too many friends, try telling them the truth.
It's easier to be alone than to be unwanted in a crowd.
One can judge their self into hell or free their self from judgments.
Ones thoughts are the only certainty one has. - 4:22:11 AM

9:31:51 AM – [1 Timothy 5:8 But if any provide not for his own, and specially for those of his own house, he hath denied the faith, and is worse than an infidel.]
This may be one of the most valuable comments outside of the remedy itself in the ancient texts and I need filler.
[But if any provide not for his own] = A parent is responsible to assist their child with the remedy after that child gets the education and this relies upon the parent first applying the remedy. The remedy is although I face the shadow of death I submit to it and this shocks the mind out of the extreme left brain state caused by the education.
[and specially for those of his own house] = This relates to the fact that every parents assist their own children with the remedy then people do not have to go around convincing people they do not know to apply the remedy. The apostles all got butchered because they appeared to be telling people they did not know what to do , which is apply to the remedy. As a parent you apply the remedy, then when your child gets the education you assist them in applying the remedy. If you are going to give them the brand of education that veils their mind then it is your duty to assist that child in applying the remedy. If you want to avoid

doing that then put your child in an education system that uses oral education instead of written and reading education.

There are schools in this world that teach oral education and oral education does not veil the mind. There are people who know how to administer this education properly so it does not veil a child's mind so you are going to have to decide if your child's mind is worth it.

[he hath denied the faith] = The faith is one that has faith after they get the written education their mind is veiled because there is no way to tell their mind is veiled after that brand of education because it is a very subtle progression. One's mind slowly starts to bend to the left over a number of years so one has to have faith years of sequential left brain education is going to bend their mind to the left so they have to apply the remedy to revert back to sound mind.

[and is worse than an infidel] = an infidel is one who does not have faith the written education brand has veiled their mind so one who is worse than that is one who does not have faith the written education has veiled their mind and they also do not bother to assist their child to apply the remedy so their child does not end up with a veiled mind. If one does not believe their mind has been bent to the left after years of left brain education that is their business and if they do not wish to apply the remedy that is their business, but if they allow their child to have its mind veiled also and then do not even offer the child the remedy they are making a life changing decision for the mental well being of their own child. It's cruel enough to bends a child mind to the left but then to not even offer them a way to get out of that state of mind is crueler, and then to blame the child for its actions after one bends the child's mind and then does not offer the remedy is crueler still. - 9:47:42 AM

6:56:19 PM – One must experience the vices to detect the virtues.

9:49:56 PM –
[Galatians 3:9 So then they which be of faith are blessed with faithful Abraham.]
Abraham was special because [Genesis 15:1 After these things the word of the LORD came unto Abram in a vision, saying, Fear not, Abram: I am thy shield, and thy exceeding great reward.] He understood the remedy the tree of knowledge, fear not or the Abraham and Isaac method. So one is faithful if they understand the remedy Abraham suggested but this is relative to that time period. Jesus suggested those who lose their life preserves it which is the same technique. Then Mohammed suggested Submit which is also the same technique. So at this time period these beings were simply repeating what was said in the Torah and also suggesting there own versions of what Abraham suggested as the remedy to the tree of knowledge.

Relative to the East, Buddha suggested, go sit in a cemetery at night alone until you feel better.

[Romans 4:8 Blessed is the man to whom the Lord will not impute sin.] Impute means charge. This comment is relative to the event when Jesus did not blame the woman for her behavior. The sign of a Lord or Master is they understand why a person is acting the way they are, because of the education left brain leaning state of mind, so they do not blame them but this is a paradox.

The comment where an apostle asked Jesus was the child to blame or the parent to blame for the child getting the education. Jesus said its no one's fault and this is relative to they know not what they do, but that is not the end of the argument because if one just says they know not what they do then all that is going to happen is they are going to keep on doing it to the children and then the entire species will destroy itself because a house/ mind divided cannot stand.

So the paradox is, the education brainwashing is no one's fault and is everyone's fault.

Ignorance is no excuse and since innocent children's minds are involved even one who is ignorant must answer for such a crime. So the burden is on the rulers or the leaders of the nations. If they allow this to happen to innocent children it is their ultimate burden because they are the only ones in the reverse world that can change it or stop it from happening.

[Matthew 23:24 Ye blind guides, which strain at a gnat, and swallow a camel.] This simply means the leaders will make a big deal about petty issues and then when this education mind altering situation comes up they just laugh at it. There is no bigger issue because all the petty problems are caused by this fundamental flaw in education which means education is a tool and not good or bad but if said tool is taught without caution and understanding to its bad mental side effects there is only disaster.

This mind altering tool is the root of all the little problems the leader makes such a big fuss about so they are straining on a gnat, the little problems, because they swallowed a camel, the root cause of all those little petty problems, improperly taught education. This comment is simply suggesting vanity. The leaders are shooting their self in the foot to save their good foot. If the leader's do not address this flaw in education every single thing they do after that is simply vanity or a symptom of not addressing the serious education flaw. This is not relative to one country this education flaw is relative to all countries. There are some who have applied the remedy and go out of their way to literally attack traditional educational institutions and now you know why.

If one applies the education properly they enrich that persons mind and if they apply the education improperly they destroy that persons mind and thus they destroy that person's potential and leave that person in a mental state of suffering and these beings of the ancient texts called that suffering, hell.

[Psalms 9:17 The wicked shall be turned into hell, and all the nations that forget God.]
Any nation that forgets what the tree of knowledge is will also not understand the remedy
to the tree of knowledge and in turn is doomed to mental hell, it is that simple. They forget
the unnamable power of right brain and that is what the education veils.

X = [Matthew 23:24 Ye blind guides, which strain at a gnat, and swallow a camel.
Mark 10:25 It is easier for a camel to go through the eye of a needle, than for a rich man
to enter into the kingdom of God.
Luke 18:25 For it is easier for a camel to go through a needle's eye, than for a rich man to
enter into the kingdom of God.] = The rich or popular or leaders in the reverse world.
[blind guides] = leaders or movers and shakers in the reversed world; the wealthy; elite;
aristocrats.

Y = [[Matthew 5:3 Blessed are the poor in spirit: for theirs is the kingdom of heaven.]
[Matthew 5:5 Blessed are the meek: for they shall inherit the earth.]] = the down trodden,
the depressed, the suicidal in reverse world.

Dante explained the X's in the reverse world are ones in limbo (first circle of hell) or ones
who are very unlikely to break out of the education induced brainwashing because they
love the reverse world.
The Y's in the reverse world are the ones close to the ninth circle of hell, treason. Treason
against their state of mind they are in, the brainwashed state, the mental hell state.

What this all means is in reverse world the wealthy are the top dogs and the poor
are downtrodden but in reality world the wealthy are the least and the down trodden are the
most valuable.
Blessed are the poor in spirit; Blessed are the meek because they are much closer to
escaping the brainwashing than the rich and wealthy in the reverse world.
In reverse world the least are the most valuable to the ones in reality world. The least
among you are the ones who are closest to escaping the brainwashing and the most popular
among you are the ones who have very little chance to escape the brainwashing. This is
relative to the antichrist or the anti-truth. This is an example of two worlds happening at
once. What is true in reverse world is not true in reality world and what is true is reality
world is not true in reverse world.
[Revelation 3:17 Because thou sayest, I am rich, and increased with goods, and have need
of nothing; and knowest not that thou art wretched, and miserable, and poor, and blind, and
naked:]

That is what this line means. A person may be materialistically wealthy in reverse world but that only means they are very low on the totem in reality world (cerebral world).

This is complex because once one applies the remedy they break the curse/ brainwashing so these comments no longer apply or have meaning. A better way to look at it is once one goes through the nine circles of hell and survives they reach heaven, break the brainwashing so the fruits of their tree is proper. Only one who commits mental treason, mental suicide, lose their life , preserve their proper mental life. What this means is their deeds after they apply the treason aspect are righteous deeds.

For example Abraham and Lot burned down those cities and killed everyone in them but that was righteous because they were trying to protect the children from being put into mental hell because the education was being taught improperly. I am mindful this sounds very harsh but the truth is, they tried to stop the curse from spreading in our species. It did not work because of this [Psalms 9:17 - The wicked shall be turned into hell, and all the nations that forget God.]

Eventually the nations forget what the tree of knowledge is and then they forget the remedy and then before you know it everyone is back in mental hell because they forgot the education is a tool and can be devastating on the mind if administered improperly.

Morphine is a good tool to control pain but if taken improperly one can die. It is no different with education at all. Education is a tool but when not taught by a master who understands it can be a dangerous tool then one is doomed to be destroyed mentally by that tool. The way the species, civilization is right now is a symptom the species is ignorant about the dangers of written language, math and reading if they are not taught properly. Everything leads back to one thing. - 10:43:59 PM

11/26/2009 12:19:05 AM –
<TRohrer> one point i make in the books is teh fact there is a subconsious, and that is right brain, so thats proof right brain is veiled
<TRohrer> its silenced or pushed to teh background and that abnormal
<TRohrer> the more one favors left brain, edcuation, teh less they favor right brain until right brain is veiled
<TRohrer> John 3:30 He must increase, but I must decrease.
<TRohrer> he = right brain I = left brain/ego
<whomasect> The Law of Inversion
<TRohrer> yes as one scale goes up the other scale goes down
Laws are simply punishment for exhibiting symptoms the education causes in the mind.

9:00:28 PM –

[Mark 1:9 And it came to pass in those days, that Jesus came from Nazareth of Galilee, and was baptized of John in Jordan.
Mark 1:10 And straightway coming up out of the water, he saw the heavens opened, and the Spirit like a dove descending upon him:]
[Matthew 14:2 And said unto his servants, This is John the Baptist; he is risen from the dead; and therefore mighty works do shew forth themselves in him.]

[and was baptized of John in Jordan.] Baptize is the same remedy in principle as the Abraham and Isaac remedy.
X = brainwashed state of mind after the education.
Y = Sound state of mind after the remedy is applied.

In the Abraham and Isaac story one will notice Isaac was not aware of what was going to happen.[Genesis 22:7 And Isaac spake unto Abraham his father, and said, My father: and he said, Here am I, my son. And he said, Behold the fire and the wood: but where is the lamb for a burnt offering?]
Isaac is saying "Father I see that knife in your hand but I do not see the lamb." What this means is one in the X state of mind has to believe they are going to die or the remedy will not work.

This is the reason this X state of mind is so devastating and also why a short period after these wise beings died the remedy was forgotten about because one has to commit treason or defeat their fear of death and this means the X state of mind has to believe one is going to die and then one fears not and they do not literally die and then they achieve Y state of mind.

So this is the comment where Jesus broke the curse or the X state of mind. [and was baptized of John in Jordan.]

So John the Baptist applied the Abraham and Isaac remedy on Jesus. John the Baptist lived in the wilderness in a cave. John would hold a person under water and when the hypothalamus started saying they were going to die that person would not panic and just allow it. It is what is called attempted murder in reverse world.
[Genesis 22:10 And Abraham stretched forth his hand, and took the knife to slay his son.]
This is also called attempted murder in reverse world.

This is what happened to Jesus after he was Baptized by John [Mark 1:10 And straightway coming up out of the water, he saw the heavens opened, and the Spirit like a dove descending upon him:]
[he saw the heavens opened] This is relative to the fact once the remedy is applied one mentally feels much better but right brain does not come to full power for about a month and that is when one gets this incredible mental "Ah ha "sensation. Everything gets very

easy relative to mental clarity, everything makes sense and that is what this relates to [he saw the heavens opened]. One starts seeing wisdom in everything.

X = brainwashed state of mind after the education; mentally dead in contrast to sound mind.
Y = Sound state of mind after the remedy is applied; quick relative to X

[Matthew 14:2 And said unto his servants, This is John the Baptist; he is risen from the dead]
[This is John the Baptist; he is risen from the dead] simply means John has applied the remedy and so John was dead, brainwashed and he applied the remedy, unveiled right brain and so he is risen from the dead. John once was blind but then he applied the remedy and now he see's. And then John was able to assist Jesus to apply the remedy and so John assisted Jesus [and was baptized of John in Jordan.] and so Jesus was [risen from the dead] also.

So John was a big fish and that explains why he was killed off so early in these texts. Simply put, John the Baptist was waking up a lot of people with his take on the remedy, baptism, and the cult of the serpent did not like that. That is what this aspect of that comment means [and therefore mighty works do shew forth themselves in him.] John was raising a lot of people from the dead, assisting them to unveil right brain, and the taskmaster would not have any slaves if they started thinking clearly, so the cult made sure to eliminate John from the picture.

So this comment [he is risen from the dead] is simply a repeat of this comment [Psalms 73:22 So foolish was I, and ignorant: I was as a beast before thee.]
A side note is [So foolish was I] should be , So I was foolish , so it is in random access and a sign post of authenticity.
This is another example of this repeat aspect in the ancient texts.
[Matthew 12:22 Then was brought unto him one possessed with a devil, blind, and dumb: and he healed him, insomuch that the blind and dumb both spake and saw.] = [Psalms 73:22 So foolish was I, and ignorant: I was as a beast before thee.]
[So foolish was I, and ignorant: I was as a beast] = [Then was brought unto him one possessed with a devil, blind, and dumb]
This comment [Matthew 4:11 Then the devil leaveth him, and, behold, angels came and ministered unto him.] is simply saying this person applied the remedy and the angels are the right brain and it unveiled and it is so fast in processing power and pattern detection and intuition and complexity one can easily suggest it ministers to them.

This is relative to an unspoken reality that once one applies the remedy no one can teach them because they are a mental giant. They can listen to what others suggest but they figure everything out their self and this is an indication of how powerful right brain is when unveiled and this is also an indication how great a crime it is to veil the right brain in a person by improperly teaching them the education improperly. I cannot explain how powerful right brain is once it is unveiled except to say its power is unnamable and it's so powerful sometimes it feels as if it is separate from the person and there is no way to test how powerful it is because it is beyond measure.

I have been able to work my way to figuring out everything relevant to these ancient texts by myself in the last 12 months and civilization has not be able to figure out these texts in 5000 years because civilization keeps veiling everyone's right brain because they have no clue about how dangerous writing, math and reading can be if not taught properly, but that is not because I am intelligent it is because right brain is intelligent when it's not veiled. I am mindful to keep telling you I am not special because we all have a right brain, I simply unveiled it after it was veiled because of the education accidentally, because I am mindful ones in the X state of mind have serious self esteem issues, they like to idolize things because they perceive they don't have good genes or a good mind, but in reality their mind is Einstein's mind they just have to undo all the damage education has done to it by applying the remedy.

If I say I am nothing you will assume I am humble. If one say's I am special you will idolize me. The only solution is for you to apply the remedy and you will understand I am not nothing nor special, I simply applied this ancient remedy, to the negate the bad mental side effects of the education by accident and unveiled right brain.

[2 Peter 3:8 But, beloved, be not ignorant of this one thing, that one day is with the Lord as a thousand years, and a thousand years as one day.] This comment is relative to no sense of time. Once you apply the remedy one day will seem like infinite time because your mind will no longer register time and this is relative to ambiguity. You will think to yourself "How long has today been?" and the ambiguity of right brain, when it is unveiled is so strong your mind will reply, infinite time and no time and it will not be able to make up its mind, so to speak, and so that is the fountain of youth. Your mind no longer registers time because it cannot make up its mind how much time has passed because of the ambiguity of right brain when it is unveiled.

[Matthew 13:39 The enemy that sowed them is the devil; the harvest is the end of the world; and the reapers are the angels.]

[The enemy that sowed them(educated them improperly with the education) is the devil(civilization, ignorant people teaching a dangerous tool and making more ignorant people, mentally veiled people)] [the harvest is the end of the world] = The end of the world as far as the end of this suffering left brain state of mind and a return to a cerebral sound mind so one is a thinker instead of in a materialistic based mind set.

[and the reapers are the angels.] = the fishers of men, the Masters who assist a person to apply the remedy, the lords, the prophets. This of course is complex because the [devil(civilization, ignorant people teaching a dangerous tool and making more ignorant people, mentally veiled people)] create so many of the unsound minded people because they educate them on an industrial scale and the remedy is difficult to apply to the full measure, so this comment is saying the angels can assist ones but that does not mean they will be able to assist as many with the remedy as civilization will mentally harm as a result of the education being taught improperly.

These texts are not suggesting rules beyond suggesting rules for the ones who have to apply the remedy because the remedy is difficult enough to apply anyway. It would be fantastic if I could walk up to you and apply the remedy for you but that is underestimating how far one's mind is bent to the left after all those years of left brain education. Simply put one cannot escape a hallucination state of mind unless there is a huge shock to the mind itself and defeating the shadow of death is what it takes, and that will never change.

A friend of mine who I knew before the accident, I sent him my books and he understands what the remedy is. He has a drug problem and is somewhat depressed and he was begging me to apply this remedy for him. He suggested I hold an unloaded gun to his head and I explained to him that will not work because you know it will be unloaded and that means you told the X state of mind by suggesting that, so the remedy will not work.

One has to trick the X state of mind into believing one is ready to die and let go. I could tell he was frustrated and I understood he was trapped by his own perceptions. He was afraid to go to a cemetery alone at night. I could read him and I could tell he really wanted to try this remedy because he was at a point he was ready to give up on life and my eyes grew black with rage, and I write in my books, I spit in the face of civilization for putting people in this mental state of suffering with your "brand" of education. You almost killed me with your "brand" of education taskmaster, and before it's all over you will wish you had, psychologically speaking, what have you, so to speak, such and such.
 I will now discuss something of value.- 10:16:57 PM

11:27:24 PM – People who apply the remedy oft are labeled as heretics by the reverse world, civilization, and that is logical because the reverse world see's the truth as lies. If you perceive the spirit of what I suggest is a lie then that is proof you got the education but have not yet applied the remedy and so you hear these words in the ancient texts but do not understand them. So before you go labeling me and digging yourself deeper into the pit you are in, you go apply the remedy and see if you do not feel better . [Luke 17:33 ;and whosoever shall lose his life shall preserve it.] The spirit of what I suggest is relative to the observer.- 11:33:37 PM

11/27/2009 8:35:43 AM – This comment [Psalms 73:22 So foolish was I, and ignorant: I was as a beast before thee.] Is relative to this comment [Exodus 22:19 Whosoever lieth with a beast shall surely be put to death.]
[I was as a beast before thee.] = had the brainwashing or was in the extreme left brain neurosis caused by being taught the education improperly.

So relative to this time period, if you were caught associating with one of the beasts they killed you. The logic being if one has a child with one of the beasts it is a very good chance that beast will sacrifice that child and make that child a beast, brainwashed, also. This is relative to the cursed beget cursed and also those who are abused tend to become abusers of their own offspring. The deeper meaning is the beast wants the children because their innocence displeases the beast and the beast cannot stand to see the light of an innocent child so it must destroy the light swiftly because it harms the beast. And one of the marks of the beast is [Galatians 4:10 Ye observe days, and months, and times, and years.] which means they sense time which is a symptom one has been brainwashed or is of the beast. The opposite of that comment is Ye is unable to observe days, and months, and times, and years. = mentally unable to sense time, is a symptom one has applied the remedy properly or to the full measure. - 8:47:10 AM

6:05:25 PM – The ones who gets the education, taught improperly, perceive a young child as imperfect. They perceive the child is imperfect because they simply are not conscious they are mentally unsound as a result of their mind being bent to the left from their education. Because of this reality they seek to mold the child in their image so they mold a mentally sound child into what they are, a mentally unsound being as a result of the improperly taught education. The educated ones see the perfect light of a young child as imperfection, so they are compelled to fix the child. The adults are trapped in this reverse "sight" where they see light as darkness and darkness as light, they see imperfection as perfection and perfection as imperfection so they are unable to escape this reverse "sight" without a major shock to their mind to bend it back towards the right so they can return to sound mind. This shock is what the remedy is all about. The remedy is not about rules or morals it is simply an ancient method one applies to return one to the sight of the sound minded, so one is able to leave the sight of the unsound minded. - 6:12:35 PM

3:53:04 AM –You have been conditioned into an unsound state of mind just like I was and you are perhaps unable to escape the mind trap, and I understand that because I escaped accidentally, so all you are doing in your life is continuing to mentally harm innocent children's minds knowingly or unknowingly, just like you did to me. You are in neurosis because of the conditioning you got as a child, and so you are mentally harming children and putting them in a mental state of hell, and you are in too deep of neurosis, mental hell, to even believe you are doing that to children. Your disbelief will not change anything. You are not looking to apply this remedy so you can brag about it. You are looking to apply this remedy so you can unveil your right brain, that has been veiled by the many years of sequential left brain education you got as a child, so you can call yourself a sound minded human being.- 4:21:53 AM

I have not yet begun to write, to fight, to have sight.

I let go of this text on 11/28/2009 8:15:31 PM

It is done. Tis well.